Gertrude F. H. Atherton

American Wives and English Husbands

A Novel

Gertrude F. H. Atherton

American Wives and English Husbands
A Novel

ISBN/EAN: 9783337349158

Printed in Europe, USA, Canada, Australia, Japan

Cover: Foto ©Andreas Hilbeck / pixelio.de

More available books at **www.hansebooks.com**

AMERICAN WIVES AND ENGLISH HUSBANDS

A NOVEL

By GERTRUDE ATHERTON

Author of "Patience Sparhawk," etc.

NEW YORK : DODD, MEAD
AND COMPANY   1898

TO
THE LADIES OF RUE GIROT
BOIS GUILLAUME

American Wives
and
English Husbands

PART ONE

CHAPTER I

MRS. HAYNE'S boarding-house stood on the corner of Market Street and one of those cross streets which seem to leap down from the heights of San Francisco and empty themselves into the great central thoroughfare that roars from the sandy desert at the base of Twin Peaks to the teeming wharves on the edge of the bay. On the right of Market Street, both on the hills and in the erratic branchings of the central plain, as far as the eye can reach, climbs and swarms modern prosperous San Francisco; of what lies beyond, the less said the better. On the left, at the far south-east, the halo of ancient glory still hovers about Rincon Hill, growing dimmer with the years: few of the many who made the social laws of the Fifties cling to the old houses in the battered gardens; and their children marry and build on the gay hills across the plain. In the plain itself is a thick-set, low-browed, dust-coloured city; "South of Market Street" is a generic term for hundreds of streets in which dwell thousands of insignificant beings, some of whom promenade the democratic boundary line by gaslight, but rarely venture up the aristocratic slopes. By day or by night Market Street rarely has a moment of rest, of peace; it is a blaze of colour, a medley of sound, shrill, raucous, hollow, furious, a net-work of busy people and vehicles until midnight is over. Every phase of the city's manifold life is suggested there, every aspect of its cosmopolitanism.

To a little girl of eleven, who dwelt on the third floor of Mrs. Hayne's boarding-house, Market Street was a panorama of serious study and unvarying interest. She knew every shop window, in all the mutable details of the seasons, she had mingled with the throng unnumbered times, studying that strange patch-work of faces, and wondering if they had any life apart from the scene in which they seemed eternally moving. In those days Market Street typified the world to her; although her school was some eight blocks up the hill it scarcely counted. All the world, she felt convinced, came sooner or later to Market Street, and sauntered or hurried with restless eyes, up and down, up and down. The sun rose at one end and set at the other; it climbed straight across the sky and went to bed behind the Twin Peaks. And the trade winds roared through Market Street as through a mighty cañon, and the sand hills beyond the city seemed to rise bodily and whirl down the great way, making men curse and women jerk their knuckles to their eyes. On summer nights the fog came and banked there, and the lights shone through it like fallen stars, and the people looked like wraiths, lost souls condemned to wander unceasingly.

When Mrs. Tarleton was too ill to be left alone, Lee amused herself watching from above the crush and tangle of street cars, hacks, trucks, and drays for which the wide road should have been as wide again, holding her breath as the impatient or timid foot-passengers darted into the transient rifts with bird-like leaps of vision and wild deflections. Occasionally she assumed the part of chorus for her mother, who regarded the prospect beneath her windows with horror.

"Now! She's started — *at last!* Oh! *what* a silly! Any one could have seen that truck with half an eye. She turned back — *of course!* Now! Now! she's got to the middle and there's a funeral just turned the corner! She can't get back! She's got to go on. Oh, she's got behind a man. I wonder if she'll catch hold of his coat-tails? There — she's safe! I wonder if she's afraid of people like she is of Market Street?"

"If I ever thought you crossed that street at the busy time of the day, honey, I should certainly faint or have hysterics," Mrs. Tarleton was in the habit of remarking at the finish of these thrilling interpretations.

To which Lee invariably replied: "I could go right across without stopping, or getting a crick in my neck either; but I don't, because I wouldn't make you nervous for the world. I go way up when

I want to cross and then turn back. It 's nothing like as bad."

"It is shocking to think that you go out at all unattended; but what cannot be cannot, and you must have air and exercise, poor child!"

Lee, who retained a blurred, albeit rosy impression of her former grandeur, was well pleased with her liberty; and Mrs. Tarleton was not only satisfied that any one who could take such good care of her mother was quite able to take care of herself, but, so dependent was she on the capable child, that she was frequently oblivious to the generation they rounded. Mrs. Tarleton was an invalid, and, although patient, she met her acuter sufferings unresistingly. Lee was so accustomed to be roused in the middle of the night that she had learned to make a poultice or heat a kettle of water while the receding dreams were still lapping at her brain. She dressed her mother in the morning and undressed her at night. She frequently chafed her hands and feet by the hour; and cooked many a dainty Southern dish on the stove in the corner. Miss Hayne, who had a sharp red nose and the anxious air of protracted maidenhood, but whose heart was normal, made it her duty to fetch books for the invalid from the Mercantile Library, and to look in upon her while Lee was at school.

Lee brushed and mended her own clothes, "blacked" her boots with a vigorous arm, and studied her lessons when other little girls were in bed. Fortunately she raked them in with extreme rapidity, or Mrs. Tarleton would have made an effort and remonstrated; but Lee declared that she must have her afternoons out of doors when her mother was well and companioned by a novel; and Mrs. Tarleton scrupulously refrained from thwarting the girl whose narrow childhood was so unlike what her own had been, so unlike what the fairies had promised when Hayward Tarleton had been the proudest and most indulgent of fathers.

CHAPTER II

MARGUERITE TARLETON'S impression of the hour in which she found herself widowed and penniless was very vague; she was down with brain fever in the hour that followed.

The Civil War had left her family with little but the great prestige of its name and the old house in New Orleans. Nevertheless, the house slaves having refused to accept their freedom, Marguerite had "never picked up her handkerchief," when, in a gown fashioned by her mammy from one of her dead mother's, she made her début in a society which retained all of its pride and little of its gaiety. Her mother had been a creole of great beauty and fascination. Marguerite inherited her impulsiveness and vivacity; and, for the rest, was ethereally pretty, as dainty and fastidious as a young princess, and had the soft manner and the romantic heart of the convent maiden. Hayward Tarleton captured twelve dances on this night of her triumphant début, and proposed a week later. They were married within the month; he had already planned to seek for fortune in California with what was left of his princely inheritance.

When Tarleton and his bride reached San Francisco the fortune he had come to woo fairly leapt into his arms; in three years he was a rich man, and his pretty and elegant young wife a social power. It was a very happy marriage. Marguerite idolised her handsome dashing husband, and he was the slave of her lightest whim. Their baby was petted and indulged until she ruled her adoring parents with a rod of iron, and tyrannised over the servants like a young slave-driver. But the parents saw no fault in her, and, in truth, she was an affectionate and amiable youngster, with a fund of good sense for which the servants were at a loss to account. She had twenty-six dolls at this period, a large roomful of toys, a pony, and a playhouse of three storeys in a corner of the garden.

Then came the great Virginia City mining excitement of the late Seventies. Tarleton, satiated with easy success, and longing for excitement, gambled; at first from choice, finally from necessity. His nerves swarmed over his will and stung it to death, his reason burnt to ashes. He staggered home one day, this man who had been intrepid on the battle-field for four blood-soaked and exhausting years, told his wife that he had not a dollar in the world, then went into the next room and blew out his brains.

The creditors seized the house. Two hours before Mrs. Tarleton had been carried to Rincon Hill to the home of Mrs. Montgomery, a Southerner who had known her mother and who would have offered shelter to every stricken compatriot in San Francisco if her children had not restrained her. Lee, who had been present when her father spoke his last words to his wife, and had heard the report of the pistol, lost all interest in dolls and picture-books for ever, and refused to leave the sick-room. She waited on her mother by day, and slept on a sofa at the foot of the bed. Mrs. Montgomery exclaimed that the child was positively uncanny, she was so old-fashioned, but that she certainly was lovable. Her own young children, Tiny and Randolph, although some years older than Lee, thought her profoundly interesting, and stole into the sick-room whenever the nurse's back was turned. Lee barely saw them; she retained no impression of them afterward, although the children were famous for their beauty and fine manners.

When Mrs. Tarleton recovered, her lawyer reminded her that some years before her husband had given her a ranch for which she had expressed an impulsive wish and as quickly forgotten. The deeds were at his office. She gave her jewels to the creditors, but decided to keep the ranch, remarking that her child was of more importance than all the creditors put together. The income was small, but she was grateful for it. Her next of kin were dead, and charity would have been insufferable.

Mrs. Hayne, a reduced Southerner, whom Tarleton had started in business, offered his widow a large front room on the third floor of her boarding-house at the price of a back one. In spite of Mrs. Montgomery's tears and remonstrances, Mrs. Tarleton accepted the offer, and persuaded herself that she was comfortable. She never went to the table, nor paid a call. Her friends, particularly the Southerners of her immediate circle, Mrs. Montgomery, Mrs. Geary, Mrs. Brannan, Mrs. Cartright, and Colonel Belmont were faithful; but as the years passed their visits became less frequent, and Mrs. Montgomery was much abroad with her children. Marguerite Tarleton cared little. Her interest in life had died with her husband; such energies as survived in her were centred in her child. When there was neither fog nor dust nor wind nor rain in the city, Lee dressed her peremptorily and took her for a ride in the cable-cars; but she spent measureless monotonous days in her reclining chair, reading or sewing. She did not complain except when in extreme pain, and was interested in every lineament of Lee's busy little life. She never shed a tear before the child, and managed to maintain an even state of mild cheerfulness. And she was grateful for Lee's skill and readiness in small matters as in great; her unaccustomed fingers would have made havoc with her hair and boots.

"Did you never, never button your own boots, memmy?" asked Lee one day, as she was performing that office.

"Never, honey. When Dinah was ill your father always buttoned them, and after she died he would n't have thought of letting any one else touch them; most people pinch so. Of course he could not do my hair, but he often put me to bed, and he *always* cut up my meat."

"Do all men do those things for their wives?" asked Lee in a voice of awe; "I think they must be very nice."

"All men who are fit to marry, and all Southern men, you may be sure. I want to live long enough to see you married to a man as nearly like your father as possible. I wonder if there are any left; America gallops so. He used to beg me to think of something new I wanted, something it would be difficult to get; and he fairly admired to button my boots; he never failed to put a little kiss right there on my instep when he finished."

"It must be lovely to be married!" said Lee.

Mrs. Tarleton closed her eyes.

"Was papa perfectly perfect?" asked Lee, as she finished her task and smoothed the kid over her mother's beautiful instep.

"Perfectly!"

"I heard the butler say once that he was as drunk as a lord."

"Possibly, but he was perfect all the same. He got drunk like a gentleman — a Southern gentleman, I mean, of course. I always put him to bed and never alluded to it."

CHAPTER III

L EE had no friends of her own age. The large private school she attended was not patronised by the aristocracy of the city, and Mrs. Tarleton had so thoroughly imbued her daughter with a sense of the vast superiority of the gentle-born Southerner over the mere American, that Lee found in the youthful patrons of the Chambers Institute little likeness to her ideals. The children of her mother's old friends were educated at home or at small and very expensive schools, preparatory to a grand finish in New York and Europe. Lee had continued to meet several of these fortunate youngsters during the first two of the five years which had followed her father's death, but as she outgrew her fine clothes, and was put into ginghams for the summers and stout plaids for the winters, she was obliged to drop out of fashionable society. Occasionally she saw her former playmates sitting in their parents' carriages before some shop in Kearney Street. They always nodded gaily to her with the loyalty of their caste; the magic halo of position survives poverty, scandal and exile.

"When you are grown I shall put my pride in my pocket, and ask Mrs. Montgomery to bring you out, and Jack Belmont to give you a party dress," said Mrs. Tarleton one day. "I think you will be pretty, for your features are exactly like your father's, and you have so much expression when you are right happy, poor child! You must remember never to frown, nor wrinkle up your forehead, nor eat hot cakes, nor too much candy, and always wear your camphor bag so you won't catch anything; and *do* stand up straight, and you *must* wear a veil when these horrid trade winds blow. Beauty is the whole battle of life for a woman, honey, and if you only do grow up pretty and are properly *lancée*, you will be sure to marry well. That is all I am trying to live for."

Lee donned the veil to please her mother, although she loved to feel the wind in her hair. But she was willing to be beautiful, as beauty meant servants and the reverse of boarding-house diet. She hoped to find a husband as handsome and devoted as her father, and was quite positive that the kidney flourished within the charmed circle of society. But she sometimes regarded her sallow little visage with deep distrust. Her black hair hung in lank strands; no amount of coaxing would make it curl, and her eyes, she decided, were altogether too light a blue for beauty; her mother had saved Tarleton's small library of standard novels from the wreck, and Lee had dipped into them on rainy days; the heroine's eyes when not black " were a dark rich blue." Her eyes looked the lighter for the short thick lashes surrounding them, and the heavy brows above. She was also very thin, and stooped slightly; but the maternal eye was hopeful. Mrs. Tarleton's delicate beauty had vanished with her happiness, but while her husband lived she had preserved and made the most of it with many little arts. These she expounded at great length to her daughter, who privately thought beauty a great bore, unless ready-made and warranted to wear, and frequently permitted her mind to wander.

"At least remember this," exclaimed Mrs. Tarleton impatiently one day at the end of a homily, to which Lee had given scant heed, being absorbed in the adventurous throng below, "if you are beautiful you rule men; if you are plain, men rule you. If you are beautiful your husband is your slave, if you are plain you are his upper servant. All the brains the blue-stockings will ever pile up will not be worth one complexion. (I do hope you are not going to be a blue, honey.) Why are American women the most successful in the world? Because they know how to be beautiful. I have seen many beautiful American women who had no beauty at all. What they want they will have, and the will to be beautiful is like yeast to dough. If women are flap-jacks it is their own fault. Only cultivate a complexion, and learn how to dress and walk as if you were used to the homage of princes, and the world will call you beautiful. Above all, get a complexion."

"I will! I will!" responded Lee fervently. She pinned her veil all round her hat, squared her shoulders like a young grenadier, and went forth for air.

Although debarred from the society of her equals, she had friends of another sort. It was her private ambition at this period to keep a little shop, one half of which should be gay and fragrant with candies, the other sober and imposing with books. This ambition she wisely secluded from her aristocratic parent, but

she gratified it vicariously. Some distance up Market
Street she had discovered a book shop, scarcely wider
than its door and about eight feet deep. Its presiding
deity was a blonde young man, out-at-elbows, con-
sumptive and vague. Lee never knew his name; she
always alluded to him as " Soft-head." He never
asked hers; but he welcomed her with a slight access
of expression, and made a place for her on the
counter. There she sat and swung her legs for hours
together, confiding her ambitions and plans, and re-
capitulating her lessons for the intellectual benefit of
her host. In return he told her the histories of the
queer people who patronised him, and permitted her
to " tend shop." He thought her a prodigy, and
made her little presents of paper and coloured
pencils. Not to be under obligations, she crocheted
him a huge woollen scarf, which he assured her
greatly improved his health.

She also had a warm friend in a girl who presided
over a candy store, but her bosom friend and confidante was a pale weary-looking young woman who suddenly appeared in a secondhand book shop in lowly
Fourth Street, on the wrong side of Market. Lee was
examining the dirty and disease-haunted volumes on
the stand in front of the shop one day, when she glanced
through the window and met the eager eyes and smile
of a stranger. She entered the shop at once, and,
planting her elbows on the counter, told the newcomer
hospitably that she was delighted to welcome her to
that part of the city, and would call every afternoon if
she would be permitted to tend shop occasionally. If
the stranger was amused she did not betray herself;

she accepted the overture with every appearance of gratitude, and begged Lee to regard the premises as her own. For six months the friendship flourished. The young woman, whose name was Stainers, helped Lee with her sums, and had a keenly sympathetic ear for the troubles of little girls. Of herself she never spoke. Then she gave up her own battle, and was carried to the county hospital to die. Lee visited her twice, and one afternoon her mother told her that the notice of Miss Stainer's death had been in the newspaper that morning.

Lee wept long and heavily for the gentle friend who had carried her secrets into a pauper's grave.

"You are so young, and you have had so much trouble," said Mrs. Tarleton with a sigh, that night. "But perhaps it will give you more character than I ever had. And nothing can break your spirits. They are your grandmother's all over; you even gesticulate like her sometimes and then you look just like a little creole. She was a wonderful woman, honey, and had forty-nine offers of marriage."

"I hope men are nicer than boys," remarked Lee, not unwilling to be diverted. "The boys in this house are horrid. Bertie Reynolds pulls my hair every time I pass him, and calls me 'Squaw;' and Tom Wilson throws bread balls at me at the table and calls me 'Broken-down-aristocracy.' I'm sure *they'll* never kiss a girl's slipper."

"A few years from now some girl will be leading them round by the nose. You never can tell how a boy will turn out; it all depends upon whether girls take an interest in him or not. These are probably scrubs."

"There's a new one and he's rather shy. They say he's English. He and his father came last night. The boy's name is Cecil; I heard his father speak to him at the table to-night. The father has a funny name; I can't remember it. Mrs. Hayne says he is very *distingué*, and she's sure he's a lord in disguise, but I think he's very thin and ugly. He has the deepest lines on each side of his mouth, and a big thin nose, and a droop at the corner of his eyes. He's the stuck-uppest looking thing I ever saw. The boy is about twelve, I reckon, and looks as if he wasn't afraid of anything but girls. He has the curliest hair and the loveliest complexion, and his eyes laugh. They're hazel, and his hair is brown. He looks much nicer than any boy I ever saw."

"He is the son of a gentleman — and English gentlemen are the only ones that can compare with Southerners, honey. If you make friends with him you may bring him up here."

"Goodness gracious!" exclaimed Lee. Her mother had encouraged her to ignore boys, and disliked visitors of any kind.

"I feel sure he is going to be your next friend, and you are so lonely, honey, now that poor Miss Stainers is gone. So ask him up if you like. It makes me very sad to think that you have no playmates."

Lee climbed up on her mother's lap. Once in a great while she laid aside the dignity of her superior position in the family, and demanded a petting.

Mrs. Tarleton held her close and shut her eyes, and strove to imagine that the child in her arms was five years younger, and that both were listening for a step which so often smote her memory with agonising distinctness.

CHAPTER IV

LEE sat limply on the edge of her cot wishing she had a husband to button her boots. Mrs. Tarleton had been very ill during the night, and her daughter's brain and eyes were heavy. Lee had no desire for school, for anything but bed; but it was eight o'clock, examinations were approaching, and to school she must go. She glared resentfully at the long row of buttons, half inclined to wear her slippers, and finally compromised by fastening every third button. The rest of her toilette was accomplished with a like disregard for fashion. She was not pleased with her appearance and was disposed to regard life as a failure. At breakfast she received a severe reprimand from Mrs. Hayne, who informed her and the table inclusively that her hair looked as if it had been combed by a rake, and rebuttoned her frock there and then with no regard for the pride of eleven. Altogether, Lee, between her recent affliction, her tired head, and her wounded dignity, started for school in a very depressed frame of mind.

As she descended the long stair leading from the first floor of the boarding-house to the street she saw the English lad standing in the door. They had exchanged glances of curiosity and interest across the table, and once he had offered her radishes, with a lively blush. That morning she had decided that he must be very nice indeed, for he had turned scarlet during Mrs. Hayne's scolding and had scowled quite fiercely at the autocrat.

He did not look up nor move until she asked him to let her pass; he was apparently absorbed in the loud voluntary of Market Street, his cap on the back of his head, his hands in his pockets, his feet well apart. When Lee spoke, he turned swiftly and grabbed at her school-bag.

"You 're tired," he said, with so desperate an assumption of ease that he was brutally abrupt, and Lee jumped backward a foot.

"I beg pardon," he stammered, his eyes full of nervous tears. "But — but — you looked so tired at breakfast, and you did n't eat; I thought I 'd like to carry your books."

Lee's face beamed with delight, and its fatigue vanished, but she said primly: "You 're very good, I 'm sure, and I like boys that do things for girls."

"I don't usually," he replied hastily, as if fearful that his dignity had been compromised. "But, let 's come along. You 're late."

They walked in silence for a few moments. The lad's courage appeared exhausted, and Lee was casting about for a brilliant remark; she was the cleverest girl in her class and careful of her reputation. But her brain would not work this morning, and fearing that her new friend would bolt, she said precipitately:

"I 'm eleven. How old are you?"

"Fourteen and eleven months."

"My name 's Lee Tarleton. What 's yours?"

"Cecil Edward Basil Maundrell. I 've got two more than you have."

"Well you 're a boy, anyhow, and bigger, are n't you? I 'm named after a famous man — second cousin, General Lee. Lee was my father's mother's family name."

"Who was General Lee?"

"You 'd better study United States history."

"What for?"

The question puzzled Lee, her eagle being yet in the shell. She replied rather lamely, "Well, Southern history, because my mother says we are descended from the English, and some French. It 's the last makes us creoles."

"Oh! I 'll ask father."

"Is he a lord?" asked Lee, with deep curiosity.

"No."

The boy answered so abruptly that Lee stood still and stared at him. He had set his lips tightly; it would almost seem he feared something might leap from them.

"Oh — h — h! Your father has forbidden you to tell."

The clumsy male looked helplessly at the astute female. "He is n't a lord," he asserted doggedly.

"You are n't telling me all, though."

"Perhaps I 'm not. But," impulsively, "perhaps I will some day. I hate being locked up like a tin box with papers in it. We 've been here two weeks — at the Palace Hotel before we came to Mrs. Hayne's —

and my head fairly aches thinking of everything I say before I say it. I hate this old California. Father won't present any letters, and the boys I've met are cads. But I like you!"

"Oh, tell me!" cried Lee. Her eyes blazed and she hopped excitedly on one foot. "It's like a real story. Tell me!"

"I'll have to know you better. I must be sure I can trust you." He had all at once assumed a darkly mysterious air. "I'll walk every morning to school with you, and in the afternoons we'll sit in the drawing-room and talk."

"I never tell secrets. I know *lots !*"

"I'll wait a week."

"Well; but I think it's horrid of you. And I can't come down this afternoon; my mother is ill. But to-morrow I have a holiday, and if you like you can come up and see me at two o'clock; and you shall carry my bag every morning to school."

"Indeed!" He threw up his head like a young racehorse.

"You must,"—firmly. "Else you can't come. I'll let some other boy carry it." Lee fibbed with a qualm, but not upon barren soil had the maternal counsel fallen.

"Oh—well—I'll do it; but I ought to have offered. Girls ought not to tell boys what to do."

"My mother always told her husband and brothers and cousins to do everything she wanted, and they always did it."

"Well, I've got a grandmother and seven old maid aunts, and they never asked me to do a thing in their lives. They wait on me. They'd do anything for me."

"You ought to be ashamed of yourself. Boys were *made* to wait on girls."

"They were not. I never heard such rot."

Lee considered a moment. He was quite as aristocratic as any Southerner; there was no doubt of that. But he had been badly brought up. Her duty was plain.

"You'd be just perfect if you thought girls were more important than yourself," she said wheedlingly.

"I'll never do that," he replied stoutly.

"Then we can't be friends!"

"Oh, I say! Don't rot like that. I won't give you something I've got in my pockets, if you do."

Lee glanced swiftly at his pockets. They bulged. "Well, I won't any more to-day," she said sweetly. "What have you got for me? You *are* a nice boy."

He produced an orange and a large red apple, and offered them diffidently.

Lee accepted them promptly. "Did you really buy these for me?" she demanded, her eyes flashing above the apple. "You are the *best* boy!"

"I didn't buy them on purpose, but my father bought a box of fruit yesterday and I saved these for you. They were the biggest."

"I'm ever so much obliged."

"You're welcome," he replied, with equal concern for the formalities.

"This is my school."

"Well, I'm sorry."

"You'll come up at two to-morrow? Number 142, third floor."

"I will."

They shook hands limply. He glanced back as he walked off, whistling. Lee was standing on the steps hastily disposing of her apple. She nodded gaily to him.

CHAPTER V

THE next afternoon Lee made an elaborate toilette. She buttoned her boots properly, sewed a stiff, white ruffle in her best gingham frock, and combed every snarl out of her hair. Mrs. Tarleton, who was sitting up, regarded her with some surprise.

"It's nowhere near dinner time, honey," she said, finally. "Why are you dressing up?"

Lee blushed, but replied with an air: "I expect that little boy I told you about, to come to see me — the English one. He carried my bag to school yesterday, and gave me an apple and an orange. I've kept the orange for you when you're well. His name's Cecil Maundrell."

"Ah! Well, I hope he is a nice boy, and that you will be great friends."

"He's nice enough in his way. But he'd just walk over me if I'd let him. I can see that."

Mrs. Tarleton looked alarmed. "Don't let him bully you, darling. Englishmen are dreadfully high and mighty."

There was a faint and timid rap upon the door.

"That's him," whispered Lee. "He's afraid of me all the same."

She opened the door. Young Maundrell stood there, his cheeks burning, his hands working nervously in his pockets. He looked younger than most lads of his age, and had all that simplicity of boyhood so lacking in the precocious American youth.

"Won't you come in?" asked Lee politely.

"Oh — ah — won't you come out?"

"Come in — do," said Mrs. Tarleton. She had a very sweet voice and a heavenly smile. The boy walked forward rapidly, and took her hand, regarding her with curious intensity. Mrs. Tarleton patted his hand.

"You miss the women of your family, do you not?" she said. "I thought so. You must come and see us often. You will be always welcome."

His face was brilliant. He stammered out that he'd come every day. Then he went over to the window with Lee, and with their heads together they agreed that Mrs. Tarleton was a real angel.

But Cecil quickly tired of the subdued atmosphere, and of the crowd below. He stood up abruptly and said:

"Let's go out if your mother does n't mind. We'll take a walk."

Mrs. Tarleton looked up from her book and nodded. Lee fetched her hat and jacket, and they went forth.

"My father took me to the Cliff House one day. We'll go there," announced the Englishman.

"I was going to take you to a candy store — "

"Nasty stuff! It's a beautiful walk to the Cliff House, and there are big waves and live seals."

"Oh, I'd love to go, but I've heard it's a queer kind of a place, or something."

"I'll take care of you. Can you walk a lot?"

"Of course!"

But like all San Franciscans, she was a bad walker, and she felt very weary as they tramped along the Cliff House road. However, she was much interested in the many carriages flashing past, and too proud to confess herself unequal to the manly stride beside her. Cecil did not suit his pace to hers. He kept up a steady tramp — his back very erect, his head in the air. Lee forgot her theories, and thought him adorable. His shyness wore off by degrees, and he talked constantly, not of his family life, but of his beloved Eton, from which he appeared to have been ruthlessly torn, and of his feats at cricket. He was a champion "dry bob," he assured her proudly. Lee was deeply interested, but would have liked to talk about herself a little. He did not ask her a question; he was charmed with her sympathy, and confided his school troubles, piling up the agony, as her eyes softened and flashed. When she capped an anecdote of martyrdom with one from her own experience, he listened politely, but when she finished, hastened on with his own reminiscences, not pausing to comment. Lee experienced a slight chill, and the spring day seemed less brilliant, the people in the carriages less fair. But she was a child, the impression quickly passed, and her interest surrendered once more.

"We'll be there in two minutes," said Cecil. "Then we'll have a cup of tea."

"My mother does n't let me drink tea or coffee. She hopes I'll have a complexion some day and be pretty."

She longed for the masculine assurance that her beauty was a foregone conclusion, but Cecil replied:

"Oh! the idea of bothering about complexion. I like you because you're not silly like other girls. You've got a lot of sense — just like a boy. Of course you mustn't disobey your mother, but you must have something after that walk. You've got a lot of pluck, but I can see you're blown a bit. Would she mind if you had a glass of wine? I've got ten dollars. My stepmother sent them to me."

"My! — I don't think she'd mind about the wine. I've never tasted it. Oh, goodness!"

They had mounted one of the rocks, and faced the ocean. Lee had thought the bay, girt with its colourous hills very beautiful, as they had trudged along the cliffs, but she had had glimpses of it many times from the heights of San Francisco. She had never seen the ocean before. Its roar thrilled her nerves, and the great green waves, rolling in with magnificent precision from the grey plain beyond, to leap abruptly over the outlying rocks, their spray glittering in the sunlight like a crust of jewels, filled her brain with new and inexpressible sensations. She turned suddenly to Cecil. His eyes met hers with deep impersonal sympathy; their souls mingled on the common ground of nervous exaltation. He moved closer to her and took her hand.

"That's the reason I wanted to come again," he said. "I love it."

The words shook his nerves down, and he added: "But let's go and freshen up."

She followed him up the rocks to the little shabby building set into the cliff and overhanging the waves. She knew nothing of its secrets; no suspicion crossed her innocent mind that if its walls could speak, San Francisco, highly seasoned as it was, would shake to its roots, and heap up its record of suicide and divorce; but she wondered why two women, who came out and passed her hurriedly, were so heavily veiled, and why others, sitting in the large restaurant, had such queer-looking cheeks and eyes. Some inherited instinct forbade her to comment to Cecil, who did not give the women a glance. He led her to a little table at the end of the piazza, and ordered claret and water, tea, and a heaping plate of bread and butter.

It was some time before they were served, and they gazed delightedly at a big ship going out, and wished they were on it; at the glory of colour on the hills opposite; and at the seals chattering on the rocks below.

"It's heavenly, perfectly heavenly," sighed Lee. " I never had such a good time in all my life."

She forgot her complexion and took off her hat. The salt breeze stung the blood into her cheeks, and her eyes danced with joy.

The waiter brought the little repast. The children sipped and nibbled and chattered. Cecil scarcely took his eyes off the water. He and his father went off on sailing and fishing excursions every summer, he told Lee, and he was so keen on the water that it had taken him fully three months after he entered Eton to decide whether he would be a "wet bob," or a "dry bob." Cricket had triumphed, because he loved to feel his heels fly.

Lee gave him a divided attention: her brain was fairly dancing, and seemed ready to fly off in several different directions at once. "Oh!" she cried suddenly, "I'm not a bit tired any more. I feel as if I could walk miles and miles. Let's have an adventure. Would n't it be just glorious if we could have an adventure?"

The boy's eyes flashed. "Oh, *would* you. I've been thinking about it — but you're a girl. But you're such a jolly sort! We'll get one of those fishing-boats to take us out to sea, and climb up and down those big waves. Oh, fancy! I say! — will you?"

"Oh, won't I? Youbetcherlife I will."

Cecil paid his reckoning, and the children scrambled along the rocks to a cove where a fishing smack was making ready for sea. Lee wondered why her feet glanced off the rocks in such a peculiar fashion, but she was filled with the joy of exhilaration, of a reckless delight in doing something of which the entire Hayne boarding-house would disapprove.

Cecil made a rapid bargain with the man, an ugly Italian, who gave him scant attention. A few moments later they were skimming up and down the big waves and making for the open sea. At first Lee clung in terror to Cecil, who assured her patronisingly that it was an old story with him, and there was no danger. In a few moments the exhilaration returned five-fold, and she waved her arms with delight as they shot down the billows into the emerald valleys. Out

at sea the boat skimmed along an almost level surface, and the children became absorbed in the big fish
nets, and very dirty.   Lee thought the flopping fish
nasty and drew up her feet, but Cecil's very nostrils
quivered with the delight of the sport, although his
surly hosts had snubbed his offer to lend a hand.

Suddenly Lee rubbed her eyes.   The sun had gone.
He had been well above the horizon the last time she
had glanced across the waters.   Had he slipped his
moorings?   She pointed out the phenomenon to
Cecil.   He stared a moment, then appealed to the
Italians.

" Da fogga, by damn ! " exclaimed the Captain to
his mate.   " What for he coming so soon?   Com
abouta."

The little craft turned and raced with the breeze
for land.   The children faced about and watched that
soft stealthy curtain swing after.   It was as white as
cloud, as chill as dawn, as eerie as sound in the night.
It took on varying outlines, breaking into crags and
mountain peaks and turrets.   It opened once and
caught a wedge of scarlet from the irate sun.   For a
moment a ribbon of flame ran up and down its length,
then broke into drops of blood, then hurried whence
it came.   Through the fog mountain came a long dismal moan, the fog-horn of the Farallones, warning
the ships at sea.

The children crept close together.   Lee locked her
arm in Cecil's.   Neither spoke.   Suddenly the boat
jolted heavily and they scrambled about, thinking
they were on the rocks.   But the Italians were tying
the boat to a little wharf, and unreefing her.   The

dock was strangely unfamiliar. Cecil glanced hastily across the bay. San Francisco lay opposite.

"Oh, I say!" he exclaimed. "Are n't you going across before that fog gets here?"

"Si you wanta crossa that bay you swimming," remarked the Captain, stepping ashore.

Cecil jumped after him with blazing eyes and angry fists. "You know I thought you were going back there," he cried. "Why, you're a villain! And a girl too! I'll have you arrested."

The man laughed. Cecil, through tears of mortification, regarded that large bulk, and choked back his wrath.

"My father will pay you well if you take us back," he managed to articulate.

"No crossa that bay to-night," replied the man.

"But how are we to get back?"

"Si you walka three, four, five miles — no can remember — you finda one ferra-boat." And he sauntered away.

Cecil returned to the boat and helped Lee to land. "I 'm awfully sorry," he said. "What a beastly mess I 've got you into!"

"Oh, never mind," said Lee cheerfully. "I reckon I can walk."

"You *are* a jolly sort. Come on then." But his brow was set in gloom.

Lee took his hand. "You looked just splendid when you talked to that horrid man," she said. "I am sure he was afraid of you!"

Cecil's brow shot forth the nimbus of the conqueror.

"Lee," he said in a tone of profound conviction,

"you have more sense than all the rest of the girls in the world put together. Come on and I'll help you along."

They climbed the bluff. When they reached the top the world was white and impalpable about them.

Cecil drew Lee's hand through his arm. "Never mind," he said, "I think I have a good bump of locality, and one can see a little way ahead."

Lee leaned heavily on his arm. "I can't think why I feel so sleepy," she murmured. "I never am at this time of day."

"Oh, for mercy's sake don't go to sleep. Let's run."

They ran headlong until they were out of breath. Then they stopped and gazed into the fog ahead of them. Tall dark objects loomed there. They seemed to touch the unseen stars, and they were black even in that gracious mist.

"They're trees. They're redwoods," said Cecil. "I know where we are now — at least I think I do. Father and I came over to this side one day and drove about. It's a regular forest. I do hope —— " He glanced uneasily about. "It's too bad we can't walk along the edge of the cliffs. But if we keep straight ahead I suppose it'll be all right."

They trudged on. The forest closed about them. Those dark rigid shafts that no storm ever bends, no earthquake ever sways, whom the fog feeds and the trade winds love, looked like the phantasm of themselves in the pale hereafter. The scented underbush and infant redwoods grew high above the heads of the children, and there were a hundred paths. The roar of the sea grew faint.

Lee gave a gasping yawn and staggered. "Oh, Cecil," she whispered, "I'm asleep. I can't go another step."

Cecil was also weary, and very much discouraged. He sat down against a tree and took Lee in his arms. She was asleep in a moment, her head comfortably nestled into his shoulder.

He was a brave boy, but during the two hours that Lee slept his nerves were sorely tried. High up, in the unseen arbours of the redwoods, there was a faint incessant whisper: the sibilant tongues of moisture among the brittle leaves. From an immeasurable distance came the long, low, incessant moan of the Farallones' "syren." There was no other sound. If there were four-footed creatures in the forest they slept. Just as Cecil's teeth began to chatter, whether from cold or fear he did not care to scan, Lee moved.

"Are you awake?" he asked eagerly.

Lee sprang to her feet. "I did n't know where I was for a minute. Let's hurry as fast as we can. Memmy will be wild — she might be dreadfully ill with fright ——"

"And father's got all the policemen in town out after me," said Cecil gloomily. "We can't hurry or we'll run into trees; but we can go on." In a few minutes he exclaimed: "I say! We're going up hill, and it's jolly steep too."

"Well?"

"That Italian did n't say anything about hills."

"Then I suppose we're lost again," said Lee, with that resignation so exasperating to man.

"Well, if we are I don't see who's to help it in the fog at night in a forest. Perhaps the ferry is over the hill, and as this is the only path we'll have to go on."

"I wouldn't mind the hill being perpendicular if memmy was at the top."

Cecil softened at once. "Don't you worry; we'll get there soon. I'll get behind and push you."

They toiled and panted up the hill, which grew into a mountain. The forest dropped behind and a low dense shrubbery surrounded them. They were obliged to rest many times, and once they ate a half dozen crackers Lee found in her pocket and were hungrier thereafter. But they forebore to discourse upon their various afflictions; in fact, they barely spoke at all. Their clothes were torn, their hats lost, their hands and faces scratched. When they paused to rest and the vague disturbances of night smote their ears, they clung together and were glad to hasten on. Lee longed to cry, but panted to be a heroine in Cecil's eyes, and win the sweets of masculine approval; and Cecil, whose depression was even more profound, never forgot that the glory of the male is to be invincible in the eyes of the female. So did the vanity of sex mitigate the terrors of night and desolation and the things that devour.

The fog was far below them, an ocean of froth, pierced by the black tips of the redwoods. On either side the children could see nothing but the great shoulders of the mountain. They seemed climbing to the vast cold glitter above.

Gradually they left the brush, and their way fell among stones, rocks, and huge boulders. Not a shrub grew here, not a blade of grass. They climbed on for a time, they reached level ground, then the point of descent. They could see nothing but rocks, brush, and an ocean of fog. Their courage took note of its limitations.

"I'm not going to cry," said Lee sharply. "But I think we'd better talk till the sun gets up and that fog melts. Besides, if we talk we won't feel so hungry. Tell me that thing about yourself—your father—I suppose you can trust me now?"

"We're friends for life, and I like you better than my chum. You're a brick. Hold up your right hand and swear that you'll never tell."

Lee took the required oath, and the two battered travellers made themselves as comfortable as they could in the hollow of an upright rock.

"There ain't so much to tell. My father and my stepmother don't hit it off—quarrel all the time. But my stepmother has the money and is awfully keen on me, so they live together usually. Besides, until two years ago my stepmother thought she'd be a bigger somebody, and my father thought he'd have money of his own one day because his uncle was old and had never married. But Uncle Basil— I'm named for him—married two years ago and his wife got a little chap right off. So that knocked my father out, and my stepmother was just like a hornet. I love her, and she's seldom been nasty to me, but I *have* seen her so that when you spoke to her she'd scream at you; and when she's in a real nasty temper I always go out. Once I got mad because she was abusing Uncle Basil — I always spent my vacations at Maundrell Abbey, and he was good to me and gave me a gun and lots of tips — and I told her she was nasty to abuse him and I shouldn't like her unless she stopped. Then she cried and kissed me — she's great on kissing — and said she loved me better than any one in the world, and would do anything I wanted. Did I tell you she is an American? My father says the Americans are very excitable, and my stepmother is, and no mistake. But she dotes on me — I suppose because she hasn't any children of her own, and no one else to dote on, for that matter; so I like her, whatever she does.

"One day, she and my father got into a terrible rage. I was in the room, but they didn't pay any attention to me. Father wanted a lot of money, and she wouldn't give it to him. She said he could ask his mother to pay his gambling debts. (Granny has money and is going to leave me some of it.) He said he'd asked her and she wouldn't. Granny and father don't hit it off, either, only granny never quarrels with anybody. Then my stepmother — her first name's Emily and I call her Emmy — called him dreadful names, and said she'd leave him that minute if it wasn't for me. And my father said she was the greatest snob in London and had gone off her head because she'd lost her hopes of a title. Then he said he'd get even with her; he couldn't stay in London any longer, so he'd go as far away from her as he could get and then she'd see what her position amounted to without him. 'You're an outsider — you're on sufferance,' he said, and he went out and banged the door. She went off into hysterics, but she didn't think he'd do it. He did though. He bolted the next day, and took me with him to spite her and granny. He's always been decent to me, so I wouldn't mind, only I'd rather be at Eton. He came here because it wouldn't cost him much to live, and he's keen on sport and knows some Englishmen that have ranches. He hopes Emmy'll repent, but she hasn't written him a line. She wrote to me, and sent me two pounds, but she never mentioned his name."

"Goodness, gracious!" exclaimed Lee. She was deeply disappointed at this unromantic chronicle. And it gave all her preconceived ideas of matrimony an ugly jar. "My papa and mamma were just devoted to each other," she said. "It must be terrible not to be."

"Oh, I expect people get used to it. And there are a lot of other things to think about. My step-mother has a very jolly time, and father doesn't come home very much when we are in London; and in the autumn we have a lot of people in the house —Emmy rents a place in Hampshire."

"Then your father isn't a lord?"

"No; Uncle Basil is."

The lord in the family was the only redeeming feature of this sordid story; he gave it one fiery touch of the picturesque. Suddenly she forgot her disappointment, and patted Cecil's scratched and grimy fingers.

"You have n't been a bit happy, like other little boys, have you?" she said, "and you are so kind and good. I'm sorry, and I wish you could live with memmy and me."

That Cecil loved sympathy there could be no manner of doubt. He expanded at once upon the painful subject, consigning the devotion of his granny, his seven aunts, his stepmother, the kindness of his uncle, and his unfettered summers, to oblivion. He could not see Lee's face in the shadow of the rock, but he felt the tensity of her mind, concentrated on himself. They forgot their anxious parents, the dark clinging night, the awful silence, hunger and fatigue. Lee forgot all but Cecil; Cecil forgot all but himself. When he had exhausted his resources, Lee cried:

"I'll always like you better than any one else in the whole world except memmy! I know I will! I swear I will!"

"Could n't you like me better than your mother?" he asked jealously.

Lee hesitated. Her youthful bosom was agitated by conflicting emotions. Feminine subtlety dictated her answer.

"I can't tell yet. When I'm a big grown-up person I'll decide."

"What's the use of doing anything by halves? I don't. I like you better than anybody."

"I'll have to wait," firmly.

"Oh, very well," he said crossly. "Of course, if

I knew some boys here, it would n't matter so much."

"Then if you had boys to play with you would n't love me? Oh, you unkind *cruel* boy!"

"No — you know what I mean; I'd like you just the same, but I should n't need you so much. There's nothing to get angry about — Now? — What? — Oh!"

For Lee was weeping bitterly.

Cecil suddenly remembered that he was cold, and hungry, and tired, and lost. And he was confronted with a scene. What Lee was crying about he had but a vague idea. For a moment he contemplated a hug, — on general principles, — but remembered in time that when his father attempted cajolement his stepmother always wept the louder. So he remarked with the nervous haste of man when he knows that he is not rising to the occasion:

"We'll stay here till morning and then I'll take your apron off and put it on the top of a long stick and somebody'll be sure to see. It's exactly like being shipwrecked."

"I never was shipwrecked," sobbed Lee; "I'm sure I should n't like it."

"We've had adventures, anyhow, and that's what you wanted."

"I don't like adventures. They're not very interesting, and I'm all scratched up, and hungry, and tired."

"We've not been attacked by a bear. You ought to be thankful for that."

Lee, who would have been comforted at once by

the hug, arose with dignity, found a soft spot and composed herself to sleep, forlorn and dejected. Cecil haughtily extended himself where he was. But he, too, was sensible of a weight on his spirits, which hunger, nor fatigue, nor cold, nor straits, had rolled there. In a few moments he took off his jacket and went over to Lee and slipped it under her head. She whisked about and caught his head in her arms, and they were fast asleep in an instant.

CHAPTER VI

LEE awoke first. She remembered at once where she was, and sat up with a sense of terror she had not experienced in the darkness of the night. The fog was gone, the sun was well above the horizon. She and Cecil were alone on a mountain peak so high above the world that the blue depths of space seemed nigher than the planet below. The redwood forest at the foot of the mountain looked like brush; on a glassy pond were hundreds of toy boats; beyond was a toy city on toy hills. Far to the South another solitary peak lifted itself into the heavens, dwarfing the mountain ranges about it. Lee glanced to the left. Nothing there but peak after peak bristling away into the north, black and rigid with redwoods.

But it was not the stupendous isolation that terrified Lee. It was a vague menace in the atmosphere about her, an accentuated stillness. Over the scene was a grey web, so delicate, so transparent, that it concealed nothing. Lee rubbed her eyes to make sure it was really there. It might have been the malignant breath of the evil genius of California. As she gazed, the mist slowly cohered. It became an almost tangible veil through which San Francisco looked the phantom of a city long since sunken to the bed of the Pacific. The sun glared through it like the suspended crater of an angry volcano. The forests on the mountain all at once seemed dead. The very air was petrified. The silence was awful, appalling.

Lee caught Cecil by the shoulder and pulled him upright.

"Something terrible is going to happen," she gasped. "Oh, I wish we were home! I wish we were home."

Cecil rubbed his eyes. He barely grasped the meaning of her words. There was a dull muffled roar, which seemed to spring from the depths of the planet, a terrible straining and rocking, and the very heart of the mountain leaped under them.

Cecil saw Lee make a wild dart to the left. Then he was conscious of nothing but a rapid descent amidst a hideous clatter of rock, and the sensation that he was sliding from the surface of the earth into space. Down he went, down, down, with the rumble below and the roar of loosened earth and rock about him. Inside of him he fancied he could hear the icicles of his blood rattle against each other. In his skull was a horrible vacuum.

The slide stopped abruptly. Cecil looked dully about him, wondering why the still trembling rocks had not ground him to pulp. He stumbled to his feet mechanically, worked his way beyond the slide, then climbed toward the cone from which he had been so abruptly evicted. His knowledge of what he sought was very vague, a primal instinct. Presently he saw Lee running toward him. Behind her was a man in the rough garb of a mountaineer.

"It was an earthquake," cried Lee, as she flung herself into Cecil's arms, "and he's going to take us home."

CHAPTER VII

BETWEEN a night of maternal agonies and an earthquake which wrenched the city to its foundations, Mrs. Tarleton's spirit was very nearly shaken out of her frail body.

Mr. Maundrell, after despatching two detectives in search of the truants, spent the greater part of the night pacing up and down the upper hall. He called upon Mrs. Tarleton late in the evening, and assured her that his son was a manly little chap, and would take good care of Lee. As the night waxed he called again. Miss Hayne was holding salts to the invalid's nostrils, and fanning her. Mrs. Tarleton implored him to remain near her; he was so cool he gave her a little courage. He consented hastily and retreated. When the earthquake came he entered Mrs. Tarleton's room unceremoniously and stood by her bed, throwing a shawl over her head to protect it from falling plaster. The chandelier leapt from side to side like a circus girl at the end of a rope, then came down with a crash which drew an exhausted shriek from the bed. The wardrobe walked out into the middle of the room, the pictures sprang from the walls. Mrs. Tarleton, stifled, flung the shawl from her head. Mr. Maundrell stood, imperturbable, beside her, a monocle in his eye, critically regarding the evidences of California's iniquity. She began to laugh hysterically, and he fled from the room and begged Miss Hayne — who had rushed out shrieking — to return.

He went down to his own rooms. It was eight o'clock in the morning. People in various stages of undress were grouped in the halls volubly giving their experiences. Not a woman but Mrs. Hayne had a dress on, not a woman had her hair out of curl-papers. The men had paused long enough to fling on dressing-gowns and blankets. They were visibly embarrassed.

Three hours later Mr. Maundrell was in his sitting-room reading an earthquake " extra." The door opened and a small boy, with a cold in his head, dirty, ragged, scratched, and apologetic, entered and awaited his doom. Mr. Maundrell glanced up. Cecil shivered.

" Go and take a bath," said his father curtly. " You are positively sickening. And kindly do not bore me with your adventures. I have really had as much as I can stand."

CHAPTER VIII

LEE went neither to school nor to her meals for a week. She nursed her mother with the ardour of maternal affection and remorse. For the first two days Cecil dared not approach that door; it seemed written large with his misdoings. On the third he knocked timidly, then put his hands behind him.

Lee opened the door, threw back her head, and half closed her eyes — to conceal the delight in them.

"Well," she said freezingly. "I am glad to see you have n't forgotten all about me — I am sure I am!"

Cecil attempted no apology. He produced a bag of candy, and an apple nearly as big as his head.

"I thought you 'd like these as you could n't go out to get any," he said with tact.

Lee almost closed her eyes. She drew back. "You are so kind!" she said sarcastically.

Cecil must have had great ancestors. He replied never a word. He stood with both arms outstretched, the tempting offerings well within the door, and under Lee's very nose.

Her eyes slowly opened. The corners of her mouth invaded her cheeks. Her hands rose slowly, fluttered a moment, then closed firmly over the tributes to her sex.

"Won't you come in?" she asked graciously.

Cecil promptly closed the door behind him.

"I'm coming every afternoon to take care of your mother," he announced.

"The idea of a boy being a nurse," said Lee disdainfully; but she brought her lashes together again.

"You go and take a nap. Which medicine does she take next?"

Lee allowed herself to be overborne, and fell asleep. Mrs. Tarleton opened her eyes suddenly to meet a hypnotic stare. Cecil did nothing by halves.

Mrs. Tarleton smiled faintly, then put out her hand and patted his.

"You are a good boy, Cecil," she said.

The good boy reddened haughtily. I'm not trying to be thought a milksop," he remarked.

"Oh, I know, I know! I mean most boys are selfish. I knew you would bring Lee safely back."

"I wouldn't mind if you said you forgave me."

"I do. I do. Only please don't do it again."

He gave her the medicine. She closed her eyes, but he saw that she did not sleep. Occasionally she frowned and sighed heavily. Finally she opened her eyes again.

"I wish you were a little older," she said abruptly.

He sat up very straight. "I'm quite old," he said thickly. "I'm much older than Lee."

"I mean I wish you were really grown and your own master, and as fond of Lee as you are now. I must die soon; I had hoped to live until Lee was grown and married, but my will won't last me much longer. It is of that I think constantly as I lie here, not of my pain."

"I 'll marry Lee if you like," said Cecil obligingly. "I like her very much; it would suit me jolly well to have her in England."

Mrs. Tarleton raised herself on her arm. Her thin cheeks fairly expanded with the colour that flew to them. The boy could see the fluttering of her exhausted heart.

"Cecil," she said solemnly, "promise me that you will marry Lee. I am a good judge of human nature. I know that you would be kind to her. I know of no one else to leave her to. Promise me."

"I promise," said Cecil promptly. But he had an odd sensation that the room had grown suddenly smaller.

"If I die before you go, take her with you if your father will consent. She has a little money and will not be a burden. If your father won't take her come back for her when you are of age. Remember that you have given your solemn promise to a dying woman."

"Yes, ma'am," said Cecil faintly. He was young and masculine and analytical; but instinct told him that Mrs. Tarleton was unfair, and he cooled to her, and to the sex through her, for the time being. He slipped out as Lee awoke.

The next day when he returned, the unpleasant sensations induced by Mrs. Tarleton had almost vanished. On the fourth day, as he and Lee were sitting before the fire popping corn — Mrs. Tarleton's nerves being under the influence of morphine — Lee remarked with some asperity:

"I wish you would n't stare at me so."

"I was just thinking," he said. "I am going to be your husband, you know."

"What?" Lee dropped the popper into the fire. Her head went back, her nostrils out. "Who said you were, I'd like to know? *I* did n't."

"Your mother asked me to marry you, and I said I would. So I'm going to."

The American girl arose in her wrath, and stamped her foot.

"The very idea! Try it, will you? The idea, the *idea* of saying you're going to marry a girl just 'cause you want to! — without *asking* her! I just won't marry you — so there!"

Young Maundrell rose to his feet, plunged his hands into his pockets and regarded her with angry perplexity. He knew what he would have done had she been a boy; he would have thrashed her. But a girl was a deeper problem than earthquakes. He descended to diplomacy.

"Of course I'll ask you if you prefer it that way."

"You just bet your life I do."

"Well —" He got very red and trembled all over. He threw his weight first on one foot and then on the other. His nails clawed at his trousers pockets.

"Well?"

"Oh — ah — that is — you can marry me, if you

like — Oh, hang it, Lee! I don't know how to propose. I feel like a rotter."

"That is n't the way," said Lee icily. She hastily reviewed her glimpses of standard works.

"You must go down on your knees," she added.

"I 'd see myself dead sooner," cried Cecil.

"You must."

"I won't."

"Then I won't marry you."

"I don't care whether you do or not."

"But you promised!"

"I 'm not going to be an ass if I did."

Said Lee sweetly: "I don't much care about the going down on the knees part. I 'm afraid I 'd laugh. Just say, ' Will you marry me? ' "

He sulkily repeated the formula.

"Now we 're engaged," said Lee complacently; "and the popper 's burnt up. But we 've got a lot popped, and I 'll make a syrup and stick some together into a nice ball for you. It 's lovely to eat when you 're in bed." She leaned forward and adjusted his agitated necktie. "You look as if you just owned the whole world when you get mad," she said.

And the male ate his sweets and was pacified.

CHAPTER IX

THE tide in Mrs. Tarleton rose once more; on Monday she was able to sit up, and Cecil took Lee for a walk; but returned betimes, having received a brief parental admonition that if he did not, he'd be caned. After that, they explored Market Street every afternoon, and on Sunday trotted off to church together.

On the following afternoon, as Lee was walking down the hill from school, she saw an excited group of boys in the street, before the side entrance of Mrs. Hayne's boarding-house. As she approached, she inferred that two were fighting, as some eight or ten others were cheering and betting.

Lee raised herself on tiptoe and looked over the shoulder of a short boy. The belligerents were Bertie Reynolds and Cecil Maundrell. Her first impulse was to scream — an impulse which she quickly repressed. Her second was to cheer Cecil. This she also repressed, remembering that she was a girl, or, as her mother would have put it, a Southerner.

She mounted a box and watched the battle, her hands clenched, her eyes blazing, her heart sick; for her Cecil was getting the worst of it. He looked as sturdy as a little oak, and he planted his blows scientifically; but his antagonist was twice his size, lean and wiry, and full of nervous fire. Moreover, the surrounding influences were all for the American: Cecil was not only English, but he had snubbed these boys of Mrs. Hayne's boarding-house for three consecutive weeks. Vengeance had been in the air for some time.

The boys fought like young savages. Their faces made Lee shudder and ponder. But that impression passed, for there was worse to come. Cecil got a huge lump over his right eye. Cecil got a damaged nose. Cecil's immaculate shirt turned an angry scarlet. Cecil got a blow under his jaw, and went down.

Then was Lee's opportunity. She leaped from the box, straight into the ring — which was giving unearthly cat-calls — and took Cecil's head in her arms.

'You just help me carry him inside, you horrid, hateful bully," she commanded young Reynolds. "Take his feet — there!"

The national instinct prompted obedience, and Cecil was safely deposited on the lower step of the side entrance, Reynolds retiring in haste before the concentrated fury in Lee's eyes and teeth and nails. She gathered Cecil into her bosom, and wept bitterly.

"I say!" murmured the wounded hero. "Don't cry! I'm all right. I've got a beastly headache, that's all."

"'Those loathsome boys!" sobbed Lee.

"Well, they know I can fight, if I didn't beat."

But his voice was thick, and there was no pride about him anywhere.

Lee's tears finished, and were succeeded by curiosity.

"What did you fight about?" she asked, drying her eyes on her ensanguined pinafore.

"They all said the United States licked England twice, and I said it did n't. They said I did n't know history, and I — well, I told them they were liars, and that Reynolds offered to fight for the crowd, and we fought."

"Don't get excited," said Lee soothingly. "Do you think you can walk up to your room? You 'll feel better if you lie down, and I can do a lot of things for you."

He got to his feet, climbed wearily to his room, and flung himself on the bed. Lee was in her element. She sponged him off, and fetched ice, and bound up his damaged face. She felt his nose to see if it was broken. It was swelling rapidly, and he shrieked as she prodded it. Lee wished that she did not feel a disposition to laugh, but her hero certainly looked funny. When she had bound two compresses about his face — his upper lip was also cut — she closed the inside blinds, and sat down beside the bed. It was her duty to go to her mother, but she was loath to leave her comrade.

"Lee," said a stifled voice, "pull off my boots."

Lee rose, hesitated a moment, then removed the boots, and threw his jacket over his feet. She walked to the window, peered through the slats, then returned to the bed.

"The United States did lick England," she said.
Cecil was on his elbow in an instant.

"It did not," he cried hoarsely. "If you were a boy I 'd thrash you."

"I finished United States history last term. We licked you in the Revolution and in 1812."

Cecil was erect on the edge of his bed, glaring at her out of his attenuated eye, over the rising sun of his nose. "I tell you you did n't," he growled. And his bandages slipped, and his wounds bled.

Lee flung her arms about him in an agony of remorse and pushed him back among the pillows.

"I 'm just horrid," she sobbed; "I don't know why I said that." And once more she bathed and bound him.

"Lee," whispered a weary voice. "Say that you did n't lick us."

Lee gave him a little hug. "Of course not," she said, as to a sick child; "of course not."

CHAPTER X

IT was something over a week later that Lee awoke suddenly in the night and sat erect, with stiffened muscles. Her skin was chilled as if her sleeping body had been caught in a current of night air. A taper burned in a cup of oil. She glanced towards the door. It was closed. Her cot was in a corner, out of the reach of window draughts. Her shoulders approached each other. Something was certainly wrong, quite different from the usual routine of night. The taper faintly illumined the large room over which her expanding eyes roved. A red light flashed across the wall like a scythe, accompanied by the dull grumble of the cable car. Everything in the room was as she had arranged or left it for the night. Even the flannel petticoat Mrs. Tarleton had been embroidering for her daughter was on the table where she had dropped it. The needle stood up straight and focussed a beam of light. It was the same commonplace comfortable room, with whose every feature Lee was intimate; yet over these features to-night rested a thin film of something unfamiliar.

Lee gave way to unreasoning terror. " Memmy ! " she called, " memmy ! "

Mrs. Tarleton was a light sleeper, but she did not answer.

Lee sprang to the floor and ran towards her mother's bed. She paused within a foot of it, her knees jerking. Mrs. Tarleton lay on her side, her face to the wall, her arm along the counterpane. In both arm and hand was the same suggestion of unreality, of change, as in the room.

Lee fled out into the hall and down the stairs to Cecil's room. His door was unlocked. He awakened to find himself standing on his feet, striking out furiously.

"It's only me," gasped Lee, who had received a smart blow in the shoulder. "Something's the matter with memmy. Come quick."

"All right, I will. You stay here and I'll go into father's room and dress."

He lifted Lee to the bed and went into the next room. Mr. Maundrell entered a moment later and lit the gas. He looked keenly at Lee's scared white face, then went out by the hall door. He did not return for some little time. When he did he met his son and Lee — who was enveloped in Cecil's overcoat — ascending the stairs. He turned them back.

"Mrs. and Miss Hayne are with your mother," he said. "Get into Cecil's bed and go to sleep. I will take him in with me."

"I never leave memmy to other people," faltered Lee; and then she put her hands to her ears, and shuddered, and crouched against Cecil. "I can't sleep," she gasped. "Don't leave me alone."

"Very well," said Mr. Maundrell hastily. "You go into the sitting-room, both of you. Cecil, you had better make her a cup of tea."

Cecil half carried Lee into the sitting-room, put her on the sofa, lit all the burners, and fell to making tea with nervous fingers and every sign of deep embarrassment. When he had finished he walked rapidly over to Lee, jerked her upright, and held the cup to her lips.

" Drink it ! " he said in his most peremptory manner. Lee gulped it down. Cecil returned to the table, drank a large measure, then went back to Lee and put his arms about her.

" Now," he said with an effort which brought his brows together and sent the blood to his hair, " you can cry if you like."

Lee promptly buried her head in his bosom and wept wildly, with abrupt and terrible insight. Cecil could think of nothing to say, but he gathered her in and gave her little spasmodic hugs. He felt very much like crying himself, and at the same time wished with all his heart that it were three days later. He concluded that a girl must get all cried out in that time.

CHAPTER XI

ALL of Mrs. Tarleton's old friends sent flowers, and many of them attended the funeral service, which took place in the death chamber. Mrs. Hayne had decided that a church funeral would be too expensive, and her boarders would have objected to the association of a coffin with the back parlour. Lee, holding Cecil's hand tightly, sat in a corner, looking smaller and darker than ever in her black frock, the novelty of which had mitigated her grief for the moment. All of the ladies kissed her and told her that she must be sure to come to see them; and Mrs. Montgomery, who had just returned from Europe, and was very much agitated, asked her to come home with her at once. But Lee only shook her head. She and Cecil had other plans.

Her cot was taken into Miss Hayne's room and she went to school as usual. Her grief waxed rather than waned, and she stooped so that Mrs. Hayne put her into braces, which confirmed her gloomy views of life. But her woman's instincts were very keen, and she knew that if she was to have the solace of Cecil's companionship, she must reserve her tears for solitude. He was very kind, and informed her that he loved her the better because she had such a jolly lot of grit and kept her back up (Lee had not mentioned the braces), and that his father — who hated Americans — had condescended to say that Lee was a jolly little thing, and had more character and good sense at the age of eleven than his own selection had accumulated in five-and-thirty years.

She and Cecil took many long walks, and rode back and forth on the Oakland and Sausalito boats, munching molasses candy; Cecil was rapidly falling a victim to the national vice. One day the father and son took her to the country on a fishing expedition. It was a very long day, and it was very hot. She sat on the bank and watched the others fish. Their concentration amounted to genius, and except at luncheon, which she prepared, they never addressed a word to her. She had never seen Mr. Maundrell look so happy, and as for Cecil, his hazel eyes sparkled like champagne. In spite of the blue sky, the warm sunshine, the beautiful depths of the red-wood forest, the singing stream, she felt lonely and depressed, and went home with a sun-burned nose, and a heart full of those obscure forebodings which assail woman when man forgets the lesson of civilisation and pays a brief and joyous visit to the plane of his sovereign ancestors.

CHAPTER XII

IT was about a month after Mrs. Tarleton's death that Cecil kicked Lee under the breakfast-table and jerked his eyebrows at his father, who sat opposite. Mr. Maundrell was reading his English mail. His pale face was flushed. His impassive features threatened a change of expression.

That afternoon, as Lee was returning from school, Cecil met her half way up the hill.

"My uncle Basil and the little chap are dead, and father's the heir," he announced.

"Is he a lord?" cried Lee, with bated breath.

"Yes."

Lee's eyes danced. Romance revived. Care fled.

"A duke?"

"No, an earl."

"Earl's much prettier than duke. I mean a prettier word."

"He's got a title of course. He's Lord Barnstaple."

"That's not so pretty."

"I——" Cecil thrust his hands into his pockets and turned very red. "I don't mind telling you — I've got a title too — what they call a courtesy title. You see my father's the Earl of Barnstaple and Viscount Maundrell. So I'm Lord Maundrell. I should n't think of mentioning it to any one else," he added hastily.

"Cecil!" Lee waved her arms wildly and danced up and down. "I never *heard* of anything so lovely. I feel exactly as if we were inside Scott or Shakespeare or something. Shall you wear a crown and an ermine robe?"

"I 'm not a king," said Cecil loftily. "Talk about *my* not knowing anything about United States history! You Americans are so funny. Fancy you caring so much about such things." His tone was almost his father's upon occasion.

"Why not? The idea! I think it 's perfectly romantic and lovely to be lords and ladies. Whole shelves full of books have been written about them — the standard works of fiction, that everybody reads. And plays, and ballads, and poems, and pictures too! I 've often heard my mother talk about it, and I used to read the descriptions out loud to her in the winter — she said it would form my taste for elegant literature. I could just see the whole thing — the kings and dukes, and the beautiful processions, and the castles and tournaments, and princesses and falcons. Oh my! Of course I care. I 'd be a silly little ninny if I did n't care. I just wish I 'd been born like all that. I 'm sure there 's nothing very romantic about San Francisco — particularly Market Street."

"Well," said Cecil, bringing down his eyebrows and consenting to establish himself at Lee's view point. "You 're going to be ' like that.' You 're going to marry me."

Lee stopped short, her mouth open. "So I am," she gasped. "So I am. Could we be married right off, do you think?"

Cecil dropped his head and shook it gloomily. "I had a talk with father to-day;" he shivered as he recalled that conversation; "and he says he won't take you back with us; that he likes you well enough, but one American in the family is as much as he can stand — and, oh, a lot of rot. We'll have to wait till I grow up, and then I'll come back for you, or perhaps some one will bring you over."

They entered the side door of the boarding-house. Cecil pulled Lee down beside him on the stair.

"Oh, Lee," he said in a high falsetto, "we're going to-morrow. And I hate to go away and leave you. I do! I do!"

"Going to-morrow!" gasped Lee, "and without me!" She burst into a storm of tears, and Cecil forgot his manly pride and wept too.

"I wish I were grown," sobbed Cecil. "And I won't be for years. I've got to finish at Eton, and then I've got to go to Oxford. I'm only fifteen and one month. I won't be my own master for six years, and I won't be through Oxford when I am. It takes so beastly long to educate a fellow. It may be eight years before I see you again."

"Eight years! I shall *die*. Why won't he take me? I can pay for myself. Mrs. Hayne says I have eighty dollars a month. Don't you think he'll change his mind?"

"He won't! he won't!"

When Lee had wept herself dry, she adjusted herself to fate. "Well," she said, with a heavy sigh, "we'll write every week, won't we?"

It was Cecil's turn to be appalled. This was a phase of the tragedy that had not occurred to him.

"Oh, Lee," he faltered, "I hate to write letters!"

"But you will?" she cried shrilly. "You will?"

"Oh, I'll try! I'll try! But only one a month."

"One a week or I won't write at all. And it's nice to get letters."

"One a fortnight then."

To this Lee finally consented, and then went upstairs and helped him to pack. Their faces were so funereal at dinner that they were the subject of much good-natured chaff. Many disapproving glances were directed at Mr. Maundrell, — with whose ascent they had not been made acquainted, — for the children had furnished the house with much amusement, and they commanded no little sympathy.

After dinner Cecil and Lee sat in one of the bay windows in the front parlour and talked of the future. Cecil good-naturedly promised that life should be exactly like one of Scott's novels, any one that Lee preferred. After some excogitation she concluded that she liked the poems best, particularly "Marmion," and Cecil agreed to qualify for the part. Lee in return vowed to go fishing and shooting with him, never to scream at the wrong time, even if a blackbeetle got on her, and never to get into rages and call him names. They also exchanged tokens. Lee gave him a little gold heart with her picture — cut from a tin-type — and a strand of her lank hair in it, and he gave her a ring cut with the arms of his house, and begged her to keep it in her pocket when his father was round.

The next morning Lee was graciously permitted to accompany the travellers across the bay. She and Cecil paced up and down the deck of the boat, too excited for melancholy; both under that spell which cauterises so many wounds. Lee was to be left behind, but she was in the midst of an event. Moreover, she was shortly to see what a Pullman car was like. She wrung one more solemn promise from Cecil to write.

Lord Barnstaple had taken a drawing-room for himself and his son, and Lee examined the ornate interior and thought it very vulgar.

"You'll be sure not to put your head out of the window, won't you, Cecil?" she asked anxiously. "And you'll hold on tight at night and not be pitched out of these things."

Cecil grunted. She had hung a camphor bag on him, and presented him with a large package of cough drops.

Lord Barnstaple took out his watch. "We start in eight minutes," he said. "You had better let me put you in the hack; I have told the man to take you home." He paused and smiled slightly. He was at peace with the world, and inclined to be gracious to everybody; moreover, there was just a chance, a bare chance, that this boy-and-girl-affair might come to something. His son had a tenacious will, and these Americans were the devil and all for getting their own way. If Lee should turn out a great heiress — he had a vague idea that all American girls became heiresses as soon as they grew up — and should fulfil her promise of even temper and sturdy character, Cecil might, of course, do worse. Far be it from him to encourage the invasion of the British aristocracy by the undisciplined American female, but if another in the family was to be his unhappy fate, as well drop into the plastic mind a few seeds from the gardens of civilisation.

"We may see you in England, some day," he said; "you Americans are always travelling. Try to make yourself like English girls. Study hard and improve your mind. A smattering is such a trial; it rhymes with chattering. Don't talk too much, and above all never have hysterics. I am sure they are only a habit and can be controlled if you begin early. And — ah — your manners are somewhat abrupt, and you have a way of sprawling. Your mother, I am told, was a very elegant woman. Try to grow like her. Mrs. Hayne says it is likely that some of your mother's friends will offer you a home. Accept, by all means; it would be quite dreadful to be brought up in a boarding-house. I believe that is all. Now say good-bye."

Cecil gave Lee a mighty hug and winked rapidly. Lord Barnstaple allowed them one minute, then took Lee firmly by the hand and marched her to the hack.

"Good-bye," he said kindly. "You are a jolly little thing — you don't make any fuss. Mind you never have hysterics."

But Lee cried audibly all the way home, secure in the pawing of the horses about her on the boat, and

in the noise of the hack on the cobble-stones thereafter. Cecil was gone, and there was no mother
awaiting her in the boarding-house. She could not
even go into the old room and cry on her mother's
bed, for strangers were there. She was very forlorn,
and life was as black as pitch.

CHAPTER XIII

AFTER several weeks' exchange of vague suggestions, Mrs. Montgomery, Mrs. Brannan, Mrs.
Geary, and Mrs. Cartright met at the house of the
former to discuss the future of Marguerite Tarleton's
child. Mrs. Cartright was the aunt of Helena Belmont, whose energies were bottled for the moment
in school. Mrs. Montgomery and Mrs. Brannan
were also preparing for the difficult rôles of mothers
of beauties. Mrs. Geary was a degree less important,
her daughter being bright rather than pretty. Mrs.
Cartright, between the imperious Helena and the
incorrigible Colonel, her brother, over whose home
she had presided since his wife's death, had long
since surrendered what little character she had
brought to California; but having a wide popularity,
and a mighty flow of words, was never absent from
the counsels of her friends. Mrs. Montgomery was
"very Southern," very impulsive, rather prone to do
the wrong thing when caught in the cyclone of her
emotions. Mrs. Brannan was merely the gorgeous
Ila's mother, but like the others of her intimate circle
was a Southerner, and had been a close friend of
Marguerite Tarleton. Mrs. Geary was the practical
wife of a millionaire. Her husband, a man from

Maine, who looked not unlike a dried cod-fish, had panned for gold in '49, bought varas and ranches in the Fifties, became a banker of international importance in the Sixties, and had succeeded in making his Southern wife as close and practical as himself. Her advice was always in demand by her more impetuous friends.

"It's just this," said Mrs. Cartright, beginning at once, "that dear child cannot be brought up in a boarding-house, even in Mrs. Hayne's. Lee is a great-niece or second cousin of General Robert E. Lee and third cousin of the Breckinridges, and Randolphs and Carrolls and Prestons, to say nothing of the Tarletons. As long as poor dear proud Marguerite lived we could do nothing, but now Lee belongs to us, particularly as dear brother Jack and Mr. Brannan are her mother's executors and Lee's guardians. Now, of course, I'd just jump at the chance of taking her, if it were not for darling imperious Helena. She will be home in a year now, and if they did n't get on it would be really dreadful. Helena is really the most kind-hearted creature in the world — but such a tyrant! Her will has *never* been crossed, you see. You don't know what I go through sometimes, although I fairly worship her. And Lee, you see, has simply managed poor dear Marguerite and done exactly as *she* pleased for eleven years. It would be really terrible if she did n't give in to Helena, and I 'm afraid she never would. And it would be almost cruel to bring her up in a house where she would have almost no individuality, although, of course, Helena may marry at once——"

"How much income has she?" interrupted Mrs. Geary.

"Eighty dollars a month. Isn't it shocking? Fancy Hayward Tarleton's daughter growing up on eighty dollars a month!"

"It's quite enough to educate and dress her, and when she is ready to come out we can each give her a frock, and help with the trousseau when she marries."

"But she's got to have a home, meanwhile; that's the point," said Mrs Montgomery, who seemed to be repressing her own eloquence, as great upon occasion as Mrs. Cartright's. "She must have a home and a mother, poor little thing. Think if it were Tiny! I have cried myself ill. And she can't grow up from pillar to post either; she would become quite demoralised, quite unworthy of her blood ——"

"The very oldest families of the South!" cried Mrs. Cartright with enthusiasm.

"That's all very well, but I can't see why she shouldn't be placed at Mill's Seminary for the next seven years," said Mrs. Geary. "Of course, she could spend her vacations in Menlo with us."

Mrs. Montgomery shook her head with emphasis. "She must have a home! She must have a mother! She's full of feeling. It would wound and demoralise her to feel a waif, with no anchor, no one in particular who took an interest in her — it is too terrible to think of!"

"It comes to this then," said Mrs. Geary: "one of us must take her."

"That is what I mean," said Mrs. Montgomery eagerly.

"If it were not for Helena——" began Mrs. Cartright, ready to recapitulate. Mrs. Brannan interrupted her with unusual firmness.

"I'm afraid I cannot," she said. "I'd really love to, and she would be such company for Coralie; but Ila is so exacting and jealous, and as imperious in her quiet way as Helena. I wait on her like a slave, and she'd fairly hate an outsider who made any claim on me. Fortunately Coralie adores her and is so sweet. It was all I could do to persuade Ila to let me come back and look after Mr. Brannan and Coralie for a few months — and I do hate Paris! I'll do everything I can in the way of a good substantial present at Christmas, and she and Coralie might study together; that would save a little on both sides, and I'm sure they'd get on, but I don't dare risk taking her."

"Of course you would take her if you could," said Mrs. Montgomery; "we all know how good and kind you are. And you, Maria?"

Mrs. Geary shook her head emphatically. "Mr. Geary wouldn't listen to it for a moment. He detests sentiment and everything out of the common, and he has a special prejudice against adopting other people's children. Besides, as you know, Marguerite used to snub him, as she did all Northerners, and he's not the kind that ever forgets. No, I haven't even thought of it. I'll make her little presents, and give her a party dress when she's eighteen, but I can't do more."

"And I'm afraid to venture," sighed Mrs. Cartright, "but Jack will do something handsome——"

"Then it's settled," cried Mrs. Montgomery. "I am to have her! The very day of the funeral I begged her to come home with me, but she would n't: she thought that heartless Englishman would take her, poor little innocent thing — but Cecil was a dear, quite as nice as any Southern lad before the war. Well, when I got home, I reflected that perhaps it was as well that Lee had refused, as I have made so many resolutions to consult my children before taking any important step — it is their right. I thought all night and finally decided that it did not concern any one but Tiny and Randolph, as the others are married. I spoke to Randolph the next morning, and he said he could see no objection; he's sixteen now, and so sensible; and after breakfast I wrote a letter of ten pages to Tiny and told her all about it, and how deeply I felt on the subject, and dilated upon the brilliant prospects of Lee's babyhood, and the distinguished blood in her veins — a Tarleton of Louisiana! to say nothing of all the others! I begged her to think it over carefully and write at once — it does take so long to get an answer from Paris! I told her I would leave it entirely to her. She has so much heart, but her head is far cooler than mine. Even when she was a child I respected her judgment, and she quite managed her elder sisters. I 've rarely seen her excited. Well! I had her answer this morning. That is the reason I asked you to come to-day and decide once for all. She is so sweet and sensible about it. She began by saying that of course it would be a great risk to take an alien into the family, no matter how well we had known the parents: for no matter how many different characters there were in a family there was always a sort of general disposition among them that carried things off. And we were all so devoted to each other, and so happy together. It would be quite terrible if Lee should turn out a strong individuality. Therefore she begged me not to take her unless Mrs. Tarleton's other friends absolutely refused to do so. But if they did refuse, then I must not hesitate — I must take her by all means and make her as much like my own children as possible — after all, she was only eleven. So it's decided! She's mine!"

"Tiny certainly has a level head," said Mrs. Geary dryly. " And I really don't see how Lee could do better, or as well, if you really care to take her. You will see that her manners are all that could be desired, and that nobody ever speaks a cross word to her; and Tiny will see that you do not spoil her, and that she acquires the family disposition."

"You dear sarcastic Maria! You know you'd just love to spoil her yourself. I'm so happy. I haven't dared go to see her, but I've sent her candy, and fruit, and a new coat and hat. I'll go straight away and fetch her."

Thus was the momentous question decided, and Lee entered upon the third chapter of her life.

CHAPTER XIV

THAT same day she was installed in the old Montgomery house on Rincon -Hill. It was a low irregularly built house, wooden, but substantial. The walls of the lower storey were panelled, and covered with portraits of Southern ancestors and relations. The furniture and carpets were worn, but as both had been bought in the golden days of Mr. Montgomery's career, before he, like Hayward Tarleton, had speculated and lost, they were of the first quality, and would last for many years to come. Moreover, his widow had picked up many bibelots and much antique furniture in Europe, which added to the reserved, aristocratic, and un-Californian atmosphere of the house. And her silver and crystal were the finest in San Francisco.

Mrs. Montgomery was no longer wealthy, but she was as exclusive as in the Fifties, when exclusiveness meant self-protection, and, if not a social power, a person whom it showed a proper pride to know. Mr. Montgomery had not lost his entire fortune, by any means, and what his wife and the unmarried children inherited was unencumbered. It was also sufficient to enable Mrs. Montgomery to indulge her passion for travelling, to educate Tiny in Paris, to give Randolph his leisurely choice of avocations, to keep up the Rincon Hill and the Menlo Park property, and to enable the family generally to live as became one of the " old families of California," *i. e.*, of the early Fifties.

The house was on the crest of the hill, and commanded a fine view of the city and mountains and water. It stood in a dilapidated high-walled garden, full of the Castilian roses, pinks, gladiolus, and fuchsias of the older time. In one corner was a large weeping-willow, and in the middle the remains of a stone fountain. The hum of the city on the plain, and on the heights beyond, never reached that quiet old garden, which symbolised a phase of California's life already remote.

Lee was given a pretty blue bedroom overlooking the city, and found her new life very pleasant, albeit her roving propensities could no longer be gratified. Mrs. Montgomery, indulgent and yielding in most things, was inexorable on all points of deportment, and gave Lee strict orders that she must never put her foot outside the gate alone. She also missed not being obliged to think for herself, to have no responsibility but punctuality at meals; even her studies were over for the summer. But she was very young; the artificial habits of the last five years fell from her, and the instincts of her nature reached forth to the conditions which had been hers during her earlier years and her mother's before her. She was never quite so young and so dependent as other children, but in less than a month she would have shuddered at the mere mention of Market Street; and she loved the repose and low-toned richness of her surroundings after the clatter and vulgarities of a boarding-house. She still mourned her mother with sudden childish outbursts, but she enjoyed the unbroken rest of her nights, and felt strong and unfatigued as a little girl should.

Randolph was a dark handsome boy — "exactly like his father, who was the picture of his grandfather, who was a perfect cavalier, my dear!" — and so polite that he made Lee feel like a Red Indian. When she rose to leave the room he opened the door. He never sat until she had placed herself, and he rose when she rose, ignoring the gulf between sixteen and childhood. He was always on hand to adjust her cape, and his attentions at table were really beautiful. He treated his mother with a deference which was surely Southern, and when Lee lamented that she was "so gawky," and that Lord Barnstaple had told her so, he assured her that the traditionally irreproachable Tiny had been quite gauche by comparison at the age of eleven. After that compliment Lee almost wavered in her allegiance to Cecil, who doubtless would have told her the truth and asked her why she bothered about "such things." But she felt that she certainly was improving, with her well-brushed hair in a tight plait, her dainty white frocks, her thin boots, and hands no longer discoloured by liniments, but washed in bran water and manicured once a week. She gave strict attention to her poses, and forbade her legs to fly up and herself to bounce down on the edge of her backbone. The mere fact that her skirts were the same length all round made her feel less awkward.

She renewed her baby acquaintance with Coralie Brannan, a fair delicate child who promised a few years of ethereal beauty before withering like a hot-house plant in the rude winds of life. She was sweet and bright and adaptable, and adored Lee at once, succumbing to the stronger nature, but companionable through the liveliness of her mind. Of course she was permitted to read Cecil's letters; and she was volubly sympathetic over every phase of that extraordinary friendship.

The summer months were passed in Menlo Park, which, although it boasted a village and a very smart railway station of the English pattern, was practically a collection of large plain substantial country houses with deep verandahs, and surrounded by grounds more or less extensive. These were scattered over an area of some six miles in the great San Mateo Valley, along whose western rim towered a mountain range covered with redwood forests. The Montgomery, Yorba, Geary, Belmont, Brannan, Randolph, Folsom, and Washington estates dated, in their present sub-division, from the early Fifties: and these families (not all of whom appear in this chronicle) may be said, for want of a better term, to have represented the landed aristocracy of California's second era — counting the arcadian episode of the Spaniards as the first.

Cecil wrote with a praiseworthy attempt at regularity. He had returned at once to Eton and to cricket. His parents were living in comparative harmony, and his stepmother had promised him a new horse and a boat. His letters were very brief, and there was the creak of protesting machinery in every line, but he rarely failed to assure Lee that her letters were "jolly," and to beg her to be faithful, as he did so love to get mail.

When Lee returned to town in the autumn, plump and strong and pink, she settled down at once with Coralie to hard study under private tutors. She was not only to be "thoroughly educated," but "highly accomplished." Her studies were conducted entirely in French. She pounded the piano daily until her back ached, covered countless pads with birds and flowers and trees, tinkled the guitar with her head on one side, attacked the German language, and took three dancing lessons a week. These studies were pursued in the old schoolroom at the back of the house, where there was always a big fire roaring, and a polished floor. Randolph and Tom Brannan attended the dancing-class when at home, and bestowed their favours impartially. Tom was fourteen, a round-faced youth with a large mouth, an amiable temper, and an inflammable heart. He sent Lee an immense package of peanuts the day after he met her, and announced himself violently in love. Both he and Randolph danced to perfection, and between the two Lee rapidly developed the inherent grace of her creole blood.

CHAPTER XV

HER life from eleven to eighteen was very monotonous and very happy. Mrs. Montgomery petted and indulged her, the boys were her slaves, and assured her, every time they came home from school, and later from their whirl at College, that she was growing up the prettiest girl in San Francisco. After Tiny's return from Paris, which was shortly after Lee entered her thirteenth year, the child caught little glimpses of the world from her secluded tower. Tiny entered society at once, and was as much of a belle as any girl so constitutionally bored and indifferent could be. But her beauty made an immediate impression; she was much entertained, and during her first winter the young men came in shoals to the house on Rincon Hill. She was very small and marvellously dignified. With a long train and a high coiffure, her fine head held well back, emphasising her fine aquiline profile, she actually had a presence. Her hair was soft and brown; her brown eyes, under their level brows, very sweet and thoughtful, her skin had the pure cold whiteness of the camellia; and her admirers swore that her feet and hands necessitated a magnifying glass. She was thin and delicate, but she had great force of character and a sweet inflexible will.   Lee conceived for her one of those girlish adorations peculiar to the impulsive and imaginative of her sex, and quite bitterly resented the rival claims to belledom of the overwhelming Helena, the sinuous tropical Ila, the clever Miss Geary, and the wealthy Miss Yorba.   When Mrs. Montgomery gave a party she was permitted to contemplate these radiant beings in the dressing-room, and preferred Miss Yorba, with her tragically plain face, because she was the only one who ever condescended to notice her.   Later, when she was supposed to be in bed, she lay prone at the top of the stairs watching the dancing and flirting.   In summer, she saw even more of the mysterious life of grown people; who appeared to live on the verandahs, and had many picnics.   When she was sixteen, men began to notice her, despite Mrs. Montgomery's efforts to keep her in the background and "a child as long as possible."   But creole blood is quick and magnetic, and long before it was time to take her place in society it was prophesied that Lee was to succeed that famous trio of belles, Helena Belmont, Ila Brannan, and Tiny Montgomery.   Her own imaginings on the subject were very satisfactory, but she studied hard and read so many books that Tiny begged her to be careful lest she be thought clever.

CHAPTER XVI

CECIL, some five months after his eighteenth birthday, went up to Oxford and entered Balliol.   Here he gave the cold shoulder to cricket, and took to the water with the enthusiasm of a man who has the honour of his college to uphold and his blue to get.   He also took more kindly to correspondence, and wrote Lee long letters on the tendencies of modern civilisation.   His letters struck his friend, used to the lighter mood of Mr. Montgomery and Mr. Brannan, as decidedly priggish, and she worried over the development not a little, — being unaware that the University youth of Great Britain must take priggishness in the regular course of measles, mumps, whooping-cough, Public School wickedness, the overwhelming discovery of his own importance as an atom of the British Empire, and cynicism.

During the second term he became profoundly and theologically religious, and Lee wept at the prospect of being a parson's wife   His excursions into the vast echoing region of spiritual mysteries nearly addled her brains, and she felt quite miserable at times to think that there was so little of the old Cecil left.   But during the spring of his second year there seemed to be a healthy reaction.   A letter dated from Maundrell Abbey informed Lee that he had been sent down for breaking windows and attempting to feed a bonfire in the quadrangle with an objectionable don. He further confided that upon the last hilarious night before his exile he had been discovered by a good Samaritan at the foot of his stairs calling imperiously upon the Almighty to carry him up to his room and put him to bed.

During the months of his exile he travelled on the Continent. His letters at this period were less like essays for posterity, and much of his old self flashed through them. When he returned to Oxford in the autumn he went in bitterly for politics, announced himself a Liberal, and made cutting references to the House of Peers. Indeed, shortly after he had been elected President of the Union, he gave full rein to his eloquence and his new-born convictions, and so scathingly and vituperously assailed the entire territorial system that he finished in a perfect pandemonium of cheers and hisses, and was pestered for months by the enterprising Socialist. During the following vacation he attempted to convert his father, who was a blue-hot Tory; and the fixity and bitterness of his convictions and his arrogant assumption of advanced thinking so irritated Lord Barnstaple that he damned his offspring for a prig; forgetting that in his own time he had been as pretty a prig as Oxford had ever turned out. Cecil's keynote at this time — frequently quoted to Lee — was Matthew Arnold's unpleasant arraignment of their common country: "Our world of an aristocracy materialised and null, a middle class purblind and hideous, a lower class crude and brutal." Lord Maundrell was for reforming all three. Unlike the great poet who inspired those lines, there was no danger of his being the "passionate and dauntless soldier of a forlorn hope, who, ignorant of the future, and unconsoled by its promises, nevertheless waged against the conservatism of the old impossible world so fiery battle." To-day the future was quite clear, that is to say, it was to be what its brilliant and determined youth chose to make it.

Lee thought these sentiments simply magnificent, and expressed her approval with such fire and enthusiasm that Cecil wrote with increasing frequency, and assured her that the way her style had improved was really remarkable.

During his last year his fads had pretty well run their course, although he was temporarily interested in "The Influence of Zola on Modern Thought," and bi-metallism. But his ideals, so he assured Lee, were leaving him. All he really cared for in life was to take a double first in Greats and History, and he was working like a horse. There were long intervals between his letters, and when he wrote it was to apologise on the score of fatigue. He was "dog tired." So were all the men. If they were n't drivelling idiots when the thing was over it was because nothing could really knock an Englishman out. Of course he was on the water more or less, and took a turn every day at cricket, which kept him in fair condition, although he was far from fit. Meanwhile Lee was to pray that he was not ploughed. He liked women to pray. Religion had gone with his other ideals, but it was a beautiful thing in a woman.

CHAPTER XVII

A RAILROAD sliced off a corner of Lee's ranch and paid her a large indemnity, which was invested by Mr. Brannan in first mortgages; and an earthquake presented another section of the ranch with a fine assortment of mineral springs warranted to cure as many ills. A hotel and bath houses were promptly erected, and a heavy patronage followed. Mrs. Montgomery insisted that every detail of her business affairs should be explained to Lee after she passed her sixteenth birthday, and that upon her eighteenth she should assume the entire control of her property.

"I want Lee to know so much that no man can cheat her, and no complication take her unawares," she said, in a memorable interview with Mr. Brannan, in which she completely routed that conservative person. "Look at the women in this town who were once distinguished members of society, and who are now getting their bread Heaven only knows how. Their husbands died involved, and they were helpless — for they had been petted dolls, nothing more."

Lee awoke one morning and found herself eighteen. It was very early, and the world was intensely still. The spring birds were silent in the willow, the stars burned low.

She was very happy and very expectant: the princess was to come down from her tower into the great hall of the castle and take part in the beautiful and mysterious drama called Life. She was quite convinced that not in the whole world was there a girl so fortunate as herself. She was lovely to look at, her manners were soft and convent-like: even the hypercritical Mrs. Montgomery assured her that they were as fine as those of the women who had been the glory of their country before the war; and her income added to her consequence and would leave no wish she could think of ungratified. She was delighted with the prospect of being a woman of affairs. She felt very important and very proud; and as the original hotel on her property was flimsy and hideous, she and Randolph, who was an architect, had already planned a new one. It was to be a huge edifice of adobe in the old Californian style, with a courtyard full of palms, and a fountain tossing the least offensive of the waters.

Lee thought of all these things this morning, and of more. In the background of her musings there was always the fairy prince. It was hard work idealising Cecil in the light of his Oxford effusions, but Lee did it; he was seven thousand miles away. And he belonged to the land of poetry and romance, crusaders, castles, and splendour; he would be the eighth earl and the eleventh viscount of his line, and the very repairs of his ancestral home were older than the stars on her flag. Deep in her imagination dwelt an ideal Cecil, a superb and lovable creature upon whom Oxford had never breathed her blight, with whom fads had never tampered, who was serious only when in love, and who would descend upon her like a god and bear her off to the abbey of his fathers. She never regretted the utter absence of sentiment and tenderness in Cecil's letters; it would have accorded ill with Cecil in the present trying stages of his development. Cecil, as a man of the world, was to be all that ever sprang from the fertile brain of a romanticist. He would not condescend to be photographed, but he could not fail to be handsome, and she could only pray that he was tall. She, with a fine instinct, had never sent him her portrait, nor alluded to her brilliant prospects. She wrote of her daily life, of the books she read, and of himself, and, having a ready pen and a generous endowment of femininity, never failed to make her letters amusing. She wondered if, as he sauntered through the moonlit gardens of Oxford — she, too, had read Matthew Arnold — or rowed alone on the Isis at night, he dreamed tender and impassioned dreams of her. If he did he gave no sign. On the other hand, there was never the flutter of a petticoat in his letters. She had asked him once if there were no girls in Oxford, and he had replied that he had too much to do to think about girls, and that she was the only one he could ever endure, anyhow. Those he met in his vacations bored him to extinction; but he liked the married women, and intended to cultivate them one of these days.

Lee yawned and sat up lazily. It was her duty to take another nap, for she was to go to her first ball to-night. But sleep was a waste of time, and her first day of young-ladyhood should be as long as possible. Her hair was braided. She shook it loose and spread it about her. It was fine and soft, and black enough to be sown with stars, but it had never a wave in it. She took a hand-mirror from the table beside her bed and regarded herself with some approval. Her skin was very white, her cheeks and lips were pink, her light blue eyes were very large and very radiant. The lashes were still short, but black and thick, and the underlid was full. The hair grew about her low forehead in a waving line, and her eyebrows, although straight and heavy, seemed, like the irregular nose and mouth, to have been made for her face alone. The short nose with its slight upward slope had a spirited nostril; what the mouth lacked in conventional prettiness it made up in colour and curves; and if the lower part of her face was square, few took note of the lines under so much beauty of texture. She knew her good points perfectly — her eyes, complexion, poise of head, and length of limb — and she already knew how to make the most of them.

She laughed, stretched herself, and slipped to the edge of her bed, where she sat for a few moments in apparent indecision. The truth was that she was in no haste to face the great fact of life, now that the door stood ajar. Until she was dressed and had gone forth into those parts of the house which were not her own exclusive bower, she still lingered in the period of dreams and anticipation, and it was very pleasant.

She thrust her feet into her night slippers, wandered about the room for a moment, then opened a window and leaned out. The perfume of roses and violets and lilacs came up to her from the old garden below and from many another about. One or two of these gardens she had full view of, others showed only a corner in the triangle of crumbling walls built about the queer old-fashioned houses when the city was young. At this early hour their secrets seemed whispering along the eaves, cowering in the dark gardens, ready to lift their heads and laugh. What Lee had not heard of the ancient history of San Francisco had not been worth repeating, for Coralie had grown up with her elders and missed nothing. In South Park, at the foot of the hill, she could see the chimneys of the Randolph House, whose tragedy seemed separated from her time by a dozen generations; so rapid had been the evolution of the city, so furious its energies. Beyond lay the plain and the steep hills bristling with the hives of human beings, who dreamed of gold, and the loud peremptory roar of Market Street. Telegraph Hill, sharp and bare and brown, passed over in contempt by the dwellers on the fashionable heights, its surface broken only by an occasional hovel, looked like an equally contemptuous old grandmother. Far across the bay, to the right of Rincon Hill, were the pink ranges of the coast; at the other end of the plain the brown Twin Peaks, as yet unhonoured by the hideous dwelling of rich and poor; and then the slopes of Lone Mountain, its white slabs and vaults grey in the dawn, the sharp cone with its Calvary behind black in the dull void.

The city looked grey and old, as if the gold in its veins had turned to lead and its uneasy head were thick with ashes.

It was the first time in many years that Lee had seen San Francisco in an ugly mood, for she was not given to early rising. She had found it beautiful from her eyrie, with its brilliant floods of winter and spring sunshine, its white mist robes and wild dust-cloak of summer. She had almost forgotten the flare and glare of Market Street; and she had rarely crossed that plain since her mother's death, — never except in the seclusion of Mrs. Montgomery's carriage. She had as seldom entered a shop. Her life in some respects had been almost cloistered. To-day all was to be changed. She should never go out alone, of course, but she was no longer to hold herself aloof from the details of life. And to-night she was to go to her first party! She hardly knew whether she was glad or sorry.

As the sun rose and the city turned pink, and a fine white mist rode in and hung itself about the sparkling windows on the heights, and the bay deepened into blue, and the bare peaks looked a richer brown, the Contra Costa range a deeper pink patched with blue, the darkness of night lingering only in its cañons, Lee decided that she was glad. The world was very beautiful out there. San Francisco, clad in her rosy gown, looked like the Sleeping Princess on her wedding-morn, but peaceful and still — and happy. Lee could hardly realise that it was a monster with a million nerves, a fevered brain, its tainted blood swarming with the microbes of every vice, of every passion; raging for gold and alcohol with a thirst that never slept; a monster that had killed her father and Mr. Montgomery, and Colonel Belmont, and Mr. Polk, and Don Roberto Yorba, and countless others whose families were scattered to the winds; that it had in its records as many terrible tragedies, as many shameful secrets as it had nails in the spires of its churches. Over there, beyond her range of vision, was a whole city of rottenness in which she would never set her foot, which counted as nothing in her carefully guarded life, and yet was crowded with beings, many of them young, not all of them wholly bad. Mrs. Montgomery would not have a newspaper in her house, but Lee knew that horrid and picturesque crimes were not infrequent in those mysterious regions known as Barbary Coast, Sailor Town, Spanish Town, and China Town, and longed for details with that kindliness for sensation inherent in the American not wholly a Southerner.

But what she could see was beautiful. She smiled indulgently into the face of that great Fact out there. For Lee was a dreamer who knew that she dreamed. In the background, ineffaced, were the hard practical years of her youth; surrounding her was the lore she had gathered from books and Coralie; to say nothing of the intellectual agonies undergone at the hands of Lord Maundrell, and the observations on the world as it is to young men settling themselves in life, with which she had been favoured by her two faithful swains, Randolph and Tom Brannan. She had helped them both to choose

their careers.   Randolph had hovered between architecture and the law, and Tom's aspirations were
directed equally towards ranching in a cow-boy outfit, and stockbrokering, until persuaded by Lee that
he was too lazy to sit a horse all day and would be
useful to her in town.

But she was none the less expectant, demanded
none the less the richest and most picturesque treas-
ures of life, its most poignant and abiding happiness.   Beyond those hills, beyond the grey ocean,
whose roar came faintly to her, was the fairy prince
— Cecil, with the faint musty perfume of the ages
about him, and the owls hooting in the ruined
cloisters of his abbey.

CHAPTER XVIII

"LEE, darling; I am afraid you will take cold."
Lee whirled about. Tiny, muffled in a pink
dressing-gown, her brown hair hanging about her
lovely imperturbable face, had entered, and was
smiling at the dreamer.

"I want to be the first to kiss you," she said. Lee
gave her an enthusiastic hug and swung her up to
the table.

Tiny laughed and made herself comfortable.
"You look for all the world like a long white lily
in your night-gown," she said; "but I do believe
you are as strong as Randolph."

Lee threw herself backward until her finger-tips
touched the floor, then writhed her slender body
until she looked like a snake uncoiling. Tiny
gasped.

"No wonder you are graceful," she said. "Who
taught you to do that?"

"Want to see me kick?"

"No, no," said Tiny hurriedly. "I don't think it
is nice to kick, dear. But I am not going to scold
you. I can't realise that you are eighteen. It
makes me feel a grandmother — I am twenty-four."

"Why don't you marry? I think it must be horrid
to be an old maid."

"How horrid of *you*, Lee.   I'm not an old maid."

"You look just sixteen; but why don't you marry?"

"Of course you will ask till you find out.   Well, Lee, considering that you are really grown-up to-day, I'll tell you something.   I'm thinking about it."

Lee gave a little shriek of delight, sat down on the floor, and embraced her knees.

"Quick!   Tell me."

"He's an Englishman."

"Tiny!"

"I met him in London two years ago, and he asked me then; but I could n't make up my mind.   It's such a bore making up one's mind.   I did n't bother much, but we corresponded, and it came about with less trouble than I thought it would: I wrote him last night definitely.   He has been so faithful — when I think of those that have come and gone meanwhile! — and he really is very nice.   Not very amusing, but, *enfin*, not too talkative."

"What is his name?"

"Lord Arrowmount."

"That makes it just perfect!"

"I wish he were not.   It will be such a bore living up to things one was n't born to.   And after the lazy freedom of California!   When I was in London it seemed to me that the poor women were worked to death.   I'd far rather have married an American — if it were a mere matter of nationality."

"They won't make you do anything over there that you don't want to," said Lee wisely.   "You

have the sweetest little face and the softest voice
in the world, but the cool way in which you walk
straight at what you want — it 's too clever!"

Tiny laughed. "It 's you that are quite too frightfully clever. Be careful, dear, that you don't talk
books to any of the young men to-night."

"I suppose I won't have any one to talk books
with till Cecil comes," said Lee with some vicious-
ness. "Is Lord Arrowmount clever?"

"No, thank Heaven! He is just a nice, quiet,
big, kind Englishman. He takes photographs, but
I don't mind that, as he does n't talk much about it;
and when I said I 'd rather not stand in the broiling
sun with my eyes puckered up for ten minutes at a
time, he never mentioned it again. I think we
shall be quite happy. Of course we 'll come back
to California every few years, or mother will come
to us."

"Of course. So shall I. I never could leave
California for very long."

"Englishmen are not so easy to manage as American men, but I believe that as soon as I understand
Arthur I shall be able to manage him quite easily.
I should simply *hate* it if he were always contra-
dicting me."

"He won't. I don't know that I should care to
manage Cecil. I think it must be magnificent to be
lorded over by a man you love; but I should want
my own way all the same. I 'd storm and beg and
cajole, and then of course I 'd get it."

Tiny laughed. "I don't know much about Englishmen, but I think you know less."

"But, you see, I shan't meet Cecil again for several years, and by that time I shall be quite experienced. Besides, I 've made a regular study of Randolph and Tom. I think it must be so interesting to understand men — and so useful."

"You look so knowing — just like a baby owl."

"There can't be such an extraordinary amount of difference, considering that we are descended from them and speak the same language. And for that matter, I 'm saturated with English literature. It 's the only one I know, and it has formed my mind. I 've scarcely read an American novel, and never an American poem — is there one? And I know English history backwards, and adore it."

"All the same, you are American straight into your marrow, and I feel surer and surer, the more I see of English people — and I have had two seasons and one autumn in England — that there are no two peoples on the earth so unlike."

"Well, I think it 's very strange," said Lee crossly. "I don't understand it at all."

"We are not even like the Americans of a quarter of a century ago. Why should we expect to be like our ancestors of several centuries back? "

"Oh, true, I suppose. And Cecil! If he 's anything like his letters he 's certainly not much like Randolph and Tom. But I had an idea he was going through a sort of freak stage, and would be just like other men (only nicer) when he got over it."

"There are, doubtless, hundreds like him; and I wish you would not use slang, dear."

"Well, I won't. What is your Arthur?"

"A baron — nothing so very wonderful; but he has a very long descent: I looked it out in Burke. And at least I am not buying him. He knows that I have very little. I believe he is wealthy. He's thirty-six; a very good age. I do hate boys."

"Is he frightfully in love?"

Tiny nodded and blushed. "When an Englishman falls in love — well!"

Lee jerked her knees up to her chin and gave a gurgle of delight. "Are you in love with him?" she asked softly. "Do tell me, Tiny?"

Tiny's massive dignity relaxed under a pink flood. " I have had other offers, you know, and some from very rich men," she said as she slipped to the floor, "and it's really commonplace nowadays to marry a title. Give me a kiss, and tell me you want me to be happy, and I'll go back to bed. I'm cold."

CHAPTER XIX

" I HAVE taken a day off in honour of the great
event," said Randolph at the breakfast table.

Lee smiled sweetly, but one of her shoulders gave
an impatient little jerk. Randolph had proposed
four times already, since his return from Europe,
three weeks ago. Mrs. Montgomery smiled approv-
ingly. She had tolerated the correspondence with
Cecil Maundrell out of respect to the wishes of the
dead; but she had long since permitted herself to
hope that the ridiculous boy-and-girl engagement
would die a natural death, and that there would be
one change the less in her happy domestic life. She
had covered the table with wild flowers, sent from
Menlo, in honour of Lee's birthday, and had ordered
three different varieties of hot bread, besides the
usual meed of griddle cakes, chicken, hash, hominy
and eggs. It was to Lee's happy indifference to the
popular American breakfast that she owed her superb
health and colour. Tiny looked as fragile as porcelain beside her; and even Randolph, although he
had achieved height and sinews, had the dull complexion and thin cheeks of the American who adds
the tax of alcohol and late hours to the decimating
national diet. He was by no means dissipated, for

San Francisco; but he worked very hard during the day, and, when free of the social claims of his family — to whom he was devoted — took his recreations with other youths by night. He had left college at the end of his first year, studied architecture for another year in New York and Paris, and had sold his first plan — for a Bonanza king's "palatial residence" on Nob Hill — three months later. Since then he had had little leisure, and had made money: he was practical, with a zigzag of originality, and planned and worked with marvellous rapidity. There were lines about his sharp nervous grey eyes, and, six months before, he had broken down, and gone to England to rest, and visit Lord Arrowmount. His manners were not what they had been in his remote boyhood, but they were still fine, and he had a certain distinction, in spite of a slight stoop and a decided restlessness of manner.

After breakfast he followed Lee to the garden, and they sat down under the willow.

"Don't propose just yet," said Lee. "I feel in a perfectly beatific humour, and I would n't be made cross for the world."

"*Not* for the world, if you don't wish it," said Randolph airily. "I will postpone it until to-morrow afternoon at six. That will give me just half-an-hour before dinner."

"I don't believe you ever are really serious. You would n't be half so nice if you were."

"It is difficult to be serious with a habit. Whenever I propose I have a sudden vision of pinafores, and braids, and angles. It takes all my mental

nimbleness to realise that you are really marriage-
able — in spite of your beauty."

He spoke in his usual bantering voice, and his eyes
smiled, but his nervous hands were pressed hard
against each other.

Lee saw only his eyes. She smiled saucily and
tossed her head. "I 'm to be reckoned with," she
remarked. "There are no pinafores on my plans for
the season."

Randolph threw back his head, and laughed heartily.
"Perhaps you suspect that you are going to be a
great belle to-night," he said in a moment.

"I? *Oh*, Randolph! how can you be sure?"

"The men have planned it between them. Don't
start out to-night oppressed with any doubts."

Lee clapped her hands. Her eyes flashed with
delight.

"Who? Who? Tell me! Of course it was you
first of all."

"You may be sure that I would do everything I
could to make you a success; and so would Tom
Brannan and Ned Geary. The others you know only
by name."

"I suppose Mr. Geary will propose to-night," said
Lee with resignation. "I am used to you and Tom,
but when the others begin I shall really be quite
frantic. I suppose I 'll have to tell them about
Cecil —— "

Randolph threw back his head and laughed again,
although he caught in his under lip. "Fancy you
marrying a little tin god of an Englishman! "

· "That 's enough! "

"I beg pardon. Don't singe me with that blue fire of yours, and I won't call him names. But you took me by surprise. I thought you had forgotten all about him."

"Why, you know I correspond with him."

"Do you still — really? I don't know that I am surprised, however: you are the kindest and most unselfish of girls, and Englishmen have a stolid fashion of plugging away at anything that has become a habit."

"Cecil is not stolid. He has changed his mind fifty times about other things. You can read his letters if you like."

"God forbid! I know of nothing in life so objectionable as the Oxford prig. But you don't mean to tell me, my dearest girl, that you consider yourself engaged to him?"

"Of course I do!"

"But, Lee, the thing is a farce. You were children. And you have not seen each other for seven years. When you meet again you will be two different beings; if you don't detest each other it will be a miracle."

"We shall find each other the more interesting; and people don't change so much as all that."

"Am I what I was at sixteen? Well, let that point go. You have n't reflected, perhaps, that there would be enormous opposition on the part of his family. The Maundrells are paupers. Old Lord Barnstaple left the greater part of his private fortune to his young wife, and the present earl soon made ducks and drakes of the rest. Cecil must marry a fortune, and yours is entirely too small; they want millions over there.   Lady Barnstaple has cut into her capital trying to keep up with smart London.   She is simply mad to be known as one of the three or four smartest women in society, and *the* smartest American; and her case is hopeless.   She has n't money enough, she never was a beauty, and now is nothing but an anxious-eyed faded pretty woman; and she has n't an atom of personality.   I was in the same house with her for a week."

"What is she like?"   Curiosity routed her irritation.

"A bad imitation of the loud English type, and fairly exudes larkiness and snobbery.   She and Barnstaple lead a cat-and-dog life.   She gives him immense sums to keep him from leaving her, for without him she 'd drop out; she has no real hold.   When she calls him a cad, he calls her a tuft-hunter, a parvenu, and a pushing failure."

"Who was she?   Cecil never told me."

"Something very common — from Chicago, I think.   She went to London a rich widow, but without letters to the other Americans in power, who are mostly New Yorkers with a proper contempt for the aristocracy of wealth in its first generation.   She worked the Legation to some extent, and managed a few easy and gluttonous titles.   But the big doors were shut in her face; she was managing herself badly, she had picked up with the wrong people, and she was about to give up the game when Maundrell and his debts came along.   They flew at each other; he was heir presumptive to the earldom of Barnstaple, and his uncle was old.   Maundrell's first wife was a daughter of the Duke of Beaumanoir, a beautiful and charming creature, and one of the most popular women in London for eight years. The present owner of her precious husband could not have made a worse move than to succeed her. Well, to return to Cecil. He won't have a penny but what his grandmother and stepmother allow him; and what he may inherit from both will not be enough to keep up the title, the way things are going now. Therefore, he must marry money——"

"Oh, bother! I don't want to hear any more."

"Answer me this—if Cecil Maundrell were out of the question, would you marry me?"

"You promised——"

"Not to propose. Fancy a man proposing at this hour in the morning, and after eight buckwheat cakes! To discuss the question in the abstract is quite another matter."

"I don't believe I could ever think of a man I had grown up with as anything but a brother."

"You could if you would. It is merely a matter of readjusting yourself mentally. I am not your brother; I have hardly seen as much of you as Tom Brannan has; and——" he hesitated a moment—"you do not know me half so well as you think you do."

Lee looked at him with a flash of curiosity, then she lifted her chin. "You want to intrigue me, as the French say. But I am not so easily managed, I know you quite well."

"You think I could never be really serious, I suppose."

"I can't imagine any man I ever met being really serious. And you are much nicer as you are. Please don't try to be."

"Why do you suppose I am working like a dog?"

"To get rich and ahead of everybody else, of course. You want to be an architect that all America talks about, and to make stacks and stacks of money."

"You are right as far as you go. I want to get to the top, and be the first in my line, and I must have wealth; but the two are ashes without the woman. I not only love you, but I should be prouder of you than of anything else that I achieved. If I made millions you could spend them, and the more you dazzled the eyes of the world the better I should like it. You should never have a duty that was repugnant or irritating to you, and never a wish ungratified."

"Would you button my boots?" asked Lee merrily.

"Of course I would."

"I don't believe you'd have time. You'll never be through getting rich, if you are like the other millionaires of San Francisco. Tom says they work like old cart-horses from morning till night, and then die in harness."

"Every man with energy and ambition wants to make his pile; and then, of course, when a man has made millions he must watch them or they will run away; but I should always *know that you were there.* That would satisfy me."

Lee made no reply. Her lip curled, her lashes approached each other, and she looked dreamily through the green lattice of the willow to the mountains beyond the bay.

"What are you thinking of?" said Randolph abruptly.

"I want more than that. I don't care for enormous wealth, and I have n't any great ambition to dazzle the world — I suppose I am not a very good American."

"What do you want?"

She turned very pink, shook her head shyly and looked down.

"You fancy you will find it with an Englishman, I suppose — with whom you would be a sort of necessary virtue, and who would have forgotten after three months of matrimony whether you were beautiful or not."

"It is too bad of you to have such a poor opinion of Englishmen when Tiny is going to marry one."

"I wish she were not, although Arrowmount is a first-rate fellow, and I like him. Besides, it is quite another matter for Tiny to marry an Englishman: she has the adaptability of indifference, and she is a born diplomatist and manager. Southern girls are not American in the modern sense, and when they are educated in Europe they practically revert to the conditions out of which their ancestors came. My mother has seen to it that Tiny is as Southern as if she had never set foot in this extraordinary chaos called California. She tried it on me, and it worked until I had to go out in the world and hustle. She tried it on you, and you are a magnificent compound of the South, California, and yourself. Before you have been out a year you will have an individuality as pronounced as Helena Belmont's; and no woman with individuality can get along with an Englishman. For the American, she can't have too much."

"Three of Tiny's friends are married to Englishmen, and they get on."

"Which is another point: when an Englishman settles down in California he sheds a part of his national individuality into the surroundings he loves. A Californian wife is part of the scheme. He loves the country first, and the woman as a natural sequence. You are not Tiny, and it is not in the least likely that Cecil Maundrell will settle down in California. I repeat what I said a moment ago, and I should like to have you think it over: as my wife you would be a queen; as his wife you would be a mere annex until you ceased to be on speaking terms ——"

"Oh, bother! I like to believe that everything in the world is beautiful, and I'm going to as long as I can. Go and get the plans for the hotel, and don't talk another word of nonsense to me to-day."

CHAPTER XX

" YES," said Tiny to Lee that night, "you are lovely — *perfectly* lovely : but it should have been white. I think it was *quite* weak of us to give way. No girl *ever* made her début in black before."

"That's why I wanted to — that, and because it's so becoming. Why should I wear a silly little white frock just because it's the custom?"

"The more you make yourself like other people, dear, the easier time you will have in this world."

Lee tossed her head. "I'm going to have my own way *in* my own way," she announced.

She was dressed for her party, in black gauze. Mrs. Montgomery had wept at the bare suggestion. Tiny had expressed herself with unusual emphasis, and Coralie, who expected to be a vision in white, had remonstrated until Lee had fallen asleep.

Lee had an instinct for dress. She knew that she would look superb in black, and merely sweet and pretty in white. She had chosen a gauze as blue-black as her hair, and ordered it to be made with a light simplicity which increased her clean length of limb and threw into sharp relief the dazzling white of her skin. She wore her hair brushed away from her face and knotted at the back of her head.

"I may not be a great beauty," she remarked, "but I *am* stunning!"

"You are a symphony in black and blue; and white and pink; your eyes are so *very* blue in that dress, and your hair, and brows, and lashes seem so much blacker than usual — one almost forgets even your complexion. You are *despairingly* pretty."

Tiny looked placidly pretty in pink and white.

"Ah! Well, I intend to be thought so, whether I am or not. If I see anybody looking at me as if they were criticising my nose and mouth I'll just blaze my eyes at them and walk across the room."

Tiny laughed. "The beauty carriage is half the battle. I've seen rather plain girls carry themselves as if they were satiated with admiration, and get far more than some modest beauty."

"Youbetcherlife — I beg pardon, Tiny; I'll never use a word of slang again — I vow I won't. Is it true that Englishwomen use a lot of slang?"

"Smart Englishwomen have an absurd fiction that they are above all laws, and some of them are as vulgar as underbred Americans — I cannot say more than that. But like other properly bred Americans — Southerners, I mean, of course — I have my own standards."

"But if you do not adopt their argot you may not get on over there," said Lee, with a flash of insight.

"I should like nothing better than to be unpopular with people whose manners I did not like, and whose race for amusement bored me. They can think me just as provincial and old-fashioned as they like. There are always charming people in every society.

The thing is to have the entrée, and then pick and choose."

".I shan't care at all about society when I'm married. Cecil and I will be frightfully in love, and live in an old castle, and stay out all day on the moors and in the woods, and climb fells and things."

"So you fancy yourself in love with Cecil," remarked Miss Montgomery. "You've been dreaming about him all these years."

Lee turned as pink as one of the Castilian roses under her window. She had been imprudent more than once to-day and betrayed her precious secret.

"Well — it *is* rather romantic. I — well, you'd think about him in that way, too — you know you would."

"Not if I had been obliged to read his letters. But if you really love him and intend to marry him, I think you should announce the engagement."

"Well, I'm not going to announce it, and spoil all my fun. An engaged girl has a simply dismal time."

"But it's not fair to other men. I do hope, dearest, that you are not going to be an unprincipled flirt."

"I don't care a bit about flirting or having men fall in love with me. I only want to have a good time. If I see any man fixing to fall in love with me — I beg pardon — I mean showing signs of it, I'll tell him, for I don't want to hurt anybody, and I'm sure it must be horrid to see men look serious and glum. But I do want to be the belle of all the parties, and have flowers sent to me, and get nearly all the favours at the germans. Surely I have a right to a girl's good time."

"You certainly have, dear. Why not break the engagement? Have you considered that it is hardly fair to Cecil?"

"What?" Lee whirled about. "Do you think *he* would wish it broken off? He's never even hinted at such a thing."

"Of course not; he's too honourable. But when you are a year older you will write and tell him that you no longer hold him to a childish compact."

"I won't! He's mine, and I'll keep him. How can you be so cruel, Tiny? It's my first party, and now I want to cry!"

"You did not let me finish. I had no intention of speaking of this to-night, and I would not spoil your pleasure for the world. I was only going to say that a year from now you will feel very differently about everything. You will have seen more of the world, and you will realise the difference between fact and fancy."

"All the same I won't give up Cecil," said Lee obstinately. "It has been my dearest dream, and I won't even think about it's being all a sham."

CHAPTER XXI

BUT a year later, as Tiny had predicted, Lee wrote to Cecil Maundrell and gave him his freedom.

It is little that a girl learns of the world in San Francisco: where the home-bred youths are a remarkable compound of guile and ingenuousness, alcohol and tea-cakes, and where the more highly-seasoned Easterner rarely tarries. But that little had taught Lee several things. She had not only been the belle of her set, but her charm was potent and direct, and she had caught more than one glimpse of the passions of men. Randolph's had waxed with her growing consciousness of her power, and upon two memorable occasions the fiery impetuosity of his Southern blood had routed his practical Americanism, his aversion to gravity. Tom Brannan, whose mouth and heart grew no smaller with the years, and who was by no means a fool, although somewhat rattle-brained, had shown himself capable of imbecility. Ned Geary, clever, versatile, indolent, who employed his larger energies in protest against his father's insistence that he should make money instead of spending it, and who was the uncertain object of many maidenly hopes, not only proposed regularly to Lee by word and letter, but

was inspired to excellent rhyme. He was famed
for breaking social engagements of the most exacting nature, and was at pains to assure Lee that the
nice precision with which he adjusted his pleasure
to his politeness whenever herself was in question
was the signal proof of the depth of his feelings.
He even answered Mrs. Montgomery's notes when
she invited him to dinner, and his fair gay face was
never absent from her "evenings." When he
pleaded his cause that face became an angry red,
and the veins stood out on his forehead, but Lee,
who was very observing, noted that when he sang
he underwent precisely the same facial changes —
contortions she phrased it — and refused to be moved.
Perhaps she was a trifle heartless at this period, as
all girls are apt to be in the first flush of their
triumphs, when the love of men is flung at their feet
and their dearest art is to dodge a proposal. Lee
liked both Ned and Tom, for their spirits were high
and they were very good fellows, and offered them
her life-long friendship. For Randolph she had
much placid affection, and she respected him, for
he had brains and rather more knowledge of books
than the average of his kind; but she prayed that
he would transfer his affections to Coralie, who
secretly pined for them.

Between the three she arrived at the knowledge
that men were practical creatures and must be
treated as such, not as dream-stuff.

When Lord Arrowmount arrived she applied
herself to the study of him, but she ran into
impenetrable dusk some few inches from the entrance

of his every avenue of approach.   He was uniformly polite, in a stiff unself-conscious way, and seemed kind, and sensible, and good, but he barely opened his mouth.   Tiny insisted that during their walks together — he arrived in summer — he delivered himself of many consecutive sentences; but her statement was regarded as an erratic manifestation of the romantic condition of her affections.   Lee, baffled at all other points, descended to pumping his knowledge of the Maundrells; but his brief comments that "Barnstaple was rather mad," and "Lady Barnstaple was going at the deuce of a pace," summed up, if not his information, at least his communications.   Of Cecil he had never heard.   When she questioned him regarding his own experience at Oxford, he looked blank, and replied that he supposed it had been the usual thing.

It seemed incredible that Cecil could ever develop into an artificially animated sarcophagus of England's greatness, but the pink atmosphere of her day-dreams faded to ashes-of-roses; particularly as Randolph, who had spent six months in England, and Ned Geary, who had spent six months in Europe, assured her that Lord Arrowmount was a "type."

After the wedding, and the departure of the Arrowmounts, she strove to reconstruct her castles and re-suffuse their atmosphere.   But her intervals for meditation were few; she was not only a belle surrounded by admirers and friends, but business claimed a considerable share of her attention.   The new hotel was almost finished, and the hungry energies of the Press had found it and its young

owner so picturesque as "copy," that the conse-
quent boom necessitated two extra wings and another
row of bath-houses.   Mrs. Montgomery was horrified
at the notoriety, and would not permit Lee to be
photographed, lest the artist should weaken under
the unholy methods of the Press; but Lee herself
found resignation possible, and even cherished a
private gratitude for the sensationalism of the rival
dailies; her income was doubled, and it was not
unpleasant to be a personage.

Altogether, she found life intensely interesting,
if quite unlike the dreams of a less practical epoch;
and although she wanted nothing on earth so much
as to marry Cecil Maundrell, when the end of the
year came, she knew that it was her duty to release
him from a boy's chivalrous promise to a dying
woman, — and did so.

Cecil was in his last year of infrequent favours,
studying mightily for his first; but his reply was
prompt enough, and of unusual length for this
period.   There was a good deal to the point, and
more between the lines. With him (haughtily) a
promise was a promise; he had never given a
thought to release, any more than he had ever
thought twice about another woman; he had taken
it for granted, of course, that they should eventually
marry; and if she stopped writing to him he should
feel dismembered; forced to readjust himself when
he needed all his faculties for the honours he was
determined to take; should, in fact, feel himself full
up against a stone wall, bruised and blinking.   His
similes were many and varied, and he seemed anxious

that his letter should do equal credit to his principles and his culture. What Lee read between the
lines was that he was aghast, that he had practically
forgotten the engagement; and had long since come
to regard his correspondent as a sort of second himself, an abstract sympathy, a repository of his corus-
cations, a sexless confessor.

Lee, who had hastened upstairs to read the letter
in her virgin bower, hung and festooned with dream-
memories of Cecil, was more miserable than she had
been since the death of her mother, and cried until
nothing was visible of her beautiful eyes but a row of
sharp black points above two swollen cheeks. Her
castles rattled about her ears, and were possessed of
imps who laughed the tenacious remnants of her
dreams to death.

When the fire was out of her brain, she wrote to
Cecil a gay matter-of-fact letter, insisting upon the
end of the engagement, but promising to write as
regularly as if nothing had happened.

" And nothing really has, you know," she added, " except
that we are no longer babies. You are thirty years older —
with your wonderful Oxford ! — than the little boy I popped
corn with and sponged after a fight for the honour of
Britain ; and I am a most practical person with not an
ounce of romance in me " — (she had less than an atom at
the moment of writing) — " and quite determined to make
no mistakes with my life. So many girls do, Cecil ; you
can't think ! Four of the girls that came out about the
same time as Tiny are married and divorced. It seems to
me quite terrible that people should marry in that reckless
manner, knowing next to nothing of the world and less of

each other ! In each case it was the man's fault — they usually drank ; but the girls, it seems to me, were as much to blame for not making as sure as one can that the men they expected to live their lives with — I suppose they did — had character and principles they could respect. I have been brought up in a very old-fashioned way, and nothing would induce me to get a divorce, so I shall hesitate a long while before I take the final step. Of course you will not misunderstand me — we are such firmly knit friends we never could misunderstand each other, I think — I know as well as if I had seen you every day for the last eight years that you would never give any woman cause for divorce ; but if we happened to have different tastes in all things, we should be just as unhappy as if you were a little Western savage. And we probably have, for our civilisations are as opposite as the poles. I have been as carefully reared as all Californian girls of my class, but those that know me best tell me that I am Californian clear into my marrow ; so I am, doubtless, as little like an English girl as if I were a Red Indian. But what is the use of all this (attempted) analysis? Of course you will come to California to see me one of these days, and as I shall not marry for years, if ever, we shall meet in plenty of time to find out whether or not we were wise to break our engagement. Meanwhile, we are both free. I insist upon that, and, you know, I always would have my own way."

Lee was extremely proud of this epistle, particularly of the touch about racial differences, and its general essay-like flavour; she was ambitious to stand well with so terrible an intellect as Lord Maundrell's. She could not fascinate him across seven thousand miles — she exchanged a glance of mysterious confidence with her mirror, her nostrils expanding slightly — but she could command and hold his attention until those seven thousand miles were wrought into the past with the years of separation. She glanced at her mirror again.

His second reply was equally prompt. He accepted her decree, of course. She had exercised her woman's privilege, and he was bound to respect it; but he held her to her promise that the correspondence should continue exactly as before; and, indeed, after the first two paragraphs of his letter, there was nothing to indicate that the correspondence had been agitated for a moment. It was not exactly relief that breathed through the letter, for Cecil's mind seemed without vulgarity; but the alacrity with which he took up the broken thread, after having tied the knot with a double loop, made Lee laugh outright.

"He's really wonderfully decent," she thought, "considering that he has been harrowed for a month with the prospect of a scrawny, yellow, and lank-haired wife. What a fright I must have been! And, of course, he has that tin-type. Fate would never have been so kind as to let him lose it!"

CHAPTER XXII

CECIL finished his Oxford epoch, taking his double first and crowning his athletic career as stroke of his college eight. He wrote to Lee that he was a wreck mentally, and was going on a tour round the world to shoot big game; he should eventually land in California, where he expected she would have a grizzly for him. He hoped for tigers in India, lions and elephants in Africa, and buffalo in the " Western " United States. He should also take a run through South America. When he had finished with the grizzly, he should feel a man once more, not a worn-out intellect.

" It would be quite dreadful not to have gone through Oxford," he confessed, " for nothing else moulds a man's brain into shape — if he 's got one. How odd and unfinished your American men must be ! I understand that few of those who go to the Universities take the whole course — which is a kindergarten compared to ours — and that the majority scorn education after eighteen ; but I am more than willing to forget all I ever knew for at least two years. After that, of course, I shall think seriously of what I am to do with my life. I did not tell you, I think, that my grandmother is dead, and that I am not quite a pauper. I feel reasonably sure that the political life will be my choice, and I shall manage to learn something of each of our colonies that I visit."

Lee understood Ned Geary, Tom Brannan and more than one other of the men who had given her opportunity to study them. At times she was sure that she knew Randolph, leaf by leaf. The habit in which the average American lives may be said to be an illuminated manuscript of himself, profusely illustrated with drawings by the author. When he is not disclosing his inmost mind, he is criticising life, within the narrow horizon of his experience, from the personal view-point; which reflections are as self-revealing as annotations by the ambitious editor of a great poet. There was no mystery about any of them for Lee, and, like all bright imaginative girls, she loved mystery. She felt that it would be long before she could understand the least of Cecil, particularly if he was anything like Lord Arrowmount. It is true that he had often written at great length, and by no means ignored the sacred subject of himself; but there was always a magnificent reach about Cecil, and a corresponding lack of ingenuousness.

She wondered if she had given him the same suggestion of a complex mind and nature, and one day re-read his letters. The first fifteen or twenty contained references to the episodes of their brief companionship. Later, these episodes seemed quite forgotten. And he not only demanded no return of confidences, he evinced no curiosity. In all his letters there was not a reference to her inner life. Occasionally he asked what she was reading, and if she were happy in her new home; that was all.

"How is one to prepare oneself for such a man as that?" thought Lee. "What does he want? An ear — nothing more? He seems different enough from American men. They seem either to understand me, or to suggest that it does n't matter whether they do or not ; I am perfect all the same. But Cecil Maundrell ! " She kicked out her little foot rather viciously. After all, why should she adapt herself to anybody? She was an individuality, more of one every month of her life, and extremely interesting to herself and other people. Englishwomen, she had been told, were very much of a pattern — the result of centuries of breeding in uninterrupted conditions. It was the very reverse that made up nine-tenths of the fascination of the American woman. When she married Cecil Maundrell — she had tossed "if" out of her vocabulary — they might take a year or two to adjust themselves to each other; but they both had brains enough to succeed in the end; and he could not fail to be charmed with a wife cut out of her own piece of cloth, and specially designed for himself.

CHAPTER XXIII

LEE spent the following winter in New York and Washington, with friends of Mrs. Montgomery, who met and made much of her Del Monte. Her social success in both places was very great, and she carried off all the honours that an ambitious young beauty could desire. She met many men-of-the-world. The species rather alarmed her at first, but, after she had posed herself, they amused her more; in their way, they were as ingenuous as the callow youth of San Francisco. She returned to California wiser than when she had left it, and a trifle more subtle, but with an undiminished vitality of spirit, and with the romantic imp in the depths of her brain as active as ever. It had been Mrs. Montgomery's intention to join Lee in the spring, take her to visit Tiny, then to the great show places of Europe — invented by a benign Providence for the American tourist; but an attack of rheumatism defeated the project, and Lee hastened home to her.

She was not sorry to return. The East quickly palls on the Californian of temperament and imagination, and before the winter was over Lee had begun to long for the mysterious Latin charm of her own country, and for its unvarying suggestion of unlimited space. Moreover, she feared to miss Cecil Maundrell if she went abroad at this time; his movements seemed very erratic, and his letters were brief and unexplanatory. He might change his plans, and come to California at any moment. Above all, she wanted to meet him on her own ground, in the country which had gone largely into the making of her; not in Tiny's drawing-room, surrounded by a conventional house-party.

Sometimes she wondered at the persistence of her desire for Cecil Maundrell, considering how little it had to feed upon, and preferred to conclude that they were held together by some mysterious bond compounded in the laboratory of Nature, whose practical manifestation only awaited the pleasure of Time. It is true that there were periods when she was rebellious and angry, and during one of Cecil's long silences — he had not written for four months — she came very close to marrying Randolph. He was ever at her elbow, with a persistence generally quiet, occasionally impassioned. He made himself useful to her in a thousand ways, and studied her tastes; reading her favourite books, and keeping up with her fads. He was clever and companionable, and would, indubitably, make a good husband. He did not interest her; she knew him too well, and her power over him was too sure, but her second winter in San Francisco had bored her; she was out of tune with the world for the moment, and very human; she was in the mood, failing the best, to hang her ideals upon the man who pleased her most, and to love him by sheer exercise of imagination; a mood that has ruined the life of more women than one.

She was balancing the pros and cons more seriously than she was aware, when she received a letter from Cecil Maundrell.

It was early spring.   The family had moved down to Menlo sooner than usual on account of Mrs. Montgomery's health, which was still delicate; and Lee was starting for a ride to the hills, when the stableboy returned from the village with the morning mail. She sent her other letters into the house, unopened, and rode off rapidly with Cecil's.   It was of unusual thickness; she had not received one so heavy since the Sturm und Drang of his Oxford days.

When she was half way down the lane that led to the hills she read his letter.   Its length was its one point of resemblance to his note-books of Oxford. Several of its pages were filled with half-tender, half-humorous reminiscences of "the happiest and most piquant weeks of his life"; the rest to the enthusiasm with which he was filled at the prospect of seeing her again, mingled with unsubtle masculine suggestions that he would take a friendly pleasure in learning that she had not committed her future to some man who was not half good enough for her. The letter was dated New York, where he had been visiting an American college friend for two weeks. He expected to start immediately for the ranch of some English friends in the "Far West," and to reach California in five or six weeks.   Would she write him at once to the enclosed address, and tell him news of herself?

Lee's horse was walking slowly up the lane between hedges of wild roses and fragrant chaparral.

She glanced about vaguely, hardly recognising the familiar beautiful scene: the green foot-hills crouched close against the great mountains that were dark and still with their majestic redwoods crowding like brush and piercing the sky on the long irregular crest; the dazzling blue sky, the soft blue haze on the mountains, the glory of colour in the fields, and on the lower slopes of the hills; for the poppies and baby-eyes, lupins, and California lilies, were swarming over the land.

What did the letter mean? Had Cecil Maundrell written it in a dream, in which she, perchance, had visited him? She read it again. It was remarkably wide-awake. And it was almost a love-letter.

She glanced about more appreciatively. The soft rich mysterious beauty of the day and of California symphonised with the flush on her cheeks, the rapt languor of her eyes, the quickening within her.

She spent the greater part of the day in the hills, buying a glass of milk and some bread at a farm-house. When she reached the redwoods on the long slopes, she tethered her horse, and wandered far into the forest. The very mystery of life brooded in those dim cool aisles, whose silence was undisturbed by the low roar of spring waters, whose feathery green undergrowth was barely flecked by the brilliant sun above the dense arbours high on the grey columns of the forest.

She lay on the edge of the bluff above the creek and watched the salmon moving in lazy and unperturbed possession of their sparkling waters, the darting trout, the wilderness of ferns and lilac and lily down on the water's edge. A deer climbed down the opposite bank and drank; owls cried to each other in the night of the forest; two hundred feet above her head the squirrels exchanged drowsy remarks; in the warm green twilight of the afternoon the very birds went to sleep.

It was not the first time that Lee had dreamed of Cecil Maundrell in this forest; she doubted if he would seem as naturally encompassed by the beech woods and fells, the ruins and traditions of his English home. Certainly this was as old, and as surely it was a part of her.

They both had unnumbered generations behind them: his were thick with men and events; hers with redwoods, whose aisles were unpeopled, in whose impenetrable depths tradition itself was lost.

She returned home late in the afternoon. Randolph, who had just come from town, was standing on the steps, and ran forward to lift her down.

"My mother was beginning to worry," he said; "you ought to take a boy with you. If you don't want a servant, I will stay down and accompany you."

Lee flicked him lightly with her whip. "Then I would n't go," she said. "I love to ride about for hours by myself. Fancy if one could never get away from men."

She spoke airily, but Randolph looked hard at her.

"What has happened?" he demanded. "There is something quite unusual about you."

Lee blushed, but Cecil's letter was safe in her bosom.

"Don't ask impertinent questions, and see that you don't talk me to death to-night; I'm tired," and she ran upstairs.

Her other mail lay on her dressing-table. She opened a letter from Coralie, who was visiting friends in New York.

"Well," it began abruptly, "I have met your Cecil. It was last night, at a dinner-party at the Forbes'. He *is* tall, you will be pleased to learn, and I fancy he might look quite athletic and 'masterful' (your style) in evening clothes that fitted him. But I believe he has been sporting round the world with a couple of portmanteaux, and avoiding polite society. He wore a suit belonging to Schemmerhorn Smith, whom he is visiting, and it was just two sizes too small. He did n't seem in the least embarrassed about it, and his manners are quite simple and natural. He does n't talk very much, but is a good deal easier to get on with than that awful Lord Arrowmount. At first I was frightfully afraid of him — of course, being the lord of the party, he took in Mrs. Forbes, but I sat on the other side of him, and Mrs. Forbes had a scientific thing on her other side, and had to give him most of her attention. Well, where was I? Scared to death in the memory of *those* letters — of course I did n't breathe that I'd read them — but he's not in the least like them — at all events not at dinner-parties. He was very much interested when I told him I was your intimate friend, although not so much as later — but wait a minute. You may be sure I said everything under Heaven in your praise, but, curiously, I never mentioned your beauty, although I dilated upon your success, and all the scalps you wore at your belt, and that you had a room whose walls were simply covered with german favours. He warmed to the theme as time went on, and said you had always been his greatest chum, and that he was going to California for two things only — to kill a grizzly and see you. He put the grizzly first, but never mind — he's English. Now comes the point. After dinner, as soon as the men came in, he made for me — I did n't tell you that I 'm sure he 's shy — and I took him straight to your photograph, which is enthroned on a table all by itself.

" ' There she is,' I said.

" He took it up. 'Who?' he asked, staring at it with all his eyes — they are nice honest hazel eyes, by the way, that often laugh, although I 'll bet he has a temper.

" ' Who? — Why, Lee, of course ! '

" He stared harder at the picture — it is the low-necked one you had taken here, in black gauze and coloured — then he turned and stared at me. 'Lee?' he said. ' *This* is Lee?' and if he were not burnt a beautiful mahogany, I do believe he would have turned pale. He 's got a mouth on him, my dear, that means things, and it trembled.

" ' She 's grown up very pretty,' he said in a moment, as carelessly as he could manage. 'I never suspected that she would — that she had. Of course some of your enterprising Americans have snatched her up. I have n't heard from her for a long time. Is she engaged ? '

" ' Not that I know of,' I said, ' although she has three or four admirers so persistent, you never know what you may hear any minute.' I thought a little worry would n't hurt him ; he looks altogether too satisfied, as if he had been born to plums, and never had anything else. All he said was ' Ah ! ' He put the picture back, and we went off to the music-room, but he managed to pass that table twice before the evening was over — and I must say, I 've seen

American men manage things more diplomatically. But there's something rather magnificent about him, all the same. He's not very entertaining — Randolph would fairly scintillate beside him — but his air of repose and remoteness from the hustling every-day world are really fine. If he had worn a potato sack instead of his almost equally grotesque get-up, he would have looked as unmistakably what he is. I hunted industriously for all his good points to please you, but give me an American every time. I never was intended for a miner, and you have to go into an Englishman's brain with a pick and shovel. Your Cecil suggests that he's got a solid mine of real intellect, developed with all the modern improvements, inside his skull; but what's the good, when you can't hear the nuggets rattle? He wouldn't even tell me his adventures — shut up like a clam, and said they were just like any other fellow's; and Schemmerhorn Smith told me that same evening that the men Lord Maundrell was with said he was one of the crack sportsmen of the day. Do you remember when Tom killed that panther that attacked him in the redwoods? We had it for breakfast, lunch, and dinner for a month. Of course a happy medium's the thing; but for my part, I don't like too much modesty. I'm suspicious of it. . . ."

So it was her beauty that had shifted the strata in Lord Maundrell's solid mine of intellect? It must have caused something of a shock to have resulted in a letter which almost committed him. It was both a jar and a relief to discover that he was much like other men. She re-read his letter. Then she glanced into her mirror.

"So much the better," she remarked.

CHAPTER XXIV

HER admirers had a sorry time of it for the next two weeks; she was capricious, even irritable, absent-minded, and at no pains to conceal that they bored her. Her appetite remained good, or Mrs. Montgomery would have grown alarmed.

The answer to Cecil's letter had required an entire day of anxious thought. Her pen ran over with the emotions he had quickened; but pride conquered, and she finally wrote him a gay friendly letter, assuring him of a welcome in which curiosity would play no insignificant part, but studiously concealing her burning interest.

She was profoundly thankful to the inspiration which dictated that letter when his answer came. It was very brief, and its only enthusiasm was inspired by the buffalo. There was not a mutually personal line in it. He concluded by remarking that if he did not write again, she could expect him any time just outside of a month. He should go to Southern California first to visit some English ranchers, whom he had known at Oxford, and to kill his grizzly.

Lee tore this letter into strips, and plunged into a desperate flirtation with Randolph, giving him an unusual meed of dances at the little parties of Menlo, making him get up at unearthly hours to ride with

her before his day in town — he detested riding —
and driving every evening to the station to meet him.
He was puzzled, but inclined to take the pleasant
caprices of the gods without analysis. He was very
busy, and it was enough to know, as he sat at his
table, his pencil working at the thousand and one
prosaic details of a huge iron building he was de-
signing, that his evenings and Sundays were to be
made radiant by the smiles of the most charming
woman in the world. He forgot Cecil Maundrell;
and the future he tenaciously desired seemed imminent.

CHAPTER XXV

"HERE comes a tramp up the avenue again," said Mrs. Montgomery, with irritation. "That makes the second this week. I shall have to build a lodge. Why can't they go to the farm-house? Tramps are very trying."

"He doesn't walk like a tramp," said Lee, "although his clothes certainly *are* —" Being a trifle shortsighted, she raised her lorgnette. She rose suddenly, turning her back to Mrs. Montgomery, and descended the steps of the verandah. Her knees and hands shook violently, and the blood rushed to her head; but she was some three minutes reaching the stranger, who had lifted his cap, then plunged his hands in his pockets, and at the end of that time her nerves were in the leash of her will.

"Well, if it isn't like you, Cecil Maundrell, to come in those awful clothes!" she cried gaily. "Mrs. Montgomery took you for a tramp."

He laughed nervously as he swung her hand to and fro. "We were burnt out last night, and they're all I've got left. I'll go on to San Francisco in a day or two and get some."

"I don't believe Aunty will let you in the house, much less sit down at the table."

"Really? How curious! I did n't know you were so conventional out here. But I 'll go on at once, if you say so."

"No, no. Only make an elaborate enough apology to Mrs. Montgomery, and she will be as nice as possible. But we 're not only frightfully conventional out here, but rather sensitive. A duke came down to a dinner-party in Menlo once in his shooting-jacket, and we 've never gotten over it."

"What a bounder. I 'll go out and eat with the farm hands. I like the rough and ready American very much."

"I don't know any, so I can't argue. You look perfectly splendid, and I 'm *so* glad you 're tall. You really have changed very little, except that you 've lost your pretty complexion — although I prefer this. You make other men look positively ill. Oh, Cecil, I *am* glad to see you!"

Her face and voice were animated by the friendliest feeling. Cecil stared hard at her, the smile dying out of his eyes. "You are very beautiful," he said abruptly.

"I hear a carriage. Some people are coming to call. Let us get out of the way — not that I 'm ashamed of you, but you don't want to meet Mrs. Montgomery before a lot of other people."

"I don't want to meet her at all — or anybody else but yourself. To tell the truth, it never occurred to me that there would be any one else, and I knew you would n't mind these old shooting rags. I do look like a tramp. I really never thought about it. I remember people rather stared at me in the train. A flashy-looking fellow in the smoking-car asked me if I was looking for work, and I told him No, I was looking for a fight. He said nothing more until we reached a station, when he asked me to get out and take a drink."

"Did you? I can't imagine your unbending that far."

"Oh, I take everybody as a matter-of-course, knocking about. I accepted the drink and stood him another. After that I went to sleep to get rid of him. Of course he wanted to talk — that is to say, monologue."

"Let us sit down here."

They had left the avenue, and crossed a side garden. There were two rustic chairs under a great oak. They took them, and faced each other.

"Did you kill your grizzly?"

"No; not one has been heard of in the neighbourhood of San Luis Obispo for three years. I never was so disappointed in my life. Now, I suppose, there is no hope; it is too much to ask of men who have been burnt out to bother about grizzlies. My other friends — the ones I've been with for the last two years — did n't come further West than Montana."

Lee had on a white summer frock, girdled with a ribbon the colour of her eyes. Her black hair was coiled loosely. She was fully aware that she looked very lovely.

"You are the only man living that would look for a grizzly first and for me after," she said with a certain arching of her brows and pouting of her lips

. . . " Cecil, you always could stare harder than any one I ever knew."

" I believe I 've thought quite as much about you as the grizzly."

" Thanks ! "

" No ; but I am serious." He looked away. Lee fancied that his triple coat of tan really paled. " I 've never been so upset in my life," he continued lucidly.

" It never did take you long to come to the point. What a relief — there are not to be a half-dozen weeks of flirtatious fencing. Do come out with it."

He laughed, but without any great amount of ease. " I 'll be perfectly frank," he said. " I saw your photograph in New York ; I nearly went off my head. I lay awake all night. It was the first time any woman had bowled me over. My two or three fancies were hardly worth recalling. You see, I put your beauty with all I knew of you mentally, and of our delightful companionship when you were older than most girls of your age — and the sweetest little thing ! — and the combination made my brain whirl. Before morning I wrote you that letter —— "

" Well ? "

Lee was twirling her lorgnette, her eyes lowered. Cecil had not removed his eyes from the horizon. He spoke jerkily, with an evident effort.

" When I cooled down, I was sorry I had sent that letter," he brought out brutally, after an instant's further hesitation. " You see, I had never thought of you in that way at all, or I should n't even have started for California. I don't believe in international marriages —— "

"But, my dear Cecil," exclaimed Lee, opening wide surprised eyes, "we're not going to marry! I settled all that long ago."

Cecil was too perturbed and too masculine to mark the rapid change of tactics. He turned his face about and stared at her. He was visibly paler, and his eyes were almost black.

"You have not settled it as far as I'm concerned," he said. "I knew it was all up with me when you came toward me down that avenue. I've done nothing but deliberate for five weeks; I've weighed every pro and con; I've recalled every scene between my father and stepmother; I've argued with myself on the folly of marrying anything under a fortune; and the moment I saw you I knew that I had wasted five weeks, and that I should marry you if you would have me."

Lee's eyes had returned to the study of her lap. Pride and passion battled again. After a full moment's silence, she looked up with so sweet a smile that he leaned forward impulsively to take her hand. But she drew it back.

"Cecil," she said, "I forbid you to make love to me until you have made me love you first. Of course I can't say if I ever shall." She looked about vaguely, her lips still smiling. "But, at least, we start fair; I don't care a straw for any one else, and I've always liked you better than anybody in the world. To-day is the twenty-sixth of April. You may propose to me again on the twenty-sixth of May."

He looked at her helplessly, his lips twitching.

"You don't care at all?" he asked. His voice still thickened when he was agitated.

"How can I, Cecil — in that way — when I have n't laid eyes on you for ten years? You admit that I was only an abstraction to you before you saw my picture. You could not expect more of me, and I never even had a glimpse of a photograph. And women don't take fire so easily as men." She prayed he would not catch her up in his arms and kiss her. "I have not even been inspired to deliberation." She gave a little laugh just tipped with malice. "What would you think, I wonder, if I accepted you on a moment's notice."

"You certainly would n't have my excuse. What a guy I must be!" He stood up with a sudden diffidence which made him look like a big awkward boy, and Lee loved him the more.

"What time does the next train go to San Francisco?" he added. He had taken out his watch.

"Twelve-ten."

"I have just time to catch it. I'll be back when I've got some decent clothes. I suppose there are tailors in San Francisco — in Market Street?"

"Go and see Randolph, Crocker Building. He will take you to his."

"Thanks. Good-bye."

He shook her hand, avoiding her eyes, and strode away. When he reached the avenue, he plunged his hands into his pockets and began to run. Lee found time to laugh at his picturesque lack of self-consciousness before she turned and fled across the lane into the friendly solitude of the Yorba woods.

CHAPTER XXVI

HE returned three days later, clad in immaculate grey, a trunk in his wake containing much smart linen and four suits of clothes, which had been ordered at the best house in San Francisco by a stockbroker who had retired from business and his country the day before Cecil, with similar measurements and similar needs, was presented to the tailor by Randolph.

Mrs. Montgomery had done the one thing possible under the circumstances — she had asked Cecil to make her house his home so long as he remained in that part of California. Her eyes were very red on the morning after his first appearance, but she made no comment to Lee, who spent the greater part of those three days by herself, but appeared quite normal when with the family. Cecil had gone at once to see and consult Randolph, who remarked, when he came home that night, that the Englishman seemed a very good sort, but that he should prefer not to walk down Kearney Street with him again until he was properly rigged out. He really did n't know why they had n't been mobbed, and two imps of newsboys had made audible remarks about "blarsted Britishers."

"I don't see why you can always tell an Englishman," he added, with some impatience. "To say nothing of his get-up to-day, look at the difference between his figure and Coe's. The clothes will fit Maundrell to perfection, but his figure is no more like Coe's than it 's like mine. He 's a lean athletic Englishman, every inch of him; Coe was thin and angular. It 's quite remarkable."

"Is he very handsome?" asked Mrs. Montgomery faintly.

"I really could n't say. He looks like an Englishman — that 's all."

Lee darted a swift side-glance; he was eating with his usual nervous haste. She knew him better than in the old days, but could detect no sign of agitation in him. In a moment he began to talk about a new pair of carriage horses he had bought his mother; and during the evening he asked Lee to play for him in the dark, as usual. Once she turned her head suddenly and caught a fixed steely gleam from the depths of his chair. She averted her eyes hastily, and gazed thoughtfully at the keys, playing mechanically, with nothing of her usual expression.

She always wore white in summer, in accordance with an unwritten law of Menlo Park, and for the evening of Cecil's second appearance she selected her softest and airiest, one, moreover, that was cut several inches below her throat, and one or two above her elbows. Full-dress, except at the rare dinner parties in honour of some-one-with-letters, was tabooed in that exclusive borough. As Cecil came from town with Randolph she left the honours of introduction to the host, and did not make her appearance until a few minutes before dinner. She found Mrs. Montgomery and Cecil amiably discussing California, and Randolph gently jeering at them for their lack of originality.

"Several volumes have been written on the ' Resources of California,' but the one to which she shall owe her permanent fame has never had so much as a paragraph. It awaits its special biographer."

"But there can be originality even on an exhausted theme," said Lee, who had shaken hands with Cecil, and was anxious to keep the conversation light. "Captain Twining's remark two days after his arrival in California is already quite famous." She glanced at Cecil, and lifted her chin with defiant coquetry. "He said that he had only heard of two things Californian before he came — Miss Tarleton and the climate."

"He was n't very polite to call you a thing," said Cecil, laughing; he seemed in excellent spirits.

"Perhaps he took her for a perfume or a flower," said Randolph quickly.

The two men measured each other with a swift glance.

"That was really very neat," remarked Lord Maundrell. "You might have blushed, Lee."

"She has had too many compliments; she is quite spoiled for anything less than downright uxoriousness."

"Ah!" observed Lord Maundrell.

They went in to dinner. Cecil was not to be laughed out of his interest in California; the grape industry had interested him during his brief sojourn in the South, and he wanted to know all about it, from its incipience to its finalities. Randolph, who knew little about the grape industry, and cared less, answered in glittering generalities, and headed him off to the subject of mission architecture. Cecil immediately instituted a comparison between the results of Indian labour and the characteristic edifices of Spain — more particularly of Granada, and then branched off to the various divergences under native and climatic influences to be found in South America. Of all this Randolph knew practically nothing. Like most Americans, he was a specialist, and had studied only that branch of his art necessary to his own interests. But his mind was very nimble, and he so successfully concealed from the Englishman his superficial knowledge of the subject, that Lee, who followed the conversation with rapt interest, did not know whom to admire most. She was wondering if Cecil could make as brilliant a showing as Randolph on next to nothing, when, in reply to a question of his host's regarding the gold mines of Peru, he replied indifferently:

"I don't know anything about them. They did n't interest me," and dismissed the subject; one upon which Randolph happened to have some knowledge. He had invested heavily in a newly-discovered mine of which one of his friends was secretary.

The conversation turned to politics. Randolph was at his best analysing and illustrating the party differences, but when Cecil questioned him about the genesis of the two parties, the constitution of the United States, and the historic significance of the various presidents, even generalities failed him, and he was obliged to confess himself nonplussed.

"Upon my word," he exclaimed laughing, "I do believe that the only thing I remember about United States history is its covert admonition to grow up as fast as I could and lick the English."

Lee and Cecil laughed simultaneously. "Have you ever told the story of my attempt to lick the United States?" asked Cecil. "That defeat rankled for years."

"Never!"

Cecil told the story very well. It was evident that his bitterness had passed, and he concluded:

"The odd part of it all is, that although you Americans beat us, it is you who are bitter, and not ourselves. It was the same way with those boys. They gave me sour disapproving glances every time they met me until I left. On the other hand, I nearly thrashed the life out of a man in Montana, and I never made such an enthusiastic friend."

"Oh, we have to be bullied," said Randolph frankly. "We love to brag and boast and swagger. You see we are such an extraordinary nation that we can't help being a little cocky, and the only man we really respect is the one who lays us on our back with a black eye and a nose out of joint. We always get up — nothing can keep an American on his back — but we go to our graves with a wondering admiration of the muscle, mental or physical, that floored us."

"That is very interesting," said Cecil thoughtfully, "very." He added in a moment: "I fancy

the bitterness would have died out by this time, in
spite of our failure to keep the finest of our colonies,
but for our diplomacy, which is a trifle too subtle
and sinuous to please the rest of the world.   I don't
know that the United States stands alone in her
antagonism."   And he laughed.

Randolph knew less about English diplomacy than
he did about the past history of American politics,
but he made a rapid calculation: if he led Cecil on,
the Englishman, with his exact and profound knowledge, would distinguish himself and win the grateful
admiration of the woman.   On the other hand,
unless he kept him talking, he should be called
upon for information which he had always considered
superfluous in an American who had but one short
life in which to "get there," and which was of no
particular interest to himself; he had cut his college
course down to one year in order to make the most
of his youthful energies, and to run no risk of losing Lee Tarleton.   Moreover, if he drew his guest
out, he should not only be doing his duty as a host,
but Lee's approval for himself would be as large as
her admiration of his rival.   There was more than
a chance, clever as she was, that she would give
him full credit for generosity and for the courtesy
of his fathers.   He made up his mind in an instant,
threw out an observation of epigrammatic vagueness
on the diplomacy of England, and in ten minutes
had Cecil monopolising the conversation, under the
impression that he was forced into an argument.

Lee forgot her dinner, and listened intensely.
She had heard men talk more brilliantly — for Cecil

had cultivated none of the graces of oratory, and of the epigram he appeared to have a healthy scorn — but she had never heard any one talk who knew so well what he was talking about, and who yet suggested that he was merely skimming up the spray of a subject whose deeps were trite to him straight down to its skeletons and flora. His knowledge of English diplomacy suggested an equally minute knowledge of the diplomatic history of every country into which England had run her horns. He talked without priggishness, rather as if he were used to discussing the subject with men who were as well grounded as himself.

As they left the dining-room, Lee lingered behind a moment with Randolph.

"It was awfully nice of you," she said. "You like to do the talking yourself, and England has never interested you much."

"I knew that it would interest you. I was bored to extinction; but it is time you had a little variety."

"You *are* good." She hesitated a moment. "He has real intellect, has n't he?" she asked.

"He knows things. He can knock the spots out of us when it comes to solid information. But in a contest of wits I 'd engage him in a match without any qualms. He 's straight out from the shoulder, and if he were stacked up against American nimbleness and adaptability for any great length of time, he 'd go under."

"He 's quick enough."

"With an answer — yes; but that 's not what I mean."

CHAPTER XXVII

THEY had remained longer at dinner than usual, and when Lee went out to the verandah, she found Mr. and Mrs. Brannan and Mr. Trennahan, a New Yorker who had recently married and settled in Menlo. Cecil was at her elbow in a moment.

"Let us take a walk," he said. "Will it be rude to leave these people?"

"Oh, no; we are very informal among ourselves, and they are Mrs. Montgomery's friends rather than mine."

They crossed the grounds, entered Fair Oaks Lane, and walked toward the hills. It was moonlight, and the redwoods on the crest of the mountain were sharp against the sky.

"Can I smoke a cigar?"

"Of course."

"Should not you have something else round you?"

"This shawl is camel's hair and very warm. How do you like Randolph?"

"A very decent chap. Is he in love with you?"

"Why is it that when a man admires a woman he fancies every other man is in love with her?"

"That 's not answering my question. Not that it is necessary. No man could grow up with you and not love you."

"You are learning to pay compliments. You will be sending me candy and flowers next."

"I'll never send you candy, nor anything that's not good for you."

"Have you spent the last three days regretting that you proposed on Monday?"

"What an ass you must think me. I proposed, and that was the end of it; my only regret was that I did it so badly. I have spent the last three days racking my brains over a different matter, not a wholly foreign one."

Lee made no reply. Her hand hung at her side. He took it in a quiet but determined pressure. "How am I to make you love me?" he asked. "I haven't the vaguest idea how to go about it."

"In the very bottom of your mind wouldn't you really rather that you could not? I, too, have been thinking hard during the last three days. Of course, I know of international marriages that have turned out very well; but that doesn't alter the fact that many have turned out badly — although, for that matter, the United States fairly reeks with divorce. It is a question to puzzle wiser heads than mine. Are most English marriages happy?"

"Probably not; but the point is that if you marry your own sort, you know where you are. If I had ever met an English girl who attracted me one half as much as you do, and had married her, we should have followed along certain traditional lines and got on fairly well, even if there were no great happiness. You see an Englishman is certain of several things if he marries a perfectly normal Englishwoman of his own class. She will obey him, she will have as many children as he wishes, her scheme of life will be his, and, no matter how bright she may be, she will adapt herself to him — which is not the least important point. An Englishman simply cannot adapt himself to anybody. It is n't in him. He can be a good husband on his own lines, particularly if he loves his wife; and if he loves her enough, and she makes herself more charming than other women, he 'll be faithful to her, and do what he can to make her happy. But she must adapt herself to him."

"You have the virtue of frankness! Are you trying to frighten me off?"

"It would not be fair of me to deceive you." He certainly looked very serious. Lee studied his profile meditatively, but she did not withdraw her hand. "I don't see why it should frighten you. We have always been most sympathetic. We really loved each other when we were little chaps, and were drawn together at once. In all these years I have had no such confidante, no one who has been so necessary to me. And you have not been indifferent; never was there so faithful a correspondent. If you loved me enough, we should be very happy. Theories go to the winds when a man wants a woman as much as I want you, and love would settle all our differences."

"I wonder!" They walked on in silence for a moment; then she said: "How brave you are! Much braver than I should be if I consented to marry you; for I, at least, know you fairly well, whereas you are merely generalising, and do not know me in the least. I might give you an exhaustive description of the conditions in which I had been brought up, from that in which my mother played no small part to the men that have been my slaves ever since I put on long frocks. I might analyse to you the growth of my individuality, describing the influence which the management of my own affairs has had on my character, the fact that I have done my own thinking all my life, and then — these three years in which I have been a real belle, and seen more than one man make an idiot of himself. I might tell you all that, and even enter into a wise dissertation on the racial differences of our two civilisations; but nothing could give you a real idea of myself, the idea you would have absorbed if you had been a part of my environment for the last ten years. Nothing could be wiser than your observation that we should marry our own sort. As far as I can figure it out, it comes to this: If I married Randolph he would spend his life buttoning my boots. If I married you, I should spend my life pulling off yours —— "

"Good heavens, no! What a little beast I was!"

He laughed heartily, although, oddly enough, his laughter did not interfere with his seriousness in the least. It would have dissipated that of any other man she knew; but he went on at once. "I should not quarrel with Fate for giving me a wife who interested me more than any woman of my own sort could do, if you were always perfectly open and frank with me. I should hate being intrigued, and I should never have the patience nor the inclination to sit

down and unravel any woman's complexities. If
you did not go to work deliberately to puzzle me, I
should soon know you, and I cannot imagine you
other than absolutely charming."

"If I pluck out my complexities — in other words,
my individuality — by the roots, and adapt myself to
you."

"You could adapt yourself to me without sacrificing the least of your individuality. I would n't have
you other than you are. Where would your charm
be?"

"You began very practically, but you are getting
rather Utopian."

"No, because we are both young. It is true that
I am twenty-five, and that my character is quite
formed — a difficult thing for a woman used to
American men to understand. But I still have all
the fresh enthusiasm of youth for anything that
interests me, and an immense capacity for affection,
which has been satisfied very little. If you loved
me well enough — that would be the whole point."

"In other words, the entire responsibility of this
matrimonial experiment would lie on my shoulders."

"Don't call it an experiment, for God's sake! It
is life and death for me. If I take you I take you
for ever, and if you decide to marry me, you must
make up your mind that we *will* be happy."

They walked on for another moment in silence.
He felt her fingers curl up stiffly, but she said quite
calmly:

"I decided long ago, when I was sixteen, I think,
to marry you, and I have never changed my mind for

a moment. I always knew that you would come. On Monday, I could not make up my mind to fall into your arms like a ripe apple; but you are so serious that you have made me serious, and I cannot coquet any longer."

Cecil had dropped her hand and stopped short, facing her.

"Is it possible that you love me?" he asked. "Is it possible?"

"I have loved you twenty times more than any one on earth for years and years, and I shall love no one else as long as I live. . . . Cecil, you *do* stare so!"

But in another second he had ceased to stare.

CHAPTER XXVIII

THEY decided to keep their engagement to themselves for a short while, but on the fourth day Mrs. Montgomery entered Lee's room abruptly.

"I must have the truth, my dear child," she said. "In the first place, unless you are engaged to Lord Maundrell, I cannot permit you to take these long walks and rides alone with him; you never did such a thing before. And in the second place —— "

"Don't cry," said Lee, fondling her nervously. "That is one reason I have n't said anything about it. I knew you would be disappointed about Randolph, and I can't even bear to think of leaving you —— "

"If you only could have loved Randolph!"

"Really and truly, I tried — two or three times. But I made up my mind long ago that I would not make a mistake when I married, if I could help it. I don't expect a bed of roses with Cecil — he 's too high and mighty, and he 's too self-centred — but at least I love him well enough to put up with anything, and nothing could make me love him less — no matter what happened."

"Oh, I hope you will be happy! — I hope you will be happy! Lord Maundrell is really most interesting and charming; his air and his manners are really — *really*. And Tiny is very happy with Arthur. But I shall be so lonely — and poor Randolph!"

"Can't you and he come to England to live?"

"I have six other daughters and five grandchildren here, remember, and Randolph is in too great a hurry to get rich to begin over again in a new country. Tiny will be here soon now for a year, and I shall go back with her. Of course, I shall see you then, but you are really lost to me."

Lee, whose tears were quick, wept passionately at this aspect; she had not thought of it before. When both were calmer, Mrs. Montgomery asked:

"Did you tell him that you had a great deal more money?"

Lee nodded.

"What did he say?"

"He was delighted, and said so as frankly as he says everything. He says we shall have three thousand pounds a year between us, and can get along very nicely; although the tug will come when we have to keep up Maundrell Abbey. His stepmother has made her will in his favour; but he says she has cut into her capital, and lately she has had to pay a tremendous amount for repairs on the Abbey. Lord Barnstaple certainly came high!"

"What a terrible marriage! Thank Heaven, there is no disgraceful commercial transaction where you and Tiny are concerned. Lord Maundrell seems clever enough for anything; why does n't he go into business and make a fortune?"

"He would never think of such a thing; he's going to stand for Parliament at the next elections. His ideas are quite fixed, and he has his whole career mapped out."

"Of course he 'll be Prime Minister. Of course he 's ambitious."

"He 's not so ambitious as he is terribly serious. He thinks it 's his duty — his vocation. A lot of his ancestors have been statesmen, although they 've generally been in the House of Lords. Cecil 's so glad he 's not going to be for ages. His father started out brilliantly, but had a great row with his party about something, and dropped out. Then, after his first wife's death, he became rather dissipated. Cecil says he began life with high ideals. His uncle Basil was a distinguished Parliamentarian, and a Bill or a Law or something is called after him — I expect to know English politics backward by this time next year."

"You will! — You will! You were made to be the wife of a great man, and he 'll be so proud of you!"

"You are the most partial person!"

"Yes, I am; but I 've always been able to see my children's faults, much as I adore them. But I don't feel a qualm about you. Your mind is so quick; and, thank Heaven, I paid such strict attention to your manners. They are simply perfect."

"Think if you 'd left me to grow up in a boarding-house! You can be sure I never forget my debts. I did n't tell you that Cecil is no longer a Radical. He 's a Conservative, straight into his marrow; his ancestors have never been anything else, and he 's outlived all his fads."

"He 's painfully mature," said Mrs. Montgomery, with a sigh. "Englishmen seem to remain boys a long time, and then to grow old all at once. I suppose it's that dreadful Oxford. Our boys are little old men who get their youth somewhere in their twenties, and are not really grown again until after thirty. It's very singular. Randolph, of course, has worked a good deal of his boyishness out of him, but he is always laughing and joking. And look at Tom and Ned — they are mere children beside Lord Maundrell. I was really mortified when they tried to talk to him last night, and I had always thought them bright."

"So they are. But if men won't cultivate their brains, what can they expect? Tom thinks of nothing but business — which he takes as a joke — dancing, and football, and Ned boasts that he has only read ten books in his life. Tom would only remain eight months at Harvard, and Ned wouldn't go at all. Both have had every opportunity, and they are full of American quickness and wit; but they have a genuine scorn for intellect. I can see that they regard Cecil as a freak. Randolph respects brains, but even he is bored."

"Yes, it's true — it's true. Will you tell Randolph? I haven't the courage."

"Yes; I'll tell him to-night — we're dining alone, aren't we? Don't worry about him. Men always get over things."

CHAPTER XXIX

THAT evening, as they were walking up the hall from the dining-room to the verandah, Lee put her hand on Randolph's arm and drew him into the parlour.

"I want to tell you something," she said nervously. "You know I have always loved Cecil Maundrell. I am going to marry him."

"So I have inferred."

The room was dark. She could not see his face.

"I am so glad you don't mind. You used to fancy yourself in love with me — that was the only thing that worried me. I'm afraid I'm hopelessly conceited."

"You have every reason to be. Maundrell has floored me. I respect him. But, as I remarked once, an American never stays on his back."

"You 'll forget me? You 'll marry Coralie?"

He brought his hand down on her shoulder and jerked her close to him. She could see his white face dimly.

"I mean that sooner or later — this year or ten years from now — I will have you, and that you will come to me of your own accord."

"I never will! What a detestable —— No matter what happened, I'd never love any man but Cecil Maundrell! I belong to him!"

" We shall see."

He left her then and went out to the verandah. Lee heard his light laugh a moment later.

" He certainly can be serious," she thought; " but I 'm sure he hates it. That laugh means either that he 's delighted to forget his momentary drop, or that he 's past master of the great national game of bluff. In his way he 's not uninteresting."

CHAPTER XXX

SEVERAL days later she took Cecil to the redwoods. Mrs. Montgomery consented reluc-
tantly — Lee had always been a little beyond her —
but put up the lunch herself. They started early,
for the weather was very warm, and as they rode
hard there was little conversation, although both
were in high spirits. When they reached the foot-
hills they were obliged to slacken speed, and Cecil
said:

"I feel exactly as if we had started out in search
of adventures again. Let us hope there will not be
a fog nor an earthquake."

They had talked old times threadbare, and, after
shuddering once more over that memory, Lee said:
"The redwoods are just the place for stories of thrilling adventures with tigers and lions and things. As
Coralie says, you are altogether too modest. I shall
insist."

"I don't mind telling you anything you like; but
to sit up by the hour and rot to other people about
oneself — it's too much like—— "

"American brag?"

"Well, I don't like to be rude, but that was what
I meant. Of course there are exceptions," he added
hastily. "Take Mr. Trennahan, for instance. I have
noticed that the American who has lived a good deal

abroad neither brags nor is in any way provincial.
And, as Montgomery says, the others have every
excuse. They would have a right to be cocky about
their country, if only on account of what Nature has
done for it."

"They are lovely, are n't they?" Lee pointed her
whip proudly to the forest above. It began on the
next slope they ascended, straggling carelessly for a
mile or more, then seemingly knit into a black and
solid wall of many tiers. Presently the hills closed
about them, the great arms of the mountain reached
down-on every side, its grass burnt golden, its redwoods casting long shadows, until their own shade
grew too heavy. As the riders ascended higher,
there was often, far down on one side of the road, a
cañon set thick with the rigid trees, and cut with
a blade of water; an almost perpendicular wall on
the other. Finally, they passed the outposts, and
entered a long steep avenue of redwoods leading to
the depths of the forest.

"I never knew anything so intensely still, nor so
solemnly beautiful," said Cecil. "Could n't we come
here for our honeymoon? Is there a house to be
had?"

"The Trennahans have one. I am sure they would
lend it to us. Oh, I should like nothing so much as
that!"

"Nor I! Fancy!"

When they felt that they were really in the forest,
they tethered their horses and sat down at once with
their luncheon. It was a very good one, and they
ate it with relish, for they had been in the saddle

several hours. When it was over, Cecil made a pillow of his saddle, and smoked a pipe.

"You look quite happy," said Lee sarcastically.

"Oh, I am! I never knew anything so jolly!"

"Would you like me to pull off your boots?"

"What an unforgiving spirit you have. I should be much happier if you would sit as close to me as you can."

Lee sat down beside the saddle.

"Now, tell me your adventures," she commanded.

Whatever the final results of her inspiration, the immediate were very agreeable. Cecil's adventures had been many, and the enthusiasm of the sportsman made him eloquent. It was soon evident that he had returned heart and soul into the past two years; and although Lee was pleased to observe that his grasp on her hand did not relax, his pipe was permitted to go out. Although his adventures did not consist of a series of hairbreadth escapes, they were novel and exciting, and Lee was thrilled.

"You always were the most sympathetic listener," he exclaimed. "Fancy my talking to anyone else like this! I do believe my tongue has been wagging for two hours."

"I don't wonder you love sport. I should, too. It was a mere name to me before. The boys go fishing once a year; they camp out in this forest; and, occasionally, they go duck or snipe shooting, or kill a few quail; but I never heard even the expression 'big game' except from you."

"And with grizzlies and pumas — fancy! What are the men thinking of?"

"Of course there are lots of old mountaineers and trappers who have shot more bears and things than they can count; but even those of our men that are not chasing the mighty dollar don't seem to take to sport."

"It's not a tradition with them. It will come with more leisure, more Englishmen, and the inevitable imitation of ourselves in that and in other things. They hate us, but the tail of their eye is always on England's big finger writing on the wall. The Eastern men copy our accent, our clothes, our customs. The New Yorkers are already good sportsmen, and they owe it to us that they are. They began with a spirit that did them little credit, but they are twice the men they would be otherwise — this generation of them, I mean. I am given to understand that, in its mad rush for money, the race has deteriorated since the Civil War. Your Californians are slower, because they are on the edge of the world, and customs take longer to reach them; but one day some idle young blood will spend a year in England, then come back and make sport the fashion,[1] and the next generation will be men with healthy bodies and healthy minds."

"And better manners! I am so glad you are not going to hustle for money. I hate the loathsome stuff — except to have it; it has so much to answer for. I should think the race has deteriorated. Look at the Southerners! Look at Randolph! The only picture Mrs. Montgomery has of her husband was

---

[1] This prediction is already being verified to some extent.

taken when he had been out here twenty years, and then his face had become very sharp and keen; but his father and grandfather were most aristocratic-looking men — full of fire, but with a repose as fine as yours. And Randolph was a most elegant boy; it is doubtful if you think him a gentleman."

"Oh, yes, yes! The American armour fairly rattles on him, and when he's old he'll look like the American eagle; but I feel jolly sure that when it came to the point, he'd never do anything unworthy of a gentleman."

"Not even to get a woman?"

"All's fair in love; but he would never do anything tricky or vulgar."

"Once he wouldn't; but he has been rubbing elbows with dishonest and common men for so many years. His standards are lowered; I can see the change from year to year."

"Blood is blood. He will never descend quite to the level of the men of one generation. I've just thought of another yarn."

"Oh, do tell it! Let us walk."

They wandered about for an hour or two, pushing through the low forest of fronds and young redwoods, sometimes silent and happy, sometimes planning out the days of their honeymoon, sometimes absorbed in the vast silence, the almost overwhelming suggestion of immensity and power and antiquity of the redwoods.

"They are a thousand years old — some of them."

"They are so new to me that I can hardly realise their age. But they make the rest of the world seem a thousand miles away, and there is something about them that agitates soul and sense, and promises — almost everything. If Trennahan won't lend us his house, we'll come here and camp out."

They went down to the flashing creek whose walls were brilliant with green and scarlet, and counted the fish, Cecil hungrily sighing for a rod.

"I'll let you fish during the honeymoon — you remember, I promised — but only one hour in the morning and another in the afternoon."

"I see you are determined to make a good wife without sacrificing your precious individuality. But, my dear, we must go."

As they descended the mountain out of the red-woods, Cecil looked back with a sigh. "If we had only *seen* something," he said. "I have talked so much sport to-day that I'm all on fire again for my grizzly."

CHAPTER XXXI

AND it was that evening at the dinner table that Randolph remarked:

"Unless you've lost your interest in sport, there's a chance for you. The grizzly's a rare bird in California, these times, but the agent of a ranch my mother has in the Santa Lucia Mountains writes me that he has seen two of late, and has been thinking about killing or trapping them. It takes him several weeks to make up his mind to do anything, so the grizzlies are yours, if you care about them."

Cecil had nearly risen from his seat. "I'll start to-night!" he said. "How do you get there?"

"If you really care to go, I'll walk over after dinner and ask Trennahan if he'll go with you. I'm sorry that I can't go myself, but I am not a sportsman, and I'm very much rushed. Trennahan is nearly as enthusiastic as yourself, and would be sure to go. You could start early to-morrow morning."

"I will indeed! How jolly of you to think of it. I really am tremendously obliged. I've seldom been so keen about anything."

Lee kept her eyes lowered. They were the feature she could least control, and she knew that they were blazing. Randolph told eighteen anecdotes of the grizzly, to which Cecil listened with undivided attention.

As they passed out into the hall, Lee tapped Cecil's arm with her fan.

"Will you come to the library a moment?" she said. "I want to speak to you."

The library was in a wing of the house; they were sure to be out of earshot. She lit the gas, and then turned her eyes upon him. He moved uneasily and raised his eyebrows.

"Are you angry about something?"

"Do you really mean that you would leave me to go to spend two weeks tracking a grizzly bear?"

"It need not be as long as that."

"It's almost sure to be. It takes nearly two days to get to the ranch, and is such a tiresome trip that you will have to rest for another before you go out. You will be gone a fortnight at the very least."

Cecil made no reply.

"We have not been engaged two weeks. Do you really mean that you will — that you can leave me for a loathsome grizzly bear?"

"I don't want to leave you, of course. Couldn't you come too?"

"And rough it? I never even camp out in the redwoods; and you have no idea what travelling in the wild parts of California means."

"Of course you mustn't come, then. But, you see, this is my only chance; and that is one of the things I came to California for — one that I started round the world after, for that matter. Surely you

would n't have me miss it! You told me to-day
that you understood my feeling for sport."

"I don't understand at all how you can leave me!
I 'm not your own sort, you see, or, doubtless, I
should."

"It is n't that only. You have led too many men
round by the nose."

"Not one of them would have left me for a
bear."

"Which does not argue that they loved you better
than I, merely that they are different. None of
them succeeded in winning you, I may observe; and
the way you treat them when they bore you makes
me blush for my sex. Yesterday you fairly swept
Mr. Geary out with a broom."

"I wanted to be alone with you."

Cecil was facing her, his hands in his pockets.
His eyes were smiling, but his jaw was set in a way
she had taken note of two days before: she had
demanded a confession of his past relations with
women, and he had merely set his jaw and made no
reply.

"Are you going?"

He nodded, still smiling. His hands were working nervously in his pockets, but she did not see
them.

She gasped slightly. "I cannot believe it," she
said.

"That I can't love you as passionately as a man
ever loved a woman, and yet leave you to complete
a record which means a good deal to me? If I were
going to live in California I would put it off for a

year — with scarcely a regret ; but it is now or never. Surely you will be reasonable. "

"You can go if you like, but you need not come back!" and she made a rush for the door.

He caught her in his arms, and held her so closely that she could not move. "I shall go, and I shall come back, and I shall marry you on the first of July. And believe this — I cannot get back quickly enough."

"I can't bear the thought of having you go, and I can't bear the thought of being put aside for a bear," sobbed Lee.

"Console yourself with the thought that you will never be able to get rid of me for more than two weeks at a time. I do not believe in matrimonial vacations."

"You will never make another long sporting tour round the world?"

"Never! I have had that. I want a home more than anything on earth."

"I wish I had more influence over you."

"You mean that I was your blind besotted slave. When you have forgotten your false ideas of the relations of men and women, and accepted the right one, you will not bother yourself about trifles; and there is no reason why anyone on earth should be happier than we."

"After I have adapted myself!"

He gave her a little shake. "When you have swung round to the old world, and the only logical point of view. A state of society is all wrong where women rule — that is to say, it is in a semi-chaotic transition period. When your greatest country on the face of the earth has shaken down, men and women will occupy exactly the same relative positions that they do in older countries. And there will be fewer divorces."

"How can you stand up here and lecture me?"

"I don't want to lecture you. I want to kiss you."

"I can't help being an American. I was made one, and I have grown up one. How can I make myself over?"

"Think less about it. You Americans — particularly you Californians — carry your individuality round like a chip on your shoulder. You are as self-conscious about it as a little boy with his first pair of trousers. I hear Trennahan's voice. I must leave you in five minutes, and I may not see you alone again. We have talked enough."

And as they were both people who did nothing by halves, they parted with fervour, and mutual assurance of the other's impeccability.

CHAPTER XXXII

THE next evening, Lee rose abruptly from her
seat between Mrs. Yorba and Mrs. Trennahan,
who had dined with them, and walked hastily over
to Randolph who sat alone in a corner of the
verandah.

"Did you send Cecil to the Santa Lucia Mountains hoping that he would be killed?" she
demanded.

"What do you take me for? — the ten-cent villain
in the melodrama? He's got the strength and the
nerve of two men, and I've written to Joe Mann not
to leave him for an instant. His precious skin is
safe enough. I merely wanted to show you what
you had to expect if you married him — a correct but
unflattering glimpse of your power over him."

"You did it on purpose?"

"I did it on purpose; and the infantile manner
in which he walked into the trap, and turned himself inside out, was really delicious."

"It's because he's as honest and straightforward
as — as your grandfather was. You are a horrid
tricky American!"

Randolph brought his teeth together, but he
answered: "All's fair in love. Moreover, if I
were entirely out of the question, I should study

your interests as I should those of my sister. You
are not married yet. Think it over carefully before
he comes back."

"Do you suppose I 'd break my engagement? I 've
given him my word, and it 's announced."

"If you had engaged yourself to me before Maundrell came, would you not have thrown me over?"

"Yes, I would."

"Your femininity is your greatest charm — to me.
Its somewhat anarchistic quality may not commend
itself to Cecil Maundrell. Better think it over."

"You can plot all you like, but I 'd marry Cecil
Maundrell if he went after grizzlies every month in
the year."

She had passed through several phases since that
morning, when she had risen at four to see her
future lord depart. The strong passion of her
nature responded with sensuous delight to the heavy
hand of the master; she was primal woman first, and
American after. But she was American "all the
same," she reminded herself with a proper pride.
She was willing to excuse Cecil from buttoning her
boots, but she would have liked him to manifest a
natural desire to kiss her slipper. Of the strength
of his passion she had no misgivings, but she was
too clear-sighted to permit herself to hope that
idolatry had any part in it. And if she had a
primal instinct for submission to the worshipped
strength of the male, she had quite as strong an
instinct for her own way. Not only had the conditions of her life fostered a tenacious will, but she
inherited a love of power and adulation from a

mother and a grandmother to whom the neck of man was a familiar footstool.

Two days later Tiny arrived with Lord Arrowmount and the Honourable Charles Edward Richard Thornton, the last in the arms of his nurse. Tiny was as pretty and as placid as ever, and Lord Arrowmount, if not so pretty, was quite as placid, and as silent as of yore. The note of command was not manifest in his voice, and it was evident that he was not on the alert.

"Have you adapted yourself?" asked Lee that night.

Tiny smiled her old inscrutable smile. "He thinks I have, so it amounts to quite the same thing."

"I wish I could manage things that way, but I can't. Cecil is horribly clever, and I don't take things calmly."

"It is all a matter of temperament, of course. Try and not expect too much, and it will be easier. An Englishman simply won't keep on telling you that he loves you — "

"Mine will, or there 'll be trouble."

"They 're so lazy about talking. I 'm afraid he won't. It 's pure laziness that has made them clip so many names, and throw all their accents backward, fairly swallowing the last syllables. When they 've told you once they love you, they don't see why you can't take it for granted ever after, and when one gets over that I 'm positive they are the most agreeable husbands in the world. They give so little trouble, and take such good care of one, and do all the thinking. Arthur is the most comfortable person. He is generous, and has no temper at all if he is not crossed, and is more than willing to think me quite perfect ·because I always look pretty, and never contradict him, and entertain all his stupid shooting friends without a grimace."

"What do you get out of it all?"

"Those things can't be analysed; he suits me. I am really very fond of him. I love people who are good-tempered and not nervous, and can be awfully fond of one without making a fuss about it. I love him well enough to bore myself in a good many ways, but I have this compensation — *I can make him do anything I choose.* We spend every winter where I want to spend it, and he's none the wiser. I entertain his friends in the summer and autumn, but I have my own in town, and we always go to at least three houses that I like."

"It is evident that Cecil and I will have to work out our own problem."

He returned in two weeks and two days with his grizzly's skin — a huge, hideous, and ill-favoured trophy. Lee lifted her delicate nose, and drew away her skirts, but assured him warmly that she was quite as delighted as he was, and so proud of him she feared every one would laugh at her.

"Trennahan got the other, but mine was the biggest," he said intensely. "It's a long and exciting story. The old chap nearly got me. Let me go and clean up, and then we'll go for a walk, and I'll tell you all about it. And that's the least of what I have to tell you."

They went for their walk, and there was no doubt left in Lee's mind that he had been in a hurry to get back to her, although he had waited until his grizzly's skin was peppered and dried.   Her doubts went to rest, and she was happy.

They were married on the first of July, in the library, in the presence of the family and intimate friends.   Coralie returned in time to be bridesmaid and to bring the wedding-dress and veil, — in which Lee looked so lovely, that, as she entered the room on Randolph's arm, Cecil put his hands suddenly into his pockets, as was his habit when his nervous fingers betrayed him.   His face was impassive, and he went through the ceremony very creditably.   So did Randolph.

After the wedding-breakfast, the newly-wed, amidst showers of rice, started for the redwoods on horseback.   Mr. Trennahan had offered his house, and their luggage had gone the day before.   Their host had asked them to remain indefinitely, as he and his wife purposed to pass the summer at Lake Tahoe.   They took the house for a fortnight.   They remained a month.

As soon as they had gone, Randolph went to town, saying he could not return until the next day. He pleaded business, and his mother, who had watched him closely, was satisfied.   He spent the night in a private room of a fashionable saloon, before a small table, drinking — drinking — drinking, his face growing whiter, the fire in his brain hotter, his ideas more lucid.   Once he took a letter from his pocket and re-read it.   It notified him that the Peruvian mine in which he had invested was several times richer than had been anticipated, and that a syndicate would offer him a million dollars for his interest.   He tore the letter to strips. When the dawn came he was still sober.

PART TWO

CHAPTER I

IT is seldom that the imagination is disappointed in
the " ancestral piles " of England. The United
Statesian, particularly, surrounded from birth by all
that is commonplace and atrocious in architecture, is
affected by the grey imposing Fact, brooding heavily
under the weight of its centuries, with a curious com-
mixion of delight, surprise, and familiarity. All the
rhapsodies of the poets, all the minute descriptions of
the old romanticists, train the imagination, bend it into
a certain relationship with the historic decorations of
another hemisphere, yet stop short of conveying an
impression of positive reality. The product of a new
world, a new civilisation, as he stands before the carved
ruins of an abbey's cloisters, or the grey ivy-grown
towers and massive scarce-punctured walls of an
ancient castle, feels a slight shock of surprise that it
is really there. But the surprise quickly passes; in a
brief time, with the fatal adaptability of the American,
it is an old story, a habit. He examines it with curiosity, intelligent or vulgar, according to his rank, but
novelty has fled.

Maundrell Abbey stands in the very middle of an
estate six miles square. The land undulates gently

from the gates to the house, woods on one side of the drive, a moor on the other. At the opposite end of the estate are several farms, a fell of great height, and several strips of woods, in the English fashion. Not far from the Abbey, on a steep low hill set with many trees, are a chapel and a churchyard.

As Cecil and Lee drove toward their home at the close of an August day the bride forgot the bridegroom in her eagerness to knit fact to fancy. The moor was turning purple, the woods close by were full of sunlight, a wonderful shimmer of gold and green; with no hint that they too, before the greed of man fell heavily upon them, may have been as dark and solemn as the forests of California. Now and again she had a glimpse of a grey pile and a flash of water.

They reached the top of a hillock of some altitude, and Cecil ordered the coachman to pause. Lee rose in her seat and looked down on the Abbey. It was quite different from the structure in her brain, but no less satisfying. All that was in ruin was a long row of Gothic arches, so fragile that the yellow sunlight pouring through seemed a crucible in which they must melt. The rest of the building was an immense irregular mass at the back, but continuing from the cloisters in a straight severe line, which terminated in a tower. Weeds and grass sprang from the arches, ivy covered the tower; before the Abbey was a lake, on which swans were sailing; peacocks strutted on the lawns. The fell behind was turning red; in a field far away were many cows; over all hung the low powdered sky, brooded the peace and repose, which, were one shot straight from the blue, one would recognise as English.

"It is the carving that makes the cloisters look so fragile," said Cecil. "They will stand a long while yet. The crypt, which is now the entrance hall, and a stone roof which once covered a part of the church and is now over the drawing-room, are all that is left of the original Abbey, except two stone staircases. The tower is Norman, and as there is a tradition that a Maundrell owned these lands before the Church, when the latter was despoiled, and Henry VIII. gave the estate to another Maundrell, it took the family name. Oliver Cromwell left precious little of the Abbey, but it was rebuilt in the reign of Charles II., and there is nothing later than the succeeding reign. That chapel on the hill dates from Henry VIII. only. We have service there on Sundays. Our vault is underneath. Only the old abbots and monks are buried in the graveyard. Well? Are you satisfied?"

Lee nodded and smiled. She was so well satisfied that she hoped to lose herself in the pleasurable sensation of a dream realised, and forget certain disappointments and tremors. She had indulged in the dream of an enthusiastic welcome by the tenantry, triumphal arches, and other demonstrations of which she had read; for Cecil was the heir of this splendid domain, and he was bringing home his bride. But they had driven from the station as unobtrusively as two guests invited for a week's shooting. Tiny had said to her the day before her departure for England:

"Make up your mind not to expect anything over there, and you will save yourself a great deal of disappointment. When you feel a chill settling over you, shake it off with the reflection that English ways are not our ways. They are the most casual people in the world, and their hospitality, although genuine, is so different from ours, that it seems at first no hospitality at all."

Lee deliberately forced these words into her mind as Cecil lifted her from the carriage and she passed between two rigid footmen into the crypt of the Abbey. The vast dim columned greyness of the crypt was beautiful and impressive, and surely it was haunted in the midnight by indignant friars, but, save for the approaching butler, it was empty.

"Are n't your father and stepmother at home?" asked Lee, as Cecil joined her.

"Father's probably on the moors, and Emmy always lies down in the afternoon," said Cecil indifferently. "We 'll go straight up to my old rooms. I hope you 'll like them, but of course if you don 't, you can take your choice of the others."

They followed the butler up an immense stone staircase, then down five long corridors, whose innumerable windows framed so many different views of the grounds that Lee felt sure nothing less than a reel of silk would guide her back and forth. The corridors were lined with pictures and cabinets and curiosities of many centuries, but Lee barely glanced at them, so absorbed was she in wondering if the Abbey were a mile square. Cecil's rooms were in the tower, and the tower was at the extreme right of the building's front, but those corridors appeared to traverse the entire

back and every wing. At length they passed under
a low stone arch, ascended a spiral stone staircase,
entered a small stone room fitted up with a desk, a
sofa, and two chairs, and Cecil said :

" Here we are."

" Well, I shall be glad to rest. Is n't there a short
cut to the grounds? If there is n't, I 'll have to take
all my exercise indoors."

" There 's a door at the foot of the tower. And
you 'll be a famous walker this time next year. You
Californians are so lazy."

He opened the door of the bedroom, a large old-
fashioned severely-furnished room with a dressing-
room beyond. Lee, who was luxurious by nature and
habit, did not like it, but consoled herself with the
charming landscape beyond the window.

" Do you think you 'll like it up here? " asked Cecil
anxiously. " I 'd never feel at home anywhere else.
I insisted upon these rooms when I was a boy, because
Charles II. hid in them once for a week ; but another
reason why I like them now is because they are out
of earshot of all the row — Emmy's house-parties are
rather noisy."

" Oh, I am sure I shall love it, and I like the idea
of being quite alone with you ; but do let me fix them
up a little ; I should feel like a nun."

" Do anything you like. And if that room is hopeless, there are any number of boudoirs to choose from.
This is the only part of the Abbey that is n't full of
windows. And your maid will sleep quite close. We'll
have a bell put in." He took out his watch. " It 's
just five. I 'll send you tea at once, and then go and

‹look up father. You 'd better lie down until it 's time to dress for dinner."

"Well, for Heaven's sake, come back for me, or I 'll not move."

Cecil pinched her cheek, kissed her, and departed. Her own maid had refused to cross the ocean, and Cecil had written to the housekeeper requesting that a new one might await them. The girl arrived with the tea-tray, asked Lee for her keys, and without awaiting orders, began at once to unpack the trunks that had arrived with the travellers. She accomplished her task so swiftly and so deftly, that Lee, with a long train of inefficient maids in mind, reflected gratefully that she would doubtless be spared any personal effort for the thousand and one details which went to make up the physical comfort she loved.

The maid laid a wrapper over the back of a chair, dragged the trunks into the antechamber, returned, and courtesied.

"Will your ladyship take off your frock and rest awhile?" she asked.

Lee gave a little jump. It was the first time she had been so saluted. It made her feel a part of that ancient tower, she reflected, with what humour was in her at the moment, — more at home. The maid undressed her, and she lay down on the sofa in the sitting-room to await the return of her lord. The maid, remarking that she should return at seven to dress her ladyship for dinner, retired.

CHAPTER II

ALTHOUGH Lee was happy, she had a hard fight with an attack of tearful repining. Surrounded all her life with demonstrative affection, each home-coming after a brief holiday an event of rejoicing and elaborate preparation, this chill casual entrance into a huge historic pile — apparently uninhabited, and as homelike as a prison — flooded her spirits with an icy rush. Cecil, who had been so close to her, seemed to have mounted to a niche in the grey stair-case, and turned to stone. The domestic machinery appeared to run with the precision of an expensive eight-day clock. Were her future associates equally automatic? She remembered the inexcitable Mr. Maundrell, and shuddered. Perhaps even " Emmy " by this time was a mere machine, warranted to have hysterics at certain intervals. Surely a woman who would not sacrifice her routine to receive a petted stepson after two years' absence and a stranger in a strange land — and so important an addition to the family as her daughter-in-law — must be painfully systematised.

"However," thought Lee, curling herself down in the hope of a nap, "I can hold my own, that is one comfort. Thank Heaven, I have been brought up all my life to think myself somebody, and that I have plenty of money; it would be tragic if I were a timid, nervous, portionless little person."

She heard a light step, and the agreeable sibilation of linings and flounces. In a second she had run to the mirror in her bedroom. Her hair was smooth, and the wrapper of white camel's hair and blue velvet sufficiently enhancing. There was colour in her cheeks, and the only suggestion of fatigue came from a vague shadow beneath her lashes. She felt that she had nothing to fear from the critical eyes of the other woman.

"May I come in?" Lady Barnstaple had rapped and opened the door simultaneously. "How do you do? Are you tired? You look abominably fresh. And how tall you are! I thought you'd be in a wrapper, so I didn't send for you. Lie down again, and I'll sit here. These chairs are stuffed with bricks."

She was a short woman, with a still beautiful figure above the waist; it was growing massive below. Her colouring was nondescript, but her features must once have been delicate and piquant; now they were sharp, and there were fine lines about the eyes, and weak determined mouth. Her cheeks were charmingly painted, her hair elaborately coiffed; she wore an airy tea-gown of black chiffon, with pink bows, in which she looked like a smart fluffy doll. Her carriage, short as she was, would have been impressive had it not been for the restlessness of her manner. If she had come to England with a Chicago accent, she had sent it home long since. Her voice was abrupt and unpleasing, but its syllabic presentment was wholly English, and her manner was curiously

like an Englishwoman's affectation of American animation. Her eyes, for some time after she entered the
room, had the round vacant stare of a newly-arrived
infant. When the exigencies of conversation removed
this stare, they flashed with the nervous irritable
domineering character of the woman. It was some
time before they were removed from Lee's face for an
instant. Lee was tired, but she obeyed the instinct
of the savage who scents a fight, and sat upright.

"You won't stay in this hole, of course — one might
as well live in a dungeon — there is one at the bottom
of the tower, for that matter. In the only letter that
Cecil condescended to write me after his engagement,
he said he wanted his old rooms to be ready for him,
and he hoped I would n't put any guests in them. But
of course you can't stand them. Fancy not being able
to turn round without falling over a man ! You 'd be
at each other's throats in a week."

" Is n't there another room underneath these that I
could fix up as a sitting-room? I like this tower."

"Fancy, now ! I believe there is a lumber-room,
or something; but what can you do with a tower-
room with walls five feet thick, and *such* windows?
Of course I don't know your tastes, but I must have
fluffy airy things in bright colours about me, and
floods of light — through pink shades, nowadays,"
she added, with a bitter little laugh. "What a lovely
complexion you have ! I had one too, once, but it 's
gone ! — it 's gone ! I don't know whether I 'm
pleased or not that you 're a beauty. Barnstaple
assured me that it was impossible you could be,
that Cecil must be mad — the English children are

so pretty; but I thought it unlikely that Cecil would sacrifice his chances of a fortune for anything less than downright beauty. Of course you 'll be a great card for me. I can make out a lot of you; but on the other hand it 's disgusting having anything so fresh forever at one's elbow. Repose is not the fashion now, and of course you are a bit of a prude — young married women who are in love with their husbands are always so fiercely virtuous! — and of course you have n't half enough money; but I can see that you will be a success. We all know that you 're clever, and they like clever people over here, and your voice is n't nasal — it 's really lovely. It 's a thousand pities — a thousand pities that you could n't bring Cecil a fortune!" Her voice gave a sudden querulous break. "He could have had one — probably a dozen — for the asking, and I think the Abbey should have been his first consideration. He won't inherit a penny from Barnstaple, and Heaven knows what I 'll have left! He can't possibly keep it up on what you and he have together — your house in town will take every penny — and he 'll either have to break the entail and sell it, or rent the moor, and cut the rest up into farms, and perhaps let the Abbey itself. I should turn in my grave, for the Abbey is the one real love of my life — "

Her restless eyes had been moving about the room; they suddenly met her daughter-in-law's. Lee had very beautiful eyes, but they were capable of a blue-hot flame of passion at times. Lady Barnstaple blinked rapidly; her own seemed scorching under that blue-fire.

"Oh, of course, it does n't signify! Nothing really signifies in this world. I really did n't mean to be nasty, but I always flare up when the Abbey is in question — and then that old superstition! — But bother! I really want to be nice! Do tell me about your clothes. If you had sent me a lining I could have ordered everything for you in Paris. I should n't have minded running over a bit."

"My things were made in New York, and will probably answer."

"Oh, of course! New York's every bit as smart as Paris, only it eats your head off. Have you many jewels?"

"Very few — compared with the shop-window decorations of New York and English women."

"We do overload ourselves," said Lady Barnstaple amiably. "I 've seen women turn actually grey under the weight of their tiaras. Still, unless you blaze at a great party, you are simply not seen. But of course the Barnstaple jewels are mine till I die, and I sold all my own after having them copied; you could wear some of those if you liked, although, being fresh from the other side, you 'd probably scorn imitations."

"I certainly should."

"Oh, you 'll get over all that! We are all shams nowadays."

"You are certainly frank enough."

"A mere habit — a fashion. Everybody shouts all he knows just now. We even talk of things at the table that would quite shock — Chicago, for instance. And as for your poor little San Francisco — there are the most amusing points of resemblance between the Americans and the English middle-class."

"Then perhaps you would not mind telling me if you would have taken the trouble to meet us this afternoon if I had brought a million with me."

"Dear me, no; not if you had arrived at such an unearthly hour. I assure you I did not intend to be rude, but I always sleep from half after four to half after five. I don't take my tea with the others."

"And there would have been no demonstration, I suppose."

"Well — yes, frankly, perhaps there would have been. Barnstaple did say something about it, but I told him I could n't think of affording it, and I could n't. Don't be bitter about it; but we need money — money — money so horribly."

"I am not bitter in the least. I merely asked out of curiosity."

"Oh, my dear, when one is young and beautiful one would be a fool to be bitter about anything. You probably think me a devil, but if you knew what my life has been! To-day I 'm in one of my moods. I'm sorry it happened so, and I hate myself for being nasty, but I can't help it. I have n't any particular reason for being; they just come down on me, and I want to scratch everybody's eyes out. I may be as cheerful as a lark, and as amiable as a kitten for a week. You have no idea what a popular little person I am!"

Lee's anger had passed, giving way to a commingling of curiosity, disgust and pity. Was this a sample of engrafted America? She asked if there were any other English-Americans staying at the Abbey.

Lady Barnstaple scowled, and the scowl routed what little youth she had left. " I 'm not on speaking terms with a single American but yourself and Lady Arrowmount, and I barely know her. I adore the English, but the jealousy and rivalry of other Americans! But I 'm sent in ahead of the ones I hate most! I am! — I am! It 's been war to the knife between three of us for years now, and I 've got to go under, because I have n't the money to smash 'em. That is one reason why I 'm a bit off my head about Cecil not having married a million. With a rich and beautiful — But here comes your maid. I must go to mine. I 'll swear you shall think me an angel to-morrow."

CHAPTER III

LEE found no time to think that night. As soon as her maid had left her, Cecil entered from his dressing-room and said that his father would like to see her for a moment before they joined the guests in the library.

"I saw Emmy for a few minutes, and she said she had been to see you — and many complimentary things."

"How kind of her!"

"Did n't you like her? Most people do."

"It's not polite to criticise your relations, but I may be excused, as she is my countrywoman first. I have been carefully brought up, and I never before met that sort of American. Of course the Middle West is very new, and it is hardly fair to criticise it, but I should think twenty years or so of England would have done something more than remove her accent."

Cecil smiled. "American women are so popular in England that I fancy they grow more and more American as the years go by. I don't know much about it."

"It is rather odd having to stand just behind a stepmother whom I should n't think of knowing at home."

"Of course there are no distinctions in regard to Americans over here; it is all personality and money. Emmy has n't much of the first in a large sense, but she knows how to make herself popular. People find her likeable and amusing — even the women, because, of course, she is so different from themselves; and she is really the best-hearted little creature in the world. I see you don't like her, but wait a little; perhaps she was nervous to-day."

"I am not going to be so commonplace as to quarrel with my mother-in-law, but I certainly shall not like her. As you would say, she is not my own sort."

"Neither am I," said Cecil laughing, "but you like me."

"We represent the fusion of the two greatest nations on earth. Why do not you tell me that I am looking particularly well?"

They were traversing one of the long corridors. Cecil glanced uneasily about, then put his arm round her and kissed her.

"I am doing my best to live up to the American standard, and tell you once a day how much I love you, and how beautiful you are. When do you think you will take it for granted?"

"Never! never! Are you proud of me to-night?"

"You never looked lovelier — except when we were married. You nearly knocked me over then."

"What a pity I can't wear a wedding-veil on all state occasions."

"I have a suspicion that as you are a bride you should wear white for a time."

"All my day summer frocks are white, and I simply

won't wear it at night. I shall take full advantage of the fact that I am an American."

She wore a wonderful gown of flame-coloured gauze, more golden than red, and so full of shimmer and sheen, that she had reflected, with some malice, it would outblaze all of Lady Barnstaple's jewels, and had concluded to wear none.

" To-morrow and the next day I am going out with the other men, and you are coming to luncheon with us on the moor — at least Emmy and the others generally come when the weather is fine: but on Sunday I'll show you over the Abbey. I'd like to do it myself, but I'm afraid we can't get into the state bedrooms until the guests are gone."

" Are they in the rooms that kings and queens and all the rest have slept in?"

"You are improving. How is it you did n't say 'kings and queens and things'? I'm afraid they are. This house is all corridors and rooms for entertaining and boudoirs; there are not more than twenty-five bedrooms. Here we are."

They entered a small room furnished as a study, and Lord Barnstaple entered from the adjoining bedroom almost immediately. He looked rather more impassive and rather more cynical, but hardly ten years older. His monocle might never have been removed. Somewhat to Lee's surprise, he not only kissed her, but shook her warmly by the hand.

"So another American is my fate, after all," he said. "You see, I suspected as much the day I left. Have you ever had hysterics?"

" Never!"

"I almost hope you have a temper — oh, you have, you have, with those eyes!" He chuckled. "Turn it loose on her! Give it to her! Gad! but I'd like to see her well trounced! She doesn't mind me, but you're a woman, and young, and beautiful, and — nearly twice her height. Gad! how she'll hate you! But trounce her — trounce her! Don't give her any quarter?"

Cecil laughed. "Why do you sow these seeds of discord in the family?"

"Oh, we'll keep out of the way. But fancy Emmy limp and worn out, and not daring to call her soul her own! 'T would be the happiest day of my life! But I'm famished."

They entered the library only a moment before dinner was announced. It was a very long room breaking the series of corridors, and only three times their width. Its panelling was black, and its books appeared to be musty with age; above the high cases were many Maundrells; even the furniture looked as ancient as the Abbey. But flooding all was a pink glare of electric light.

The room was full of people, who regarded the bride with descriptive curiosity. Lady Barnstaple was flitting about, her expression in perfect order, her superlatively smart French gown quivering with animation. She came at once toward Lee, followed by a tall good-looking young man, whom she presented as Captain Monmouth.

"What a love of a gown! I'm so glad you know how to dress!" she exclaimed. "You are to go in with Miss Pix," she added to her stepson.

Cecil drew his brows together. " Why do you send me in with Miss Pix ? " he muttered angrily. " You know she bores me to death."

" To punish you for not marrying her. You can't get out of it; she expects you."

Lee overheard the conversation. So did Lord Barnstaple, who was laughing softly at his son's discomfiture. She had no time to question him, for they went down at once to dinner, and his attention for a time was claimed by the woman on his left. Cecil was on the other side of the table, some eight or ten seats down. Lee studied his partner attentively while talking with Captain Monmouth, who sat on her right.

The immense room looked like the banqueting hall of kings, but, so far as Lee could judge — and she had one half of the guests within her visual range — the young woman with the dreadful name looked more the traditionally cold haughty aristocrat, for whom such rooms were built, than any one present. The others appeared to have nothing of the massive repose of their caste; they seemed, in fact, to vie with each other in animation, and they certainly talked very loud and very fast. But Miss Pix had that air of arrested development peculiar to the best statuary. Her skin was as white as the tablecloth, her profile was mathematically straight, suggesting an antique marble or a sheep. Her small flaxen head was held very high, and her eyelids had the most aristocratic droop that Lee had ever conceived of.

"Who is she ? " the bride asked her companion, who appeared to be an easy and untraditional person.

"And why is she so different from the rest — with that name? She looks like one of Ouida's heroines — the quite impossible ones."

Captain Monmouth laughed. "Her father was a brewer, disgustingly rich. Her parents are dead. She and her brother — dreadful bounder — have been trying to get into Society for years — only been really successful the last three. Lady Barnstaple took "em up, for some reason or other. She 's usually rather nasty to new people. Only girl, and has three millions, but does n't marry and is n't popular — scarcely opens her mouth, and has never been known to unbend. Fancy it 's rather on her mind that she was n't born into the right set. So she fakes it for all it 's worth, as you Americans would say. I do like American slang. Can you teach me some? "

"I know more than I 've ever dared to use, and you shall have it all, as my husband disapproves of it. I think Miss Pix has done rather well. She is what we would call a good 'bluffer.'"

"Quite so — quite so. The women say all sorts of nasty things about her — that all that white is put on with a brush or a sponge or something, as well as that haughty nostril; and that she has had the muscles cut in her eyelids — ghastly thought, ain't it? Nature gave her that profile, of course; can't have the bridge of your nose raised — can you? — even with three millions. It 's the profile that made all the trouble, I fancy. She 's livin' up to it. Must be deuced aggravatin' to be born with a cameo profile and a Lancashire accent. No wonder she 's frozen."

"Has she got rid of the accent?"

"Oh, rather! She was educated in Paris with a lot of swagger French girls. She's quite correct — in a prehistoric way — only she overdoes it."

His attention was claimed by the woman on his other side, and Lee asked Lord Barnstaple:

"What did Lady Barnstaple mean? Did she want Cecil to marry that Miss Pix?"

"Did n't she! She never worked so hard for anything in her life. She was ill for two weeks after Cecil went off. It would n't have been a bad thing. I 'd have wanted it myself if she had n't. I like you — always did — but I wish to gad you had more money! Don't you think you 'll discover a gold mine on that ranch of yours some day?"

Lee laughed, although the sensation of dismay induced by Lady Barnstaple's visit returned at his words. "I 'm afraid not. Sulphur and arsenic and iron are as much as can be expected of one poor little ranch."

"Perhaps we can sell the springs to a syndicate — who knows? Syndicates are always buyin' things and givin' seven figgers for 'em. I 'll tell you what we 'll do. The next old Jew or brewer that wants to get into Society we 'll send for and tell him that the ranch at seven figgers is our price for a week's shooting at the Abbey and three dinners in town," and he gave his ungenial chuckle.

"You are n't all really as bad as that over here, are you?"

"Oh, we 're mixed, like you Americans. We 're all right so long as we don't need money; but, you see, we need such a cursed lot of it — several thousand times more than the nobodies who sit outside and criticise us. It's in our blood, and when we can't get it one way we try another. We all cling to certain ideals, though: I've never gambled with a parvenu. It's true I made an ass of myself and married one, but I pulled up just after. Miss Pix is the only other that has got inside my doors. That's the one point Emmy and I agree on: I have my ideals"— he laughed again—" and, like all upstarts, she despises other upstarts. Monmouth is the only person in the house except Miss Pix without an hereditary title, and he's grandson of a duke, and a Guardsman. Some of the smartest women of the day are untitled, but Emmy won't have 'em. Wonder who she'll have this time five years?— Second-rate actors and long-haired poets, probably."

Lee wondered at even a dilapidated set of ideals, and at a pride — and pride was written all over him — which would permit him to live on a woman's money. Of course he may have argued that Lady Barnstaple was paying a fair yearly rent for the title and the Abbey, but it was an old-world view-point, to which it would take a long period of habit to accustom the new. She wondered if she had any right to despise a man who was a mere result of a civilisation so different from her own, but felt unindulgent. In the United States, if a penniless man married for money, he had the decency to affect the habit of the worker, if it were only to write alleged poems for the magazines, or to attach himself to a Legation.

After dinner she went with the women into another immense room, also panelled to the ceiling. Each panel was set with a portrait, several of which she knew at a glance to be the originals of bygone masters. Their flesh tints were uniformly pink: Lee glanced upward. The stone ceiling, arched and heavily carved, was set with electric pears. It was an irritating anomaly.

Lee thought the women looked very nice, and wondered if she was ever to be introduced to anybody. Emmy was flitting about again — rather the upper part of her seemed to flit as if propelled by the somewhat unwieldy machinery below. She looked indubitably common, despite her acquired " air " and the exquisite taste of her millinery; and Lee wondered what these women — who, well-dressed or ill, loud-voiced or semi-subdued, delicately or heavily modelled of face, intensely modern all of them, looked what they were, and as if they assumed the passing fad in manners, even the fad of vulgarity, as easily and adjustably as a new sleeve or a larger waist — could find in this particular American to their fancy.

" Do sit here by me! " A young woman on a small sofa swept aside her skirts and nodded brightly to Lee. She had sat opposite at dinner, and spoken across the table several times to Captain Monmouth, whom she addressed as " Larry." She had a large open voice and a large open laugh, and, to use an unforgettable term of Lord Barnstaple's, she rather sprawled. But she was exquisitely fine of feature and cold of colouring, although charged straight up through her lithe figure with assumed animation or ungoverned nervousness, Lee could not determine which. The bride sat down at once.

"You are Lady Mary Gifford," she said smiling. "I asked Captain Monmouth who you were."

"Oh, did you ask who I was? How nice! I wish everybody in the room was talking about me as they are about you. But my day for that is past. Would you guess I was twenty-four?"

Lee shook her head, smiling. In spite of the persistent depression within her, she found her new friends very interesting.

"Twenty-four, not married, and only sixty pounds a year to dress on! Is n't it a tragedy? I wish I were an American. They 're all so frightfully rich. At least, all those are that come over here; they would n't dare to come if they were n't."

"I have dared, and I am not — not as you count riches."

"No — really now? But of course you 're joking, Cecil Maundrell simply had to marry a ton——"

Lee laughed, with a nearer approach to hysteria than she had ever known. "Would you mind not talking about that?" she said. "If ever I know you as well as I hope I shall, I'll tell you why."

"Fancy my being so rude! But I 'm quite horribly outspoken, and Cecil Maundrell 's so good-looking, of course he 's been discussed threadbare. Of course we all knew the Abbey must go to another American, and we 've been so anxious to see you. Emmy is a duck, but she 's not a beauty — few Americans really are, to my mind. They just 'chic it' as the French painters say. Everybody is simply staring at you, and you 're so used to it, you don't appear to see them.

You're going to be a great success. I know all the signs — seen 'em too often ! "

" Well, I hope so. I suppose an American failure would be painfully conspicuous."

" Oh, *would n't* she ! Tell me, is it really true that you have different grades of society, as we have — an upper and middle-class, and all that sort of thing? Some of the Americans over here have always turned up their noses at Emmy, and it seems so very odd — you are only a day or two old; how *can* you have so many distinctions? Of course I know that some are rich and some are poor, which means that some are educated and some are not, but I should think that would make just two classes. But Emmy is — has been — awfully rich, and yet she has had a hard fight with two or three other Americans that are dead against her. She has n't it in her, poor little soul, to be quite as smart as Lady Vernon Spencer and Mrs. Almeric Sturt — you could be ! — but she 's ' popular,' and unless the Abbey burns down — oh, it 's the sweetest thing in England, and the shootings are famous ! But do explain to me."

" About our social differences? Of course to be really anybody you must have come from the South, one way or another."

" What South ? — South America ? "

Lee endeavoured to explain, but Lady Mary quickly lost interest, and made one of her dazzling deflections: it was evident that more than three minutes of any one subject would bore her hopelessly. But Lee had realised in a flash the utter indifference of the English to the most imposing of the new world's family trees.

The haughty Southerner and the raw Westerner were "varieties," nothing more. She might be pronounced better style than her stepmother, and doubtless would be more respected, but no one would ever think of looking down the perspective of each for the cause. She felt doubly depressed.

CHAPTER IV

SHE awoke late next morning, after a restless night. Cecil had risen without disturbing her and gone to his grouse. In a happier frame of mind she would have indulged in a sentimental regret at this defection, but now she only wanted to be alone to think; and to think she must get out-of-doors.

The maid was in the outer room awaiting orders, and went for her tea at once. Lee hurriedly dressed herself, and while she was attacking her light breakfast told the girl to go down to the foot of the tower and see if the outer door could be opened. At the end of a half-hour the rusty key and hinges had been induced to move, and Lee, having convinced herself that no one was in sight, left the shelter of her tower and went hastily toward the woods.

The air had a wonderful softness and freshness, and the country showed a dull richness of colour under a pale sky. The woods looked black as she approached them, but within they were open and full of light. There were no majestic aisles here, no cavernous vistas, but, in their way, they were lovely, as many trees massed together with a wilderness of bracken between must always be.

Lee selected as secluded a spot as she could find, and sat down to think. She was terrified and depressed and homesick, and longed passionately for some one of her " own sort " to whom she could present the half of her troubles, and with whom dissect her uneasy forebodings. Cecil was not the man to whom a woman could take her daily worries. He would be a rock of strength in the great primary afflictions of life; he looked after her as carefully as if she were blind and lame; and she had not been called upon for an independent decision since the day of her marriage. Moreover, she was firmly convinced that no man had ever loved a woman so much before; but, she had admitted it with dismay more than once, there was a barrier. It was humiliating, almost ridiculous, that she, Lee Tarleton, should live to confess it, but she was just a little in awe of her husband. Why, she had not been able to guess until yesterday, for he had been the most enamoured of bridegrooms; he had even yielded laughingly to more than one whim (tentative, each), and he had been rather less high and mighty than before marriage; but, and he had given her many opportunities to look into him, at the end of each of his vistas there was something terrifyingly like a blank wall. It had not worried her deeply in the redwoods, where she had been as happy as mortals ever are, nor yet on their long journey home, monotonous and uninteresting as it had been, but she had instinctively refrained from talking over her own small affairs with him, as had been her habit with Randolph and the other members of her family; and it was not until the flat disappointment of the drive from the station yesterday, that she had suspected what this deprivation would mean to her.

And it was not until she had looked down upon the Abbey that she had begun to understand. Centuries had gone to the welding together of Cecil Maundrell, and he was as coherent and unmalleable as the walls of his historic home, as aloof in spirit, as self-contained as if he no more had mingled with men than had the Abbey altered its expression to the loud restless fads with which it so often resounded. His wife might be the object of his most passionate affection, she might even be his companion, for he was the man to satisfy the wants of his nature, but it was doubtful if he was capable of opening the inner temple of his spirit, had such a thing ever occurred to him. He would want so much of a woman, and no more. He was English; he had been born, not made. And the men within whose influences her mind and character had developed had been little more than liquids in a huge furnace whose very moulds were always changing.

But Lee put this new interpretation of Cecil aside for the present, realising that it would torment her sufficiently in the future, and that she had better shut her eyes as long as she could, and linger over the pleasant draughts of the moment.

But it was of the future that she thought, and she longed for wings that she might fly to California for a day. England was beautiful, and it satisfied her imagination, but its absolute unlikeness to California, combined with the incidents of her brief sojourn, filled her with a desperate home-sickness. It might have been dissipated in a moment if she had had one Californian to talk to — Mrs. Montgomery, or Coralie, or Randolph. On the whole, she would have preferred

Randolph, not only because she had run to him with most of her troubles during the last ten years, but because his advice had always been sound and practical.

His assertion some years before that the Maundrells needed millions, and Cecil's subsequent graceful remark that he had argued with himself on the folly of marrying anything under a fortune, had been mere words to her. It is difficult for a Californian who has not known grinding poverty or the suicidal care of vernal millions to realise the actual value of money. In that land of the poppy, where the luxuries of severer climes are a drug in the market, where the earth over which people sprawl their tasteless "palatial residences" is, comparatively speaking, inexpensive, where a man with a hundred thousand dollars can live almost as smartly as a man with a million, where there is little inclination for display, even among the fungi, and where position is in no wise dependent upon the size of one's income, one never conceives the most approximate idea of the absolute necessity of great wealth to men born to other conditions of climate, race, and to the enormous responsibilities of territorial inheritance.

To Lee, millions had always been associated with vulgarity, as belonging exclusively to low-born people whom Mrs. Montgomery would not have permitted to cross her door-mat. It is doubtful if her father or Mr. Montgomery or Mr. Brannan had ever been worth eight hundred thousand dollars, although they had been stars of the first magnitude in their day. Colonel Belmont had left little more, and the Yorbas and

Gearys were the only families of the old set who were known by their riches. The great wealth of these had meant nothing to Lee; Mrs. Montgomery lived quite as well, and entertained far more brilliantly. Her own income had seemed very large to her, her jump from eighty dollars a month to nearly a thousand one of the glittering romances of California. She had sincerely pitied the people whose malodorous opulence made them the target of the terrible Mr. Bierce, and whose verbal infelicities had contributed standing jests to those outer rings of Society which had opened to them. To-day she was almost ready to envy them bitterly, to barter her honoured name and illustrious kin for their ungrammatical millions.

Lord and Lady Barnstaple and Lady Mary Gifford, even the speechless Miss Pix, had succeeded in making her feel as guilty as if Cecil were a half-witted boy whom she had entrapped. One of the great homes of England — one, moreover, to which he was passionately attached — was the price he had paid for his wife. She was too charged with the arrogance of youth and beauty to wonder if he would live to regret his choice; but she was far-sighted enough in other matters, and she was as certain of his capacity for suffering as for deep and intense affection. The day he lost the Abbey he would cease to be Cecil Maundrell.

And she had cause to bitterly reproach herself; Randolph had begged her to sell her ranch and invest in the Peruvian mine. She had replied that she " had enough," in tranquil scorn of the United Statesian's frantic lust for gold. If she had only known! She conceived a humble and enduring respect for a metal that meant so much more to man than the response to his material wants and his greed.

She went to the edge of the wood, and looked down on the Abbey. Its lids seemed lowered in haughty mute reproach. She saw a thousand new beauties in it, and knew that she should shake and thrill with the pride of its possession, exult in the destiny which had made it her home, were it not that the stranger bided his time at the gates.

Had Cecil Maundrell been mad? Were all men really mad when they loved a woman? Or had it been that he, too, had but an abstract appreciation of the value of money? This splendid estate had fitted him too easily, and he had worn it too long, for it not to seem as inevitable as the stars, in spite of much desultory talk; and his personal wants were simple, and had always been liberally supplied.

She turned her back on the Abbey, which seemed actually to lift its lids and send her a glance of stern appeal, and returned to her nook. What should she do? There was not a cell of morbid matter in her brain; she contemplated neither suicide nor divorce — in favour of Miss Pix. There seemed but one solution of the difficulty. She must find a million — dollars, if not pounds. The latter were desirable, but the former would do. She decided to write to Randolph that very day. He had a genius for making money, and he must place it at her disposal.

She heard the sound of many voices rising with the slight ascent between the Abbey and the wood, and hastily sought the deceptive shades beyond.

These people had been very charming to her the night before, and she had no doubt that she should, in time, like all good Americans, fall under their spell; but at present she rather resented their failure to differentiate between herself and "Emmy." And she was harassed, and they were not her "own sort."

CHAPTER V

SHE escaped from the wood into her tower, and wrote a letter to Randolph. She made no attempt at diplomacy; she told him the truth. Randolph loved her, and she was a woman of sufficient humour, but there was no one else to appeal to, and she argued that he would respect her frankness; and it had been his habit for many years to obey her commands. Moreover, in the sequestered recesses of his brain he was a Southerner, chivalrous and impulsive. She believed that he must by now have accepted the fact that she was another man's wife, and she believed that he would help her.

After breakfast, which she took in solitude, as she was very late, she went to call on her mother-in-law, who had graciously intimated the night before that she would be visible at twelve. The maid conducted her to a suite of apartments removed from Lord Barnstaple's by almost the width of the building, and Lee wondered if he had caused the walls to be padded. The bedroom was certainly very pink, and as fluffy as much lace and fluttering silk could make it. Miss Pix, in a white serge tailor-made frock, was seated in a large carved chair, with her profile in bold relief. Lady Barnstaple, in a pink peignoir, looked like a ball of floss in the depths of an armchair. She smiled radiantly as Lee entered.

"So good of you to come!" she said. "Lee, dear,

this is my intimate friend, Miss Pix. How perfectly brilliant you look! Of course you have been out. I almost went myself. I feel *quite* fit to-day; one would think I'd never had a nerve. Victoria, my beautiful daughter-in-law has been such a belle in the States, and has had an unheard-of number of offers, three of them from immensely wealthy members of the peerage, Lord Arrowmount's friends. But it was an old boy-and-girl affair between her and Cecil, and I think it is all too romantic and sweet! I've felt ever so much younger since she came. I never had one spark of romance in my life. Men are in the way, though — we'll have ever so much nicer times a year from now when you and Cecil have learned to exist without each other — not that I can complain that Barnstaple was ever in my way. Things might have turned out differently if he had been occasionally, for I was young enough, and romantic enough, when I married him; but he always was, and always will be, the most cold-blooded brute in England. Once I cared, but now I don't. I'm content to have got the upper hand of him. It was that or being simply ground to powder myself. But, to say nothing of the fact that he sold himself in the most bare-faced manner, I soon learned that when I played a tune on my nerves he'd give in at any price; there are more ways of getting ahead of an Englishman than one. Still he was a fascinating creature — but that's passed. Cecil always was sweet to me, and I've always simply adored him. If *he'd* been his father — well! It would have made me simply ill if he hadn't married a woman worthy of him. I believe he's the only human being I've ever really loved. And he simply adores — but I shan't be personal. Your clothes are really perfect — "

She rattled on, with brief intermissions, for nearly an hour. It was evident that her mood had undergone a metamorphosis in the night, and that she desired to be amiable. Lee could understand her "popularity"; her manner and certain intonations were most fascinating, and she constantly swept little glances of suffering appeal and voiceless admiration into her disciplined orbs. Her tiny hands fluttered, and from head to foot, in a pink light, she pleased the eye. Her smile was rare and dazzling. Lee wondered why, when she was young, Lord Barnstaple had not loved her.

Miss Pix made one or two sensible remarks in a low excellent voice, which had evidently received scientific training. When Cecil was flashing among his stepmother's conversational pyrotechnics, her cheek looked less like paper for a moment, but her profile stood the strain.

Suddenly Lady Barnstaple jumped up. "You must dress and I must dress," she said to Lee. "We're going out to luncheon on the moor, and afterward we'll stay and watch them shoot, if you like. Of course, everything will interest you so much — I envy you! I'm sick to death of shooting-talk myself! One doesn't hear another topic from the twelfth of August until the first of November, and then one has hunting and racing for a change. I live for the London season — and the Riviera. I've had to give up dear, delightful Homburg. Well, ta, ta! '

CHAPTER VI

A FORTNIGHT later Lee scanned her new boudoir with complacency and pride. The large tower room beneath the suite above had been cleared of its rubbish, and she had availed herself to the full of Lady Barnstaple's careless permission to take what she liked. Lee liked beautiful things, and, having been surrounded by many during the greater part of her life, regarded the best that could be had as her natural right. Therefore her stone walls had disappeared behind ancient tapestries, which she had thoughtfully selected from different rooms, that they might not be missed. Round two sides of the room ran a deep divan, made by a village carpenter, which was covered with Persian rugs, and cushions of many, but harmonious styles. Persian rugs also covered the floor. Some of the furniture was carved, high-backed, and ancient, cut with the Maundrell arms; other pieces were modern and luxurious. In two of the window-seats, which were five feet deep, were cushions, in the others noble marbles and bronzes. The room was further glorified by a writing-table which had belonged to Charles II., a wonderful brass and ivory chest with secret drawers which had been the property of Katherine of Aragon, an ancient spinet with a modern interior, a table inlaid with lapis-lazuli, a tortoise-shell cabinet, and a low bookcase curiously carved. On the mantel, heavily draped with the spoils of an obscure window, and on the top of the bookcase, were not too many bibelots, selected after much thought and comparison. The tapestries could meet across the narrow windows at night, but flat against the glass were silk curtains of a pale yellow colour, as a background for the marbles and bronzes. Altogether, Lee felt that she had some reason to be proud of her taste.

She sat down to await her father-in-law. He was kept at home by a sprained wrist, and she had invited him to be the first to pay her a call. He entered in a few moments, raised his eyebrows, then gave vent to a chuckle of unusual length.

"What amuses you?" asked Lee, rather tartly. "Don't you think my room is pretty?"

"Oh, it's charming! It's close to being the prettiest room in the house. I congratulate you. You have excellent taste — and you are delicious!"

Leé never expected to understand her father-in-law, and felt little inclination to attempt the dissecting of him; she merely begged him to take the most comfortable chair, placed a cushion under his elbow, and sat down opposite him with an expression of genuine welcome; she liked him so much better than she liked Emmy that she was almost persuaded that she loved him. And he had been consistently kind and polite to her, whereas her mother-in-law had twice been the victim of a " mood," and cut her dead in the corridors.

" It 's just as well to tell you," said Lord Barnstaple, " that if Emmy happens to come to this room when she 's in one of her infernal tempers, she 'll raise the deuce of a row, and order you to send these things where they came from. If she does, stand to your guns, and tell her I gave 'em to you. They 're mine, not hers. Don't refer her to me, for God's sake! You 're quite able to take care of yourself."

" She shan't have them — and thanks so much. You can smoke if you like. I 'll light it for you."

" Upon my word, I believe this will be the pleasantest room in the house — a haven of refuge! Well, how do you like us? What do you think of us? You 're an interesting child. I 'm curious to hear your impressions."

" I must say I do feel rather like a child since I came over here " — Lee made this admission with a slight pout — " and I thought I was quite a person-of-the-world after two winters in San Francisco and one in the East."

" Oh, we 're pickled; you 're only rather well seasoned over there. But do you like us?"

" Yes — I think I do. The women are very nice to me, and although I don't understand half they say, and they are quite unlike all my old ideals, and I 'm never exactly sure whether they 'll speak to me the next time they see me, I feel as if I 'd get on with them. I must say, though, I don't see any reason why I should attempt to make myself over into a bad imitation of them, like Emmy —— "

" Some of them — your countrywomen — are such jolly good imitations — that they no longer amuse the Prince of Wales. Emmy happens to be a fool."

" The men look as if they'd be really charming if they could talk about anything but grouse, and I had one last night at dinner who was so tired he never made one remark from the time he sat down till he got up."

" Men are not amusing during the shooting season; but, after all, my dear, men were not especially designed to amuse women."

" That's your way of looking at it."

" Do you expect Cecil to amuse you ? "

" Cecil has stayed home with me three whole days, and we've roamed all over the place, and had the jolliest times imaginable. He has a lot of fun in him when he has nothing on his mind."

" I never attempt to discuss men during those periods when they are engaged in proving the rule. Cecil is in love. Long may he remain so " — he waved his uninjured hand gallantly — " but unless I am much mistaken, the longer you know him the less amusing you will find him. It is the prerogative of greatness to be dull. England is the greatest nation on earth, and is as dull as befits its dignity — mind you, I don't say stupid, which is a wholly different quantity. Conversely, many of the most brilliant men living are Englishmen, but they are not great in the national sense. Read *The Times*, and you will see what I mean."

" Do you think Cecil has it in him to be great ? " asked Lee eagerly.

" Sometimes I've thought so. He has as good a

brain for its age as there is in England, and I believe he 's ambitious.   Do you think he is? "

" I can't make out.   I don't think he knows, himself."

" He 'll find out as soon as he 's in the running.   Just now I fancy he imagines himself oppressed with the weight of family traditions, which I have neglected.   But there are no half measures about him, and if he develops ambition he 'll make straight for the big prizes.   It will be all or nothing."

" I hope he 's ambitious."

" Ah!   Ambition is an exacting mistress — a formidable rival! "

" I 'd not be afraid of that; I don't know that I can explain."

" Do — try."   Lord Barnstaple could be very charming when he chose; he tossed aside his cynical impassivity as it were a mask, and assumed an expression of profound and tender interest.   His son was the only living being that he loved, and he had planned for an uninterrupted interview with Lee in order to ascertain, as far as was possible, what were Cecil's prospects of happiness.   He liked and admired his daughter-in-law as far as he knew her, but he despised and distrusted all women, and he had heretofore hated Americans with monotonous consistency.

Lee was very susceptible to a warm personal interest, and this was the first she had experienced in England.   And she was in a surcharged state of mind to speak out freely at the first sign of unmistakable sympathy. Lord Barnstaple took the one step farther that was necessary.

"I am not given to sentimentalising, but I love Cecil. And next to him, I want you to regard me as your best friend in England."

He was rewarded and somewhat taken aback by an enthusiastic hug and a kiss on either cheek. He laughed, but he felt more amiably disposed toward Americans.

"Now, tell me," he said, "why do you want Cecil to be ambitious? Do you want a great political *salon?*"

"I should n't mind a bit, but that 's not the reason. The more Cecil wanted of life, the more he 'd be dependent on me for consolation and encouragement — the most successful have so many disappointments. If he went through life animated by duty alone, content with the niche he drifted into, he 'd close up at all points, become a mere spoke in the wheel, without a weak spot that I could get at. And then he *would* be dull. It 's in Cecil to become terribly solid or to spread out in several different directions. I want him to spread out."

"Ah! I see you have done some thinking, if you are a mere child."

"I 'm no child — really. I took care of my mother and did all her thinking for five years, and I have been treated like an individual, not like an Englishman's necessary virtue, ever since. I 've managed my own business affairs; I 've read more books than any woman in this house; I 've had heaps and heaps of men in love with me; and I 've done a lot of thinking — particularly about Cecil."

Lord Barnstaple in another moment might have smiled, but for the present his concern had routed his cynicism.

"You look as if you 'd merely been made to fall in love with," he said gallantly. "But I am surprised and gratified. Tell me what you have been thinking about Cecil."

"I 'd day-dreamed for years about him before he came, but it was all romantic and impossible nonsense. I don't think I ever realised that he was the author of his own letters, and I persisted in imagining him a mixture of Byron, Marmion, Robert Dudley, Eugene Wrayburn, Launcelot, and several of Ouida's earlier heroes. Of course, my imagination wore down a good deal after I came out and saw more of the world; nevertheless, when Cecil did come, he was wholly unlike anything I had concocted. But, somehow, he seemed quite natural, even in the first moment, and I would not have had him otherwise for the world. He seemed made for me, and it did n't take me a second to get used to him."

"Well?" Lord Barnstaple was watching her closely; the slightest acting would not have escaped him. She spoke with some hesitation, her eyes turned aside.

"He only stayed a little while, and I did n't see him again for three days. During those days, and during two weeks a little later when I was alone again — he left me for a bear! — I did harder thinking than I 'd ever done before. I realised two things, especially the second time: I was frightfully in love with him, and the whole happiness of our future was in my hands. Cecil had told me, with his usual frankness, that I 'd have to do the adapting — he could n't.   I 'm sure he had no idea of being egoistical; he always looks facts in the face, and he merely stated one.   And there 's no doubt about it ! He 's made for good and all — he 's centuries old. That threw the whole thing on me."

"Considering that you look things in the face with something of the intellectuality of a man, you have undertaken no light responsibility."

"It 's the less light because I am a Californian, and we have twice the individuality and originality of any people in the United States.   We always get quite huffy when we are spoken of as merely Americans.   Of course we take enormous pride in our Southern descent, but we are — those of us that were born there — Californians, first and last."

"These fine distinctions are beyond me at present. Of course you will be good enough to initiate me further."

"You need not laugh.   Cecil did at first, but now he quite understands that it is the United States *and* California.   What I was going to say was this: it 's the harder for us to adapt ourselves, in spite of the fact that we are malleable and made of a thousand particles.   Compared with Englishwomen, who — who — are much more conservative and traditional, we are in a state of fusion.   But the fact remains that we have tremendous individuality, and that we are — as Cecil says — self-conscious about it."

"And you don't fancy adapting yourself to anybody.   Quite so."

"It irritated and worried me at first, for I 'd not only been on a pedestal, but I 'd been a fearful little tyrant with men. You would n't believe the way I used to treat them. Now " — she paused a moment, then blurted out: "I 'm so much in love that I don't care a rap about my individuality. I don't care for a thing on earth but to be happy. Of course, before I married, I had made up my mind to make the best of many things I probably should n't like, and not to attempt the impossible task of making Cecil over. But there is so much more in it than that. I am determined that my marriage shall be a success. I have had already enough happiness to want always more and more and more. I 'll live for that. I buried my private ambitions in the redwoods. It is a curious contradiction, that happiness is the one thing people really want, and that it is the one thing nearly everybody misses. I believe it is because people do not concentrate on it. They wish for it and make little grabs at it. I intend to concentrate on it, and live for nothing else. And of course that means that Cecil will be happy too. I 'll simply fling aside the thought of certain attributes I would wish Cecil had, and make the most of what he has. And, Heaven knows, Nature was not niggardly with him!"

Lord Barnstaple held his breath for half a moment. His interest had ceased to be speculative, and even, for the moment, paternal. He was in the presence of elemental passion and a shrewd modern brain, and the combination was a force from which he received a palpable shock. There was so profound a silence for several moments that Lee stirred uneasily, wondering if she had tried his interest too far. When he spoke, it was in his most matter-of-fact tone.

"If I were a younger man I should say many pretty things to you, notably one which I don't doubt Cecil has said very often — that you are the sort of woman a man imagines he could cheerfully die for. I am no longer young, but I recognise the type." He hesitated a moment. "My wife belonged to it. Now, I am going to give you some hard practical advice. If you adopt it, I believe that, taken in connection with your purpose and with what Nature has been kind enough to do for *you*, it will insure your success if anything can. Identify yourself with every one of Cecil's pleasures and pursuits. By the first of October the guests will have gone, and Emmy with them; she spends the rest of the autumn and early winter in London, and in a round of visits further South. Cecil and I always stay on here for the pheasants, and I usually ask two or three men down at a time. There will be no other women here until next August. Come out with us, learn to shoot, stay out all day, and —— *learn to like it*. I doubt, though, if you could help it. Then comes the hunting season. We always spend the month of November in Warwickshire at Beaumanoir, my brother-in-law's place — you will remember he was here when you came. Cecil tells me that you are a fine horsewoman. You will learn to ride to hounds in no time, and Cecil is particularly keen on hunting. So much for his pleasures; and you will soon learn that you cannot know too much about sport of every sort.

In December we must return here. Parliament may be prorogued for elections at any moment after February, and Cecil must begin as soon as possible to nurse his constituency. It's been nursing for him in a way for several years, for it has always been understood that Cecil was to succeed old Saunderson, who has now had enough of it, and practically notified the Division. Nevertheless, Cecil has work of his own to do, for the Liberal element has been gaining strength here for some time. He must make speeches, open libraries, or whatever else demands the grace of his presence — and I believe several things of the sort are finishing. He must do everything he can to make himself known and liked, and to inspire confidence. And he will have to study very hard — will study, for he does nothing by halves. You must go about with him, and also visit a little among the village people. You will be a great help, for the lower classes love the compound of beauty and rank; and if it is known that you will sit on the platform while he speaks he will be doubly sure of a large audience. He may give an occasional lecture or preside at a magic-lantern show at the village schools. It is expected of us, for some six or eight villages skirting the estate were once ours. I, too, have been an oracle in my day. The bare thought bores me now, but it will amuse you and Cecil. And — here is another point — study with him. That will not be so interesting; in fact, it will bore you —— "

"No, it will not. I'm immensely interested in English politics already."

"You'll find it something of a pull, tramping through Blue Books, Reports, Public Speeches, Statesman's Year-Books, and all the data on the great question of the Landlord *v.* the Farmer. But if you have the brains and the energy to stick to it — and I believe you have — you will succeed in getting closer to Cecil than you ever would in any other way. He will be flattered at first, and pleased with the prospect of companionship; later, you will become his second self, and he could no more do without you than without one of his legs or arms. It's a risky thing to say to a woman, but to live comfortably with an Englishman you've got to become his habit, and to be happy with him you've got to become his second self. Englishwomen are the first from tradition. When they have brains they usually bolt in the opposite direction. That is because they are deficient in passion. Let me see what you will make of the combination. I believe you will succeed. Thank Heaven, here comes the tea! I've never talked so much in my born days, and I'm as dry as a herring."

They took their tea cosily in the dim beautiful room, and Lee, being a woman of tact, dropped the subject of herself, and attempted the seemingly impossible task of amusing Lord Barnstaple. She succeeded so well that he discarded his usual chuckle, and laughed heartily no less than five times.

"I foresee that you and Cecil and I shall be three jolly good comrades. Of course I shan't see quite so much of you in London; you and Cecil will have to take a house of your own, and I've got to live

under the same roof with Emmy, for decency's sake.
But here we can be a really comfortable family
party. This year we'll be here till April, and after
that, of course, you'll have to move up to London
in January. Do you look forward to being the beauty
of a London season? What a question!"

"Of course I want to be admired; and what is
more, I don't intend to let Cecil forget that I can
be, when I choose. I suppose I'll look horrid in a
shooting outfit."

"I am sure you will look charming; and, I don't
wish to be rude — Cecil will not know whether you do
or not. But that's not the point, and you can make
yourself fascinating at dinner. Tea-gowns ——"
He waved his hand vaguely.

Lee's eyes sparkled. "I have a delightful sensation of novelty," she said. "I want to get right into
the middle of it all. It may not be like my old
dreams, but it glitters, all the same. I love doing
new things."

"Novelty is the half of many battles," observed
Lord Barnstaple dryly.

The conversation drifted again to other matters,
but as he was leaving her a half-hour later, he turned
at the door, and said:

"Cecil is very much under your spell. Keep him
there."

"I intend to." Lee's eyes rarely failed to express
what leaped into the foreground of her mind. As
Lord Barnstaple picked his way down the dark and
winding stair his smile was much as usual.

CHAPTER VII

AS Lee sat alone, pondering deeply over her father-in-law's advice, her American mail was brought up. She opened a letter from Mrs. Montgomery. After several pages of lamentation in many keys for her lost child, and several more of advice, the good lady got down to news.

"And I 've lost another, for a whole year at the very least — I 'll join him somewhere in Europe when Tiny goes back, and then, of course, he 'll come with us to England, and has almost persuaded me to take up my real abode in Europe and pay visits to California. Of course I mean Randolph, darling. He decided, after all, not to sell his share in the mine, but formed a syndicate — himself, Mr. Geary, Mr. Trennahan, Mr. Brannan, and others of unimpeachable integrity — and now they own the mine, and Randolph says he 'll be worth five millions at least. As soon as it was all settled he told me that as there was nothing in particular for him to do he should go abroad. I could n't believe my ears when he said : 'I never want to hear the word " business " again. I am sick of being a hustling American. I want the repose of the old world, and all it must be able to give and do for a man. I want to read and study, too. I feel half-educated, half-baked. If I could only have got a million out of the mine I should have been satisfied, and turned my back on money-grabbing just the same, but of course my instincts were too strong to take one million where there was a chance of five.' So he's gone! I've cried until I can't see, for, although Arthur's the best of men, and I love him like my own son, he's not Randolph, and even Tiny couldn't call him entertaining. When I tell him my troubles, he merely says, ' Ah! ' at regular intervals. But I'm glad, for one reason : I 've always *hated* money-*making ;* money was never made for anything but to spend with an open hand without asking for change, and I could never shut my eyes to the fact that Randolph was not what his grandfathers were — and his father when the latter was a young man. And he looks so like his paternal grandfather — the very image, and old Colonel Montgomery always looked as if he'd just come from a private audience with the king — of course there wasn't any king, but he made one think there was. Europe does wonders for people. I never saw an American woman go over for one year that she didn't come back improved. The men don't usually stay long enough, but when they do — look at Mr. Trennahan. I'm sure it will give Randolph just the one thing he needs. . . . "

Lee dropped the letter in dismay. If hers ever reached Randolph, would he interrupt his first real holiday to attend to her affairs? And it would be a year at least before he arrived in England. For a few moments she was nervously excited and very depressed. Then she bethought herself of her resolution to worry about nothing she could not alter. Both her parents-in-law would, in all probability, live for many years to come, and Lady Barnstaple seemed by no means at the end of her resources. By hook or by crook she would get the money before it was needed; but until she could take her next step she would agitate herself no further about it.

Her mind wandered to Randolph. It was on the cards that he would be much changed and improved the next time they met. He inspired her with quite a new interest, and she anticipated his advent with a lively curiosity.

She opened a letter from Coralie:

"I am going to marry, too," announced Miss Brannan; "Ned Geary. I used to fancy myself rather *éprise* with Randolph, as you know; but really one's affections can't thrive on disinterested friendship, so I 've transferred mine, bag and baggage, to the uncertain Teddy. I don't believe Randolph will ever marry. I 'm light and Ned is light, like the North American atmosphere and Californian claret; but Randolph is the kind that takes things clear down to his boots. He 's as blue as paint, and it 'll be a long while before he spruces up. However, he 's got several millions to console him, so I expect he 'll pull through."

Lee felt a slight irritation at the rapid consolement of Mr. Geary, and smiled at the assurance of Randolph's unaltered devotion. Then, out of her fuller knowledge, she sent him a little sigh of pity, and shortly after dismissed him from her mind.

In a few moments she went out to meet Cecil on his return from the moors. On the top of a hillock she turned and looked back at the Abbey. During the last fortnight she had studied it in every light and from every side. She understood why even Emmy loved it, and why Cecil had cared for no other home, even when a child, and with a bare prospect of inheritance; she herself had conceived a feeling that was almost a passion for it. Cecil had rehabilitated its past, and the tales were heroic and dramatic and ghostly enough to satisfy even her girlish imagination; small wonder that she loved the Abbey as the one thing that had been wholly without disappointment, and had made no demands upon her powers of adaptability.

It was nearly half an hour before she met the brakes with the returning sportsmen. The undulations of the moor soon hid every other feature of the landscape. It was a vast and lonely expanse, as primitive and as widely lonely as any prairie of the New World. And it was so beautiful that Lee was faithless to her redwoods; for it came to her with something of a shock that the expression " purple twilight " was not a mere poetic felicity. Whether or not the atmosphere absorbed the heather's colour, all the light on the moor, and on the mountain beyond, was purple. She had read of the dreary moorland, and had pictured it a dun grey thing; possibly it was in winter. But in its autumn purples it was mysterious and enchanting. And it gave the impression of shouldering the horizon on every side — of possessing the Earth. Far away was a solitary hut; near by a pond of ugly traditions. It was all as it should be, Lee reflected with a quizzical smile. Within the walls of the Abbey Emmy held romance by the throat, but out here on the moor it was impossible to realise her existence, or anything but the England of the poets.

CHAPTER VIII

WHAT Lee did at all she did thoroughly, volatile as she was in some respects; original force of character, fostered and augmented by certain conditions, overbalanced for long periods the lighter qualities of her native atmosphere. She had wanted Cecil for the greater part of her life, and she had got him; to be completely happy with him, and to be all to him that it is given to one mortal to be to another was her fixed purpose, and she applied herself to it with the energy and concentration which have carried many men to their pedestal in a public square.

Cecil was not disposed to desert the grouse after the last of the guests had left the Abbey, and she went out every day with him and the keepers — Lord Barnstaple was still nursing his wrist; and, having a quick eye and a steady hand, occasionally managed to bring down a bird. It was true that walking on the moor was much like walking on a spring-mattress, and, being the child of an earthquake country, she was never quite able to rid herself of an uneasy anticipation of collapse; but so great was the enthusiasm of her nature that she was not only interested, but delighted with this, as with other novelties of her present life.

Shooting in the covers was a more difficult matter, and when she scratched her face or caught her hair on a briary branch, she said things under her breath which would have shocked Mrs. Montgomery or Cecil; but there was no doubt that sport, if one went into it with one's entire brain, was really exciting, and, had it not been, Cecil's delight in his wife's latest development would have sustained her.

In hunting, she took an unqualified pleasure. No Englishwoman had a finer seat in the saddle than she, and, having always loved riding for itself, the additional incentive of pursuit, and the picturesque appearance of the field, made the pastime quite the most perfect she had ever known. Before the season was far advanced she rode as straight as any woman in the county; and perhaps Cecil's compliments at this period were the most spontaneous of his life. There was no doubt that he was very proud of her, and once he went so far as to hint that he felt rather sorry for the majority of men.

The month at Beaumanoir was rather fatiguing, but very gay — at least, everybody laughed a great deal, and seemed full of energy. Emmy came for a few days, and Lady Mary Gifford remained a fortnight, and bestowed much of her society on Lee.

When they returned to the Abbey there was still more or less shooting and hunting, but Cecil applied himself seriously to the imminent elections. As time passed, and the defeat of his party loomed large in the possibilities, Lee noted that his interest became less impersonal and considerably more acute; his latent ambitions and energies felt their first prick.

He spoke frequently at this time, and as the roar

of the storm grew nearer, his own accents lost the cold deliberation of the first weeks and became impassioned and convincing. He had little doubt of his own election, but the threatened downfall of his party harassed and angered him. It was then that his wife discovered that he had not outlived his boyish love of sympathy; and the boudoir in the tower and the lonely moorland were the scenes of many long and intense conversations, until it became his habit to demand the sympathy of his wife for every strait, great and small, in which his country and his party found themselves.

If a solid winter of politics bored Lee, her husband never knew it. Neither did Lord Barnstaple, who watched her critically; he had no more intimate talks with her. But although she was destined to find much in English politics more interesting than Home Rule, the present crisis was certainly exciting. And the two facts, that Cecil was expanding, not solidifying, and that he showed signs of becoming almost dependent on her, were satisfying alike to the pride of her purpose and to the might of her affections.

On the first stormy day, Cecil announced his intention to begin the course of study he had planned, and was surprised and gratified when his wife invited him to bring his tomes to her boudoir.

" I 'm tired of novels, and I 've nothing else to do, and I 'm so tremendously interested myself, that I think I 'll read with you," she said, as Cecil littered her lapis-lazuli table. "Would it bore you to explain things to me?"

"You are sure it wouldn't bore *you?*" Cecil looked across the ugly volumes at his beautiful wife, his eyes sparkling as eagerly as when she had, ten years ago, at the Cliff House, put into words his half-formed desire for an adventure. "I should like it —above all things."

"I should be much more bored roaming round the Abbey by myself, or sitting here twirling my thumbs. I think I can understand. I've read *The Times* every morning for three months, and I feel equal to anything." She did not add that at each finish she invariably stuck a pin up to its head into the pride of England, lest her surcharged spirits find vent upon the gentlemen of her household.

"You can understand anything," replied Cecil, who did not appreciate the humour of her remark. "And I'll get along twice as well myself if I have somebody to talk things over with. But you mustn't tire yourself." And he went over to the other side of the table.

They read together the long winter through, seeing Lord Barnstaple only at the table and in the evenings: he had congenial spirits in the neighbourhood, and he paid several visits to London. The conversation between the three was invariably of politics. When the weather was fine Cecil and his wife spent two or three hours of every day out-of-doors, and occasionally attended a meet.

The fascination of politics, when the mind has fairly opened to them, is indubitable; and Lee not only felt proud of herself that her understanding and her patience stood the strain of this mass of facts

—whose skeletons fairly rattled—which mounted higher and higher on her lapis-lazuli table and encroached upon the divan and all of the ancient chairs, but she took a keen mental delight in the acquiring of knowledge; and what knowledge to the alert modern mind can equal the charm of current history? Although her primary purpose was to bind her husband to her by every fetter she could devise, she occasionally saw herself the centre of a political *salon*, when the world had pronounced her the brilliant wife of a great man.

It was not later than the beginning of the second month of their close mental intercourse that Lee made one of her most important discoveries regarding her husband; he had intellectual heights and depths which she would never touch. She had cleverness far above the average of her sex, and, had she chosen, she would have had every right to pose as an intellectual woman; but she had distinct limitations, and one proof of her cleverness was that she recognised and accepted them. The discovery arrived in the wake of a pleased reflection that it was certainly a privilege to be in constant contact with a mind like Cecil Maundrell's, and that she was distinctly grateful for it. For a time she was mortified and depressed, for it was her first intimation that she was not all that the gods or man could desire; but it was her mental habit to face facts and digest them, and when this was disposed of she considered its possible results. Her conclusions soothed her. She knew something of men. When Cecil tasted to the full the sweets of masculine superiority over the mate with whom he was so delighted, and of whom so justly proud, there would be still another bond between them. Far be it from her to attempt to throw dust into his keen eyes by feminine blandishment and subterfuge; she admitted the truth, whenever the opportunity offered, with spontaneous bursts of admiration; and if Cecil had not been flattered he would have been less than human.

"I don't see how I shall ever be permitted to become discouraged," he said one day with some humour, looking into the rapt and beautiful eyes opposite him. "I believe if I made an egregious ass of myself in the House, you would persuade me that I was too great to be understood by my fellow-men."

"I'm not a goose, thank you. But you'll never make an ass of yourself, so it doesn't matter. Of course you'll be a great man."

"I wish I could believe it."

"It's plain enough to every one else. All you need is ambition, and I can see that growing already. If your party is defeated, so much the better for you. You can devote your energies and your gifts to putting new life into it. You're just what the old fogies need. I don't see how you could start out more favourably, and I don't see what is to prevent your being the next great man."

Cecil's nostrils quivered suddenly. He looked for an instant longer into the eyes that had expressed many more things to him than admiration for his intellectual equipment, put out his hand impulsively and took hers, then returned to his studies.

CHAPTER IX

THEY moved up to town on the third of April. Lady Barnstaple had taken a tiny and costly house for them in Green Street, and as there had been much correspondence on the subject, and many samples had travelled from London to Yorkshire and back, it was almost in order when the young couple arrived to take possession.

"For goodness' sake, have it light and bright," Lady Barnstaple had written. "London is such a grimy hole, people simply love colour. Don't mind bothering me; if I were poor I'd be a house decorator. The only fault I had to find with the Abbey was that it was furnished."

Lee found her doll's house a delicious nest of colour and luxury after the feudal severity of her tower; and although Cecil was even more serious than when he had married, she managed, during that first spring in London, to make him feel that they were playing at keeping house and at the lighter side of life. She could always amuse and interest him when she thought it wise to do so.

They went out very little, for he detested crushes in hot ill-ventilated rooms, and large dinners were not more to his taste; but he liked the play, and they were always to be seen at Tattersall's on Sunday afternoons, and often in the Park, which had not yet been vulgarised as a promenade. In the mornings they rose early and rode either through the Park with the many of stereotyped habits, or out into the country; occasionally to Richmond, where they breakfasted at the Star and Garter, and tried to imagine that it was still brilliant and wicked. Sometimes, of an afternoon, they traversed three or four " At Homes," where Lee had an enchanting sense of being in the great world at last, and Cecil kept his eyes longingly on the windows. At the play they always took a box, as Cecil became restless in the narrower confines of the stalls, and Lord Barnstaple and Mary Gifford usually accompanied them. Lady Barnstaple, although she sang her daughter-in-law's praises in a loud high key, flatly refused to elevate her passing charms into a box of which Lee was the radiant and novel star. Lee was greatly admired, and knew that she could have been the bride of the season, had Cecil permitted; but although she felt some natural regret, especially when her mother-in-law expostulated, and Lady Mary Gifford commiserated, on the whole she did not care. Cecil barely let her out of his sight, and once he sulked for an entire day because she went to a luncheon; she was happy, and nothing else mattered. When she was stared out of countenance at the opera and theatre he took it as a matter of course, but the newspaper comments were less to his taste, and he peremptorily forbade her to give her photograph to any of the illustrated weeklies, or to be the heroine of certain enterprising " lady-journalists," who wished to exploit her beauty and her many delectable gowns. Her semi-seclusion gave her a touch of mystery, and one woman's magazine would have made her known to fifty thousand provincials; but Cecil was disgusted at the bare idea of sharing his wife with the public, and flung the artful request for an interview into the fire. Lee was much amused, and assured him that Mrs. Montgomery had brought her up to regard notoriety with horror.

"And after all," she said to Lady Barnstaple, "suppose I did become a professional beauty, that would place Cecil in a contemptible position, and I'd rather be a desperate failure than do that."

"Oh, bother! But it's no use talking to a woman in love. You'll sacrifice your youth to a selfish brute of a man and spend your thirties regretting it and your forties making up for lost time. I love Cecil, and of course I'm glad to see him happy, but he's as selfish as all men, and you're making him more so. I don't say you won't keep him. I believe you will, for he's the sort that would rather be faithful to his wife than not — does n't take after his illustrious parent — but he'll soon take you as a matter of course, and then you'll realise what the world could do for you. God knows what I should have done without it, and if I ever have to go under, a dose of laudanum will do the rest."

But Cecil gave no sign of taking his wife as a matter of course. It is true that he took all and gave nothing — except his love. That Lee might have an inner life of her own never crossed his mind; that it had ever crossed any one's else that she was fitted

for a career more or less apart from his own, however parallel with it, he would have resented as an
insult to them both; and he had long since dismissed
from his thoughts certain complexities which had
puzzled and worried him during the weeks of their
engagement. He was perfectly satisfied with her;
although he had begged to be released from paying
her compliments, and had received his discharge, he
would have had her changed in nothing. Her beauty
and passion held him in thrall, and he was more than
grateful for the companionship she offered him, to
say nothing of the incense. He would have liked to
be rich that he might have had the pleasure of making her many beautiful presents, but he was philo-
sophical, and wasted no time in regrets. And he
was not wholly an egoist, for he occasionally reminded
himself that he was the luckiest chap alive; and when
he glanced along the future, and reflected that for each
of the severe trials, mortifications, and disappointments of his public career he should find solace, and
even forgetfulness, in his home, he felt that there
were indeed no limits to his good fortune.

Did he ever think of Maundrell Abbey at this
time? He gave no sign. But possibly he saw no
reason for anxiety. Emmy was entertaining magnifi-
cently, and had informed her family that Chicago had
taken a sudden leap in the direction of certain of her
town lots, and trebled their value. Lee, in spite of
the gossip with which Lady Mary Gifford regaled her
concerning almost every woman in Society, was not
inclined to think evil spontaneously of any one, but
she overheard one woman say to another, with a

shrug of the shoulders, that "Lady Barnstaple had taken up with the wrong man," and she was surprised at the constant presence of Mr. Algernon Pix in her mother-in-law's house. Mr. Pix had none of his sister's aristocratic beauty, although he was good-looking in a common way; he was very dark, with eyes set close together, and he had a neat little figure. His manner was polite to exaggeration, but his accent was fatal, and three years of Society had not curbed his love of diamonds. In truth, his position was very precarious. Some women liked him, but the men barely accepted him, despite the determined bolstering of several of Victoria's powerful friends; and as he had never even attempted to handle a gun, and feared a horse as he feared the snub of a Duchess, his social future ran off into vague perspectives. He was wise enough never to accept invitations to the country, and Lee had not met him until she moved up to town. He was the sort of man whom she had heretofore associated with drapers' counters and railway trains, and inevitably she snubbed him.

"I'd be very much obliged to you if you'd treat my friends decently," said Lady Barnstaple sharply, when they were alone.

"Surely he is not a friend of yours."

"His sister is my very most intimate friend; and as for him — well, yes, I do like him — immensely. It means something to me, I can tell you, to have a man show me the thousand and one little attentions that women love — and to think me still beautiful; _and he does._ I don't say he would if I were not the Countess of Barnstaple, and miles above him socially

— I'm no fool — but that he can be really dazzled means a great deal to me, and when you're my age you'll know why."

Lee reflected that probably the bond between them was the commonness of both, and that " Emmy " was a striking instance of heredity, then dismissed the subject from her mind. Lord Barnstaple, who never took a meal in his wife's house, except in company with many others, and took many at the little house in Green Street, was apparently unaware of the existence of Mr. Pix, although he commented freely, and with caustic emphasis, upon the idiosyncrasies of his legal wife.

CHAPTER X

ON June twenty-eighth Parliament was prorogued for the elections, and Cecil and Lee went to Yorkshire at once.

Lord Maundrell made a number of speeches, made himself agreeable to many men whom he would have preferred to kick, and received his nomination. The contest was bitter and exciting, and Lee designated her husband during this period, for want of a better term, as " less English " than she had yet known him. There were times when he let her see just how perturbed and excited he was, carefully as he secluded his inner mind from others. Lee, in the little stone villages, that looked as if they might have been built by the heirs of the cave-dwellers, played the part made familiar to her by the novel and the stage, and, for the life of her, could not take herself seriously. Her difficulty was increased by the fact that she could not understand two words in ten of the Yorkshire dialect. The villagers understood her as little, but there was no doubt that her uncommon beauty and her gracious and magnetic manner duly impressed them.

Cecil was returned, but his party was defeated; and he convinced Lee that without her his melancholy would have lasted fully a month.

There were still two weeks before the twelfth of August, and they took a run over to Normandy. After their return, life until December was precisely what it had been the year before. The same people, almost without exception, came in four instalments to the Abbey for the six weeks which followed the opening of the grouse season, and it seemed to Lee that they talked about precisely the same things. The men spent the day on the moors, and at dinner talked when they felt like talking at all, of the bags which had been made, the condition of the birds and the moor, and the weather prospects, occasionally indulging in reminiscences of other years. The women played tennis and golf, rode or drove, or sat about the Abbey. After dinner the men roused, and permitted themselves to be flirted with, either in historic boudoirs or across the billiard tables, and there were many who played high and late. Cecil and Lee usually started on their long walk to the tower about midnight after a long and fatiguing day.

When Emmy's guests had gone, Lee went out with Lord Barnstaple, her husband, and half a dozen other enthusiasts, and persuaded herself that sport was really absorbing whether one had been brought up to it or not. It was certainly preferable to wandering all day long by oneself over an immense and echoing Abbey, or driving to neighbouring estates, and taking tea with women who rarely went up to London.

When the hunting season came, although the novelty of riding hard after a yelping pack with some twenty men in beautiful pink coats, or even of dancing with the latter at hunt balls, was no longer a part of her pleasure, she felt that the chase would wear when other things had palled, although she would have been glad to return to the Abbey for December. They visited, however, and they hunted, and they shot; they graced farmers' balls and hunt races with their presence, and they even attended a great magic-lantern show; only returning to the Abbey for a few days at Christmas. Lord Barnstaple went to Paris, and the young people were alone. It was a blessed interval of rest, during which Lee exacted from Cecil a solemn promise that he would not mention sport, adding hastily that she adored it, but was horribly jealous, and did not want him to think of a thing but herself for an entire week. And to his credit it must be said that he seemed to find no difficulty in humouring her.

In January they went to Paris for a fortnight, as Lee's wardrobe needed replenishing, and in February Cecil's parliamentary duties began, and they settled down in London when it was at its dreariest and ugliest, and the rest of England was moist but beautiful. Lee was alone now, for the greater part of the week, from three in the afternoon until midnight or the small hours of the morning, although she frequently went to the Ladies' Gallery of the House and brought Cecil back to dinner; or took tea with him on the Terrace, which she thought very interesting. There was always — for a reasonable time — at least one distinguished man to be pointed out, and she liked to conjure up the days when the Thames was gay with the barges of sovereigns and their courtiers, instead of mildly picturesque with penny boats and queer-looking water vehicles for which Cecil had no name.

When the young member was not too busy they still rode or walked in the morning, and attended the play or the opera at night. Occasionally they went to a dinner or a party, and as Emmy's entertaining this year took the form of morning concerts, with divas and tenors to beckon the fickle world, Cecil made a martyr of himself upon these occasions as gracefully as he could.

On the whole, Lee, although she left a good many cards and received on Tuesdays, saw less of Society than during the preceding season, and learned of its doings and of what faint interest it still felt in her from Lord Barnstaple and Mary Gifford, who came frequently to luncheon or tea. However, she assured herself that after the late hours of the autumn and early winter she was glad to get her beauty sleep again, and went to bed at ten o'clock.

When there was an important debate on in the House she always attended, and more than once came home with Cecil at two in the morning. Such speeches as she did not hear she read next morning, as well as the comments thereon in no less than six different newspapers; and she frequently assured herself that her political education was comparable with that of any Englishwoman born. Her enthusiasm undoubtedly had its reward, for not only was Cecil pleased and grateful, but when they attended dinners of more or less political significance she invariably incited her partner to speech, no matter how silent Heaven had made him. One, and he was famous and stout, and had buried conversation with other follies of his past, surprised himself by informing her that she could talk politics with her eyes more eloquently than any woman in England with all the resources of a large vocabulary and all the ambition inspired by the heroines of Disraeli.

Lord Barnstaple laughed when she related this anecdote.

"Oh, you will be wanting a *salon* next," he said. "It is quite natural you should picture statesmen crowding your rooms — I am making no reflection on the size of your house — and whispering their secrets in your pretty little ear — or seeing themselves upside down in your eloquent eyes."

Lee coloured and lifted her chin in a manner which even a father-in-law must find charming. "I could have one if I liked — and that quite satisfies me, thank you."

"I'm sorry you can't go out more, though," he said tentatively. "You are young and admired, and of course you like what women call pleasure."

"I don't care a rap about it," she said with emphasis. "I am sure one hard London season would bore me to death."

"Quite so. Quite so. It's just a beastly grind, nothing more. You're really far better off in the way you have chosen. I am glad to see you so happy. Cecil is certainly a lucky dog."

"You gave me some good advice that day." She smiled brilliantly into his watchful eyes.

"Oh, you were quite clever enough to have arrived at the same conclusions without my help. Of course if you had wanted a flashing career of your own, or had been a silly woman, greedy for admiration and intrigue, it would have been a different matter — a terribly different matter for Cecil. But you wanted happiness, and there is only one way to get it."

CHAPTER XI

IT was not long before Cecil's abilities were recog·
nised. Something was expected of him, for he
came of a line of able Parliamentarians; and as he
was already famous as a sportsman, he commanded
an interest by no means inspired by the average
young man of an illustrious house.

When the time came for him to make his first
speech, shortly before the end of the Session, Lee sat
in the gallery with an icy exterior surrounding a furious nerve storm. The day was dark and depressing.
Those long rows of faces had never looked more
apathetic; it was enough to make a novice feel, as he
rose and confronted the bored old veterans, that he
was on trial for his life. If Cecil failed Lee felt that
she could hate him, not because the world would curl
its lip, but because Cecil, mortified, stammering, a
failure, would be an ideal in collapse. She might
oust these unworthy sentiments later, and sympathise
with him in his distress, but she could never quite
rehabilitate him. He might be defeated in the most
significant climaxes of his career, his party might
turn upon and rend him, and she would pour all the
wealth of her nature at his feet, but if he made a fool
of himself, she'd never forgive him.

But Cecil had no intention of making a fool of
himself. Moreover, his training at Oxford, when

the Union had rung with his salad eloquence, made itself manifest among the other foundations of his mind and character. He was neither nervous nor too diffident. In fact he opened so easily that Lee thrilled with pride and excoriated herself. When he got his first "Hear!" her knees jerked; she realised how excited she was, and glanced about the gallery hastily; but in that dim cage she had little to fear. He demanded the attention of the House for something over an hour, and he would have scorned to amuse it; but his speech was terse and packed with his own thought; it had not a platitude in it, nor a time-honoured sentiment. He might or might not become a brilliant speaker when he had acquired sufficient practice and confidence to let himself go, but that he was a Maundrell to be reckoned with had been conceded long before he sat down.

Lee was with him in the lobby when he received the congratulations of men many years older than himself, and the next morning she brought all the newspapers, and pasted the highly laudatory articles on the rising sun into a scrap-book. She cunningly persuaded him to be photographed, and as his reputation waxed she supplied the weekly papers with his distinguished profile. He was moved to wrath, but his wife's fervid admiration was very sweet to him, and when she pleaded it as her excuse for taking a step without consulting him, he forgave her instantly.

They could not get away in time for a trip abroad that year, much to Lee's disappointment; for the

Continent was one vast romantic ruin to her, varied with shops and the picturesque costumes of peasants. The late summer and autumn and early winter were precisely like the summer and autumn and early winter of the year before. They entertained the same people, visited the same houses; and this time Lee had the novel feeling of amazement for a people who were just as much pleased and just as absorbed as if a benign Providence had gifted them with the instinct for variety.

"No wonder they are great," she thought, with a sigh.

In January the London *maisonnette* was open again, and as gay as flowers and upholstery and lamp shades could make it. Cecil for some time past had meditated a Bill for the relief of certain manufacturers, and had worked at it on odd days during the recess. He introduced it, and it failed, for it was practically a demand for the exclusion of much that was "made in Germany," and was regarded as a covert and audacious attack on Free Trade. His Speech in its behalf was the most brilliant he had yet made, and he was bitterly denounced by the Liberal and Radical press next morning. Nor did their attentions cease with their comments on his Bill and Speech. From that time on he was regarded by the Opposition as a man to be sneered into the cooler regions of private life. His constituency was warned by that section of its press whose principles he did not represent, and he was accused of having pledged his abilities, "such as they were," to a lifelong fight against progress, and of a criminal indifference to Home Rule and to the unfortunate Armenian.

Of these jeremiads — which Cecil refused to read, having made up his mind and being at peace with his conscience — Lee was as proud as of the many compliments which the young member received, and she pasted them dutifully in the scrap-book. Of Society she saw something less than ever, although her mother-in-law adjured her not to "make a fool of herself." She admitted that she should like to go to some of the great parties, and to an occasional supper at the Savoy, under Lady Barnstaple's wing; for her evenings were lonely, and politics would have been even more interesting if seasoned with variety. She asked Cecil, with an apologetic blush, if he would mind.

He plunged his hands into his pockets.

"Are you very keen on it?" he asked.

"Oh, I'm not mad about it, but I have n't seen much of London Society, and it interests me; and I have so much time on my hands."

"I'm afraid you must get rather bored. I'm sorry I have to be so much away from you. But — I hate to see women running about without their husbands. Besides it's always the beginning of the end — when a woman goes her way and a man his. It's selfish of me, but I like to think of you as always here. As you know, I break away sometimes, and come home unexpectedly —— "

"You have n't this year."

"We've been so confoundedly busy. But I often think of you, and I like to picture you in this room with a book, or asleep when other women are baking their complexions."

Lee smiled. "That was very astute. You would rather I did not go out, then?"

"I feel a selfish brute. Let me know what you particularly want to go to, and I'll try to pair and take you myself."

But Lee knew that he hated the very thought of it, and he was more and more absorbed in his work. Of his ambition there was now no question; he had even gone so far as to half admit it to her. He did not return to the subject, upon which their conversation had, indeed, been so brief that he might be pardoned for forgetting it. Lee attempted to find oblivion in the mass of data elucidative of colonial history, past and present, to which Cecil, with his usual thoroughness, was devoting his leisure. It had been his purpose, from the moment he had decided upon his career, to achieve a full and sympathetic understanding of the colonies. He had given no little attention to politics in India and South Africa, as well as to their peoples, during his sporting tour, and he intended to revisit these and other parts of the Empire as soon as he felt reasonably sure of his footing at home, and had mastered the enormous bulk of colonial conditions in the abstract. He had no belief in home-made theories for governing the alien millions of the English race.

Lee looked forward to these journeyings with some interest, although she would have preferred to explore the crumbling and rather more picturesque civilisations of Europe. Travel would be more comfortable, and the Continent was a superb theatre, under superb management — to take it seriously was out of the question; but although it did not appeal to the soul, it was a delight to the imagination. But neither the one change in her programme nor the other seemed imminent; Cecil found too much to do in England. The present routine bid fair to last for three or four years to come.

And to have argued that social success would have conduced to her husband's advancement would have been a waste of words, for Cecil was a man of ideals and regarded meretricious connectives with scorn. He was very much elated at this period, for there was every indication that the Liberal tenure was a brief one, and that his party was regaining all it had lost, and more. He intended to speak throughout the North, pending the next elections, and he had good reason to anticipate that his services to his party would be rewarded with that first stepping-stone to power, an Under-Secretaryship. Lee was to go about with him, of course; he would as soon have thought of leaving one of his members at home, and she looked forward to the variation of the usual autumn programme with some enthusiasm. She was tremendously proud of her gifted and high-minded young husband, and when disposed to repine, forced into her mind her ten years of unremitting determination and desire to marry Cecil Maundrell, and her girlish hopes and dreams, some of which had certainly been realised.

It was just after the Easter recess that he began

to feel the need of a secretary, for he was doing certain work outside the House. Lee disliked the idea of a stranger in her *maisonnette*, to say nothing of the fact that she would see less of her husband by many hours, and offered herself for the post. He was surprised and delighted, for he was reserved almost to secrecy with every one else, and had contemplated admitting a stranger into the privacy of his study with much distaste.

"Are you sure it won't tire you?" he asked fondly. He was always very careful of her.

"Of course not! And I haven't a thing to do, now that all my clothes are made. I'm sick of the sight of Bond Street. You know I love to feel that I am of use to you."

"You are always that, whether you are doing anything for me or not. I'm quite selfish enough to accept your offer, if you really mean it. I simply hated the thought of an outsider. But if I find it tires or bores you, we can put a stop to the arrangement any day."

It bored her, but he never knew it. As she had an exuberant vitality, it did not tire her, although she sometimes felt very nervous. She marvelled at the greatness of the masculine mind which could master such details and find them interesting, and wondered if she were a real politician after all. Somewhat to her amusement, she found herself looking forward with pleasure to the sporting season; it would be an interval of comparative liberty and rest. She enjoyed the sensation of being useful to her husband, and the increased companionship; but

it was trying to spend so much of the morning
indoors, and to sit up by herself copying, when she
preferred being in bed, or reading such novels as
were clever enough to satisfy a mind now quite
tuned to serious things.   The theatre was neglected
during the last two months of the Session, for Cecil
grew busier and busier, and worked late on his off
nights.   Occasionally he examined his wife's lovely
face anxiously to see if she were losing her colour,
or acquiring any little fine lines, and when he could
discover no outward symbol of injured health he
begged her to tell him if she were really equal to
the strain.   When she assured him that she was
profoundly interested, and had never felt better, he
assured her in return that she was, indeed, a wife of
whom any man might be proud.   Sometimes she
wished, with a sigh, that his wants were more
spiritual.   She might revive her enthusiasm if he
had need of sympathy and solace, but the world was
treating him very well, and he was satisfied and
happy.   She wondered if he had ever been anything
else; he certainly seemed one of the favoured of
earth.

CHAPTER XII

A DAY or two before the end of the season Lee received a letter from Mrs. Montgomery which suggested another variation in the autumn programme. That lady and Randolph were leaving France for England, and after a brief visit to Tiny they hoped to be welcome at Maundrell Abbey. The junior Gearys, who were taking a belated honeymoon (Mr. Geary had died a week after the wedding), would arrive in England in the latter part of August.

Lee had seen nothing of her old friends since her departure from California. Lord Arrowmount had amused himself with a ranch until a month ago, when he had returned to England with his family, and gone straight to his place in the Midlands. Mrs. Montgomery had remained in California with them for two years, and spent the last year with Randolph, who had bought a *château* in Normandy and seemed to be devoting himself to the pleasures of the *chasse*. For two years he had sauntered leisurely about the world, and had finally made his home in France, as the sky and air reminded him of California and the life did not. He had written Lee a brief note occasionally, in which he said little about himself, and gave no indication that his sentiments towards her were other than fraternal. Nor could she guess what changes might have been wrought in him, although he remarked once that the longer he remained away from America the less he ever wanted to see it again. Out of the chaos of Mrs. Montgomery's letters Lee gathered that he was improved; but she hoped that he was not too much changed, for with the prospect of her old friends' advent came a lively desire for something like a renewal of old times. To her letter in behalf of Maundrell Abbey he had never alluded, and she had not revived the subject, for she had expected him to appear at any moment.

She went at once to the house in Upper Belgrave Street, and asked her mother-in-law to invite the entire party to the Abbey for two or three weeks in August and September. Lady Barnstaple happened to be in a particularly gracious humour.

"I shall be delighted to see some new faces," she announced. "One gets sick of the same old set year after year. I quite liked Lady Arrowmount, what little I saw her — rather prim and middle-classy, but, *enfin*, quite *convenable;* one must not expect too much of the ancient aristocracy of San Francisco. You 've improved so much, dearest. You never look shocked any more, and you 've quite lost your provincialisms. When you came you were like a sweet little wild flower that had got lost in a conservatory. Now you are *tout à fait grande dame*, and it is quite remarkable, as you go out so little. But you always could dress, and the Society papers actually mention your frocks, which is also remarkable. As a rule one has to be *en évidence* all the time to retain any sort of interest.   But you are pretty, and Cecil is so clever — a selfish beast, though.   How long are you going to keep this thing up?"

"Oh, I am a mere creature of habit now.   Who else is going down for the twelfth?"

"Mary Gifford — could n't you marry her to Randolph Montgomery?   It's really tragic the way she hangs on!"

"Her sisters have married, so I suppose she could. I don't think she wants to marry.   Under all her loudness she's a queer porcelain-like creature, and rather shrinks from men."

"Fiddlesticks!   She's waiting for eighty thousand a year!   And she's quite right.   Whether she'll get it or not —— she's a real beauty, and the way she keeps on looking just eighteen!   Well, let me see: there will be the Pixes —— Mr. Pix has really consented to come at last; never breathe it, but he's been taking private lessons and has actually learned how to shoot as straight as anybody.   I think Mary has her eye on him, but she'd better not!"

"Why not — since you are interested in her future?"

"Because I'm positive he's the only man living that does n't see my wrinkles, and in my pocket he'll stay.   Well — there will be the Arrowmounts, Montgomerys, Gearys, Pixes, Mary, and sixteen or eighteen of the usual crowd: the Beaumanoirs, Larry Monmouth, the Duke and Duchess of Launcester, Lord and Lady Regent, and, oh, the ones one has to have or drop out.   But I'd like to shake them all for one year."

"I thought you adored English people."

"I do and I don't. I get mad sometimes at all the trouble they give me. Look at Mary Gifford! She has n't a penny, does n't lift her finger, and she 's in and out of every great house in England."

"Well — surely; she belongs to them. She 's related to half of them — her father was a Marquis ——"

"That 's just it," said Lady Barnstaple, with a heavy scowl. "She belongs to them. I don't. I can't complain that they have n't even run after me, but I 'm not intimate, not dead intimate with one of 'em, all the same."

"What does it matter? You had ambitions and you 've satisfied them. There must always be something beyond one's grasp."

"There 's a good deal beyond mine," said Lady Barnstaple with a sigh. "I can't be young again; and when I had youth I made so little of it."

"Well, you dazzle Mr. Pix," said Lee lightly. "Let that console you."

CHAPTER XIII

LORD ARROWMOUNT and Randolph wrote to Lady Barnstaple that they would arrive at the Abbey on the eleventh; Mrs. Montgomery was indisposed, but hoped to come a week later with Lady Arrowmount. The Gearys wrote from Paris to expect them any time during August.

Lee laughed as Lady Barnstaple tossed her back Coralie's letter with a sharp exclamation.

"They are both spoiled children, you know, and Ned has ignored social obligations all his life."

"He can't take any liberties with me if I am an American — or was."

"Oh, you 're quite English."

Lee and her mother-in-law exchanged hooded sarcasms occasionally, but on the whole were excellent acquaintances. Lady Barnstaple had never paid a second visit to the tower, and was ignorant of her daughter-in-law's depredations; no other excuse for a quarrel had occurred. Lee having made up her mind to accept "Emmy" — there being no alternative — veiled her with philosophy, and saw as little of her as possible. Lady Barnstaple forgave the younger woman her beauty, as, according to her lights, it might as well have blossomed in Sahara; and she uneasily respected the obvious will beneath that lovely exterior, and frankly admired Lee's genius for dress.

On the evening of the eleventh Lee selected her gown with unusual care. During the past three years she had dressed for no man but her husband, who occasionally informed her that she always looked exactly the same to him no matter what she had on, and she had been as indifferent to the admiring glances of other men as a beautiful woman can be. She had not indulged in so much as a dinner flirtation, and had kept her ideal of matrimonial bliss so close to her eyes that she had occasionally received a hint of myopic dangers and a benumbing of certain mental faculties. Her glance, rising on the wing of a phlegmatic fancy, sometimes strayed to the right or left of the steel track she paced, but it returned submissively; and the only alteration in her face was a slightly accentuated determination in the curves of her mouth. During the last six months she had been conscious of a certain restiveness, but had refused to analyse it.

It was quite natural to dress for Randolph, for he was an old and valued friend; and it was certainly a pleasure to dress for him, for he appreciated every detail and his taste was exquisite. She therefore selected the sort of gown in which he had always most admired her, a black gauze made with the dashing simplicity which suited her so well.

He would arrive about five. She sent him word to dress early and come to the tower. She knew that he would doubtless be detained by Cecil in the library for a time, but she was in her boudoir before seven. Her flutter of excitement was very agreeable. As it trembled along her nerves it brought with it an admitted desire for a whole series of sudden and brilliant changes. She wished that Randolph had come straight from California, for she could have fancied the wild winds of the Pacific blowing about him. She had learned to keep California out of her mind for many months at a time, but to-night as she stood in her tower looking through the narrow ancient window on the calm beauty of the English landscape, she shook with homesickness for that land which seemed to have all space just above it, and as many moods and features as the imagination of Byron. The sudden nostalgia was as much of the body as of the spirit. Her very veins seemed full of tears; in her brain was a distinct sensation of nausea. She was a child of the redwoods, not of the landscape-garden.

Randolph came up the stair with a slower step than of old, but with as light a foot. Lee was conventional at once.

"You have been long enough crossing the Channel to see me," she said gaily, and shaking him warmly by the hand; "but you know I never harbour malice, and now — I am simply delighted to welcome you."

"It was my mother that kept me in France after I got within crossing distance of the Channel; her health is really broken, I am afraid."

They talked of Mrs. Montgomery for some time, while studying each other. Lee hoped that if he found her changed his surprise and approval would equal her own. He had transformed himself into what he would have become years since had his mother taken him to Europe while he was still a boy, and kept him there.   His restless Americanism, his careless stoop, the nervous play of his features, even the lines about his eyes and mouth had gone. His erect and graceful carriage made him look almost as tall as Cecil Maundrell.   He was a trifle stouter than when he had left California; and he was, in his new habit, so handsome and so distinguished, that Lee thrilled with the pride of the Montgomerys, and of the South before the War.   His manner was scarcely fraternal, nor did it hint of the lover, discarded and tenacious; it was merely that of an amiable man-of-the-world pleased to renew an intimate friendship with a charming woman.

"Am I as much changed as you are?" asked Lee impulsively.

"Am I changed?   You — I will tell you when I have been here a little longer.   There is a difference — although that gown makes you look very natural.   I cannot decide what it is.   You are more beautiful than ever, if that could be possible."

It was so long since Lee had received a vigorous compliment that she blushed with delight.

"I'm so glad you've come, Randolph," she exclaimed.   "Do talk to me about old times and California, even if you do hate the thought of it."

"I hate the thought of it?"

"Well, you hate America."

"Why will even the cleverest of women add so many little frills?   I am immensely proud of the United States; I would have been born under no other flag. What I do hate is the modern spirit of the country as typified by New York, Chicago, and San Francisco. I love California, and am beginning to get a little homesick for her. I fancy it won't be long before I shall suddenly pack my trunk and go back for a year."

"Oh, if I could go! If I could go!"

"Could n't we all go back together next year?"

"Cecil cannot leave England. I suppose you have not heard —— "

"That great things are expected of him. I take several London papers; and, when travelling, they are always at the clubs. How proud you must be of him."

"I am;" but she was thinking of California; and there seemed to be a hundred things to be talked about at once. There had been a time when she had talked to Randolph about nearly everything that passed through her mind. That time came sharply back to her.

"That is one of the changes in you," he was saying. "You have the least little more pride in your carriage. You never were very humble, but this is a sort of double duplicated pride, as it were. And — yes — you are more intellectual looking. It is that which has dissipated your girlishness without ageing you a particle."

"Oh, I am intellectual! I 've been on one long intellectual orgie for the last three years. I 'm ready for a change. If you 've been cramming your brain, don't you try to impress me; and don't you dare to mention politics."

Randolph laughed. "I should not think of such a thing. My interest is too cursory to burden my conversation. And as for books — I've read a good many on rainy days since I saw you last, and am better for them; but I have spent the greater part of the time living books of many sorts."

"Have you grown serious? You used to take life so lightly. So did everybody. So did I."

"I am afraid I still take life with reprehensible lightness. I have got an immense amount of fun out of the old world."

"Do you remember how we used to roar — you and Coralie and Tom and I? And about nothing! We *were* such good laughers!"

"I hope you have n't forgotten how."

"Not much! But I 'm out of practice. Let 's go up on top of the fell to-morrow, and sit down on the ground and shriek."

Randolph threw back his head and laughed so heartily that Lee caught the infection of it, and in a moment was leaping from peal to peal. She caught herself up.

"I shall have hysterics. And it 's nearly dinner-time. I 've got to go down and talk grouse prospects and the tantalising peculiarities of that loathsome bird for two hours. I don't know if I dare put you on my other side. I 'm afraid I 'd giggle like an idiot all through dinner if I did. I suppose it 's reaction, but I really feel on the verge of idiocy."

"The result of my sudden appearance. I am immensely flattered."

"Oh, you would be if you knew! Cecil is simply perfect; don't think I am casting the faintest reflection on him. It's the life! Oh, I must! I must! I always did tell you things, Randolph, and you always were so sympathetic. Have you read many English novels that aim to initiate the outside world into the life of our class — the truth without any frills, and all that sort of thing? After I'd been here two years I made a terrible mistake: out of curiosity — to see the influence of England on the imagination circumscribed by conscience — I read, one after the other, about twelve novels of that sort — the sort that might be called the current history . of social England. Then I realised what I had got into — that unchanging, inevitable, mathematically precise *mise en scène*, that wheel that goes round and round with never a change of spoke nor of speed. You know — begin with the twelfth of August: house parties for grouse shooting. Men — same men — out all day. Women — same women — at home. Sporting talk at luncheon. Sporting talk varied with politics at dinner. Little gambling, little flirting, a rowdy game or two in the evening. Next month same thing in other houses for partridge and pheasant shooting. Next two months hunting and hunting talk for a change; otherwise the same, only a little more hard work for the women. Races and race talk thrown in all along the line. Then the Riviera for some, and for me two months of life in grime and fog and mud. Then the roasting crush of the London season, in which everybody works like a horse, and the women are reduced to a mere combination of bones and paint. Then more races, a few days' breathing space, and again the Twelfth of August. I wish I had n't read those books; I would n't have realised it so soon. But really, I 've hardly admitted it before to-night. My own programme is slightly varied. I shoot, and I don't go to the Riviera, and I 've had no chance to get tired of London Society. But it surrounds me — that automatically shifting *mise en scène. I know it is there.* I am a part of most of it — a fly on its paint. I may get the whole thing any day. That is one reason I don't really rebel against being out of it in London. Politics are the best there is in the whole thing, because there is some variety, and there is always the promise of some tremendous excitement — only there has n't been any yet."

She sprang to her feet, overturning her chair.

"Damn it! Damn it! Damn it!" she cried, her eyes blazing, her voice pitched high with delight. "Do you remember how you and Coralie and Tom and I used to lock ourselves up in the schoolroom, and swear as loud and as fast as we could when Tiny had been primmer than usual, or Aunty had been holding forth on the South before the War? Well, that 's the way I feel to-day, and I 've been feeling that way for a long time, only I did n't know it."

She stopped for want of breath. Randolph had risen too, but his back was against the light. If his voice was not as steady as it had been she was too excited to notice it.

"You certainly ought to return to California," he said. "We are all half savage — the strongest of us

Californians. The great civilisations fascinate us, but they don't satisfy, and in time they pall."

"I'd like to put dynamite under the whole business, and then take Cecil and go and shoot bears with him in the Santa Lucia Mountains and sleep under the redwoods without so much as a tent. I believe I'd be willing to eat acorns." She sat down and glanced up at him with all her old coquetry.

"You don't think I've made an idiot of myself, do you?" she asked anxiously.

"You could never be other than the most charming woman in the world."

"Will you pay me three compliments a day, Randolph?"

"I shall probably pay you twenty."

"I hope to Heaven you will! I need them — I do really *need* them. Now go and wait for me in the library: I must go up and put some powder on; I feel that I have the colour of a dairy-maid. It's so nice to order you about — and I couldn't speak out to a soul on earth as I have to you! I should have burst if you hadn't come soon. If you get lost in those everlasting corridors ring a bell."

The promptness with which Randolph obeyed her command, with the little laugh that had always saved his dignity, was the first of his signals that the old Randolph still flourished within that mellowed and polished exterior.

Lee ran up to her room. The door of the dressing-room was open; Cecil was ready for dinner, and alone. Her conscience hurt her, and she was still excited. With all her old impulsiveness she ran in, flung her arms round her husband's neck and kissed him.

The " Imp of the Perverse " is always hovering near to man awaiting the more subtle climaxes of his life. Cecil adored his wife, but he liked to do the love-making; and Lee, long since, had accepted the submissive and responsive rôle her beloved autocrat demanded. And he was a man of moods, which were deep and showed little on the surface. To-night he was keen for the sport of the morrow, for a renewal of the brief and congenial conversation he had had with his men guests before dinner; and if his wife were to be too absorbed in her friends for several days to give him a moment he should not miss her. He had had a hard Session and the reaction to sport and open air was violent, that was all.

He returned Lee's kiss politely, and took up a hair brush.

" You seem nervous," he said. " Do calm yourself before dinner. It is always a relief to me that you do not talk as loud as the rest of the women."

And when his wife rushed out and banged the door, he frowned, then shrugged his shoulders, and went down to the library.

CHAPTER XIV

" IN other words," said Randolph, " loving an Englishman means hard work and plenty of it."
They were on top of the fell and had been roaming
about all the afternoon. Randolph had begun by
amusing her and putting her into the best of tempers,
then he had led her on to speak of her long and
determined struggle to be many things foreign to her
disposition and habit, evincing so deep and genuine
an interest that Lee's ego, so long the down-trodden
subject of her imperious will, had leaped hilariously
to its own and confessed itself steadily for two hours.

" I 'm not disloyal for a moment, and you 're really
my brother; and I could not speak to any one else
living like this: the others I know as well would not
understand. I don't see why I complain. I 've got
almost everything I ever imagined myself wanting."

" You 've surrendered your individuality. It is that
that gnaws, and almost devitalises you."

" Perhaps. I don't know. I could be very quickly
spoiled and get it all back; but that would mean
that I should not be happy in the same way, nor
Cecil either."

" Are you happy?"

" I thought I was until lately — the last — oh, it is

hard to say exactly. But I never was intended for quite such hard and fast routine. I feel positive that in certain conditions I should not mind being a mere second self to Cecil. When you love a man nothing much matters up to a certain point; and after that, nothing would matter at all if the nerves could be made to hum occasionally to something like uncertainty. This cut-and-dried life of England's leisure class, which reminds me of a grandfather's clock in magnificent running order, may suit many temperaments, but not mine. As you say, the old civilisations fascinate us who are two-thirds made up of the unruly instincts of the new, but they don't satisfy, and they certainly do pall. Three years more of this and I shall be a machine without a nerve, or — I shall hate Cecil Maundrell. I've been horribly upset ever since you came; you actually brought an earthquake with you, and I've thought and thought and thought —— "

" Well ? " he said gently.

" If I've relapsed into the national monologue it's your fault."

" Have you been fashioning your mental habits on an up-to-date novelette ? People always monologue in private life. Do go on."

" You know I never had a morbid nor a hysterical moment; but there must come a time to all strong natures when all they have inherited and all they have been in their plastic years finds itself in violent conflict with an alien present. The problem would be solved if we could get away, if Cecil's genius could make a leap into other lines. If I could only have had a finger in the moulding of our two destinies Cecil would have been a great pioneer, an 'Empire-maker,' like Cecil Rhodes. There would have been no stagnation then; I should have felt all the stimulation of trampling down obstacles and defying the prejudices of a million little minds in opening up a new and savage country by the sheer insolent force of one great man's personality. And then the excitement of not knowing what would happen next, where we or the whole country would be this time next year! And in a new country, where civilisation is still in the making, man is greater than the State, and he is much more alive and individual, much more primitive and at the same time many-sided than when he is the slow and logical result of a rounded and fagged civilisation which has caught him fast. But there is no hope. . . . Even if Cecil discovered the instinct of the pioneer in him he would not listen to it, for he is very proud and very ambitious. When a man towers in an isolated field like Mr. Rhodes, every man who plants his heels in the same field in the same epoch is a moon to Jupiter. And no two men in a century will ever have all the gifts of the Empire-maker united in one brain. Cecil is highly gifted, and he has enormous energy, but his gifts are on the old conservative lines."

Randolph, who had been absently tearing up the heather by the roots, his eyes apparently absorbed in his task, extended himself at her feet.

"What are you going to do about it?" he asked.

"What can I do? It has been an unspeakable relief to talk to you — have I bored you?"

" I 'll not answer such a foolish question. Do you still love your husband? "

"Oh, I 'm sure I do, down deep; but my brain is in a chaotic state; the whole of me is an ugly rebellious temper. We 've had our first real misunderstanding these last two days, and Cecil is so absorbed in grouse he does n't even know it."

Randolph laughed so heartily that Lee was forced to smile. " If that were all," she said with a sigh.

" I can think of no better temporary remedy than that you should come back to California with us for a year. You might find that England had weaned you after all, and California was an idealised memory. And as for your husband — there is nothing like an occasional vacation. Mother is already homesick: we 'll return this year."

" Cecil would never consent. He 's really devoted to me."

" I should hope so. But English wives are not slaves, I suppose. If you asserted yourself he would neither tie you up nor divorce you."

" He really needs me tremendously. If I were not a little beast I 'd be contented with my lot. And as I 've tried to make him happy for purely selfish reasons for three years, I don't see that I have the right to make him miserable because I have wheeled about and want something that he can't give me."

" Or awakened? "

" It 's not only that. I shut my eyes deliberately to a great deal at the first — that I could not be everything to him, that there were depths in his nature that were way beyond me."

"My dear child, no woman can be everything to
a man; that would be Utopia."

"He could at least be more to me."

"Ah, that is another matter," said Randolph
softly.

They returned to the subject many times. Randolph spent but a part of the day on the moors. He
was an admirable shot, and took care to distinguish
himself, but was at no pains to conceal his lack of
enthusiasm. On the fourth day of his visit, as Lee
was showing him over the Abbey, she said abruptly:

"Did you ever get a letter I wrote to you the day
after I arrived here?"

"The day after——"

"It was all about the Abbey. I told you that
Emmy might leave nothing, and that everybody had
expected Cecil to marry a fortune, or else lose his
inheritance. They wanted him to marry that Miss
Pix, and they all seemed to think I was a criminal
for not being worth a million. I felt a fool, I can
assure you, for not investing in the Peruvian mine."

"And you wrote to your old slave to make a million for you. I did not get the letter, but I can see
every word of it."

"I don't think I should have the same assurance
to-day, but I'd be very thankful if you'd advise
me."

"Oh, you have changed! It's really tragic!"

They were in the crypt of the Abbey, an immense
rambling and shadowy vault. Lee put her hands to
her face suddenly and began to cry. Randolph took
her in his arms and patted her gently.

"Don't worry," he said. "I'm not going to make love to you. I'm only your big brother. But you must come back with me to California."

"Oh, I want to go — the more I think of it, the more I want to go. The first time I have a chance I'll speak to Cecil about it; but he comes home just in time to dress and is so tired he's asleep before he's fairly in bed and in the morning he's gone before I'm awake."

"You were certainly never intended for a sportsman," said Randolph dryly. "I have written to mother to urge you to return with us. And as for the other matter, we'll see to it when we get there —— "

"I am serious about that. I love the Abbey. I should think I had been born to some purpose if I could save it. And I look upon it as almost my mission; for should Cecil lose it, it would be through me. I'd never forgive myself."

"It strikes me that Cecil would have no one to blame but himself. He was no raw stripling when he married you, but a man with a remarkably mature mind —— "

"But he was frightfully in love."

"And never wiser. However, if you wish to make the Abbey your mission in life you can command my services, as always. I will take the matter in hand as soon as I get back."

" *Will* you?"

"Yes, but you must come too. It takes a month to get a letter answered from here, and business secrets cannot be cabled."

"I will go then. A double object gives me double

courage. But I've bored you long enough. You listen to my woes by the yard, and you never talk about yourself except to amuse me——"

"I came to England for no other purpose but to see you and to hear you talk."

"Well, I can tell you then, that you were inspired by the real missionary spirit, for I needed you badly."

CHAPTER XV

AFTER dinner that night, Lee and Lady Mary Gifford, instead of following the other women, strolled along the corridors for a quiet chat. They were not intimate, for they had too little in common, but they admired each other and Lee had seen something more of Lady Mary than of any of the Englishwomen whom she received in her little drawing-room on Tuesdays or maintained a community of interests with during that division of the year allotted to house parties.

"I like your cousin, or whatever he is," announced Lady Mary, clasping her hands behind her. "He does n't talk through his nose and he 's quite at his ease. . As a rule I detest American men as much as I like the women. Of course he 's rich — you can always tell."

"He 's very rich."

"Now don't jump — I 'd like you to marry me to him."

Lee did jump. "Really ? " she said dryly.

"I 'd rather never marry: if I had a talent I 'd go and set up a studio in Kensington, or take chambers and write a popular novel. Of course I could make hats or open a florist's shop, but neither is to my taste ; and I really can't hang on any longer —

twenty-seven and my ninth season — it's positively sickening. I have had one or two good offers — in the long ago — but I hated the thought of marrying then more than I do now — when a thing has to be it never seems quite so bad. Of course I could get any numbers of parvenus, and I'd almost made up my mind to Mr. Pix, but I should feel quite reconciled to Mr. Montgomery."

"That is very amiable of you, but I don't see what you are offering to Mr. Montgomery; and as he is almost my oldest friend I have his happiness to consider. He would not care a rap for your title ——"

"Wouldn't he? How very odd. But I'd make him quite happy. You know I am fascinating. Some men have gone quite off their heads about me."

"If you send Randolph off his head he'll undoubtedly propose to you. You will have plenty of opportunity."

"I see you don't like the idea ——"

"You are quite mistaken. I have had no time to think it over. Of course if I thought you would be happy together ——"

"Oh, I'm sure we'd arrange everything quite amicably. I have immense tact, you know, and American men are said to make such indulgent husbands; and he's really distinguished-looking. And of course he'd be quite sure of me. I'd scorn to do the things most women do. That's one reason why I like you so much — you haven't a lover."

Lee laughed. "I can't see the superior virtue of selling oneself."

"My dear, we must each do what is best for ourselves, whether it is money we want or love. Standards have never insured happiness yet. We must do our own thinking and try for what we most want. Here is a secret for you to keep — until a year ago I expected my godmother's fortune. She had all but promised it to me and that is the real reason I never married. She died without a will. I *can't* be a stranded old maid living off my alternate relations. And perhaps you can imagine what it would mean to me to marry a man like Mr. Pix."

Lady Mary had drawn in her wide voice, and it vibrated slightly. It was the first time Lee had known her to display anything like feeling, and she softened at once.

"I'll do what I can," she said. "Randolph is a gentleman, and very clever. Try to fall in love with him, and make him fall in love with you."

"You *are* good. And Emmy can keep her Pix and welcome; by the way, I suppose you have noticed, there's not so smart a crowd here this year as usual — except the Beaumanoirs, and Larry Monmouth and the other single men."

"I had not — there is not, come to think of it."

"The Launcesters and Regents can be got by anybody that will feed them ——"

"What are you driving at?"

"I mean that Emmy has been a little too careless this last year. People simply won't swallow Pix —

the men hate him so. There was a little doubt before, but of course there's none now. She let him go to the Riviera with her."

"Are you trying to make me believe that Mr. Pix is Emmy's lover?"

"You don't mean to say you are an infant in arms?"

"Of course I'm well enough used to women and their lovers, by this time; but somehow one never thinks that sort of thing can happen in one's own family. It is plain enough, I suppose. She might at least have chosen a gentleman."

"She might indeed; that's her crime. Pick up with the wrong man, and Society is on its hind legs in no time. I've seen it coming for an age. She certainly must know that she's got off the track as well as any one can tell her, and considering the way she's worked for one thing for five-and-twenty years, it's rather surprising; but the trouble is, she's in love with him, I fancy."

"I don't think there's any doubt about it; but if her original commonness demanded a mate she certainly could have found a bounder with a little more gilding. There are one or two with the titles she adores."

Lee spoke with heat and bitterness. She had the indifference of familiarity to many things that had horrified her youthful ideals, but a lover under the family roof filled her with protest.

"Emmy's a curious contradiction——" began Lady Mary.

"What's to be done? Of course it can't go on.

Lord Barnstaple or Cecil could put a stop to it, but
I can't tattle on any woman ——"

" My dear, I don't advise you to put a stop to it
unless you want to see the Abbey put up at public
auction."

" Mary Gifford ! "

" Now don't shriek out; but I have more than one
reason to think that I 'm right."

" And perhaps we 're eating his bread? "

" I don't know that it 's as bad as that, but I am
positive that she borrowed from him first and mort-
gaged her properties heavily — he was over in
America last year. Now, he is certainly in love with
her. He would marry me, of course, because I
could give him what Emmy cannot — but — however ! Better not say anything, my child. Lord
Barnstaple has always been too indifferent to give
two thoughts to his wife's private affections; but if
he were made to know anything, of course he 'd
have to kick the man out. And he and Cecil would
have to break the entail, and the Abbey would go
to the highest bidder — who would probably be one
of the Pixes. Victoria the Silent has never stopped
wanting it from the day she first saw it; nor Cecil
Maundrell either, for that matter."

" Well, she won't get it. What a ghastly business !
I wish you had n't told me."

" I wish I had n't, but it never occurred to me that
you could n't see the length of your nose."

" Something has to be done; it 's a horrible position for Lord Barnstaple and Cecil."

" What they don't know won't hurt them — it is

though. What's the use of platitudinising? Everybody else knows — or guesses, and it *is* rough on them. But let things drift along for a little. Who knows what may happen?"

"If you don't mind, and if you will make an excuse for me, I'll go up to my room. I'm tired out, and I'd like to be alone."

"Do go, that's a dear; and don't bother too much about other people. Almost everybody's too selfish to be worth it!"

She returned to the great drawing-room of the Abbey, where people were hovering about many little tables, smiled brilliantly on Randolph, and marched him off to a charming boudoir where she detained him agreeably for the rest of the evening. Her young blue eyes were very keen and she took pains at once to assure him that Lee would be visible no more that night.

CHAPTER XVI

L EE went to her bedroom, and, in accord with
some curious feminine sympathy of mental
and material habit, immediately took off her gown
and put on a wrapper. Then she sat down, and, to
use her own phrase, endeavoured to take hold of
herself. It was the first time that she had been alone
for several days, and she had a good deal of thinking
to do.

The most gifted of men are successful in analysing
women up to a certain point only; when they find
themselves confronted with utter unreasonableness,
perversity, and erratic curvatures of temper, they
solve the problem with a baby, and pass on. A
woman may be in superb condition, she may be leading the most normal of lives, she may not have a
care worthy of mention, and yet she may find herself
in a state of nervous and rebellious antagonism to the
whole scheme of creation. The women who work
and exhaust their brain vitality with a certain regularity are less prone to such attacks, but the woman
of leisure is liable to them at any moment. For the
feminine imagination is a restless and virile quantity,
and a clever woman is often its victim to an extent
which no man can appreciate. That men are, on the
whole, so patient with what must often confound and

incense them, constitutes their chief claim to the forgiveness of many sins.

If Lee was by nature neither morbid nor hysterical, she felt that she was doing her best to overcome the deficiency. Randolph's appearance had shattered the routine of her married life, and with it her self-control. She was aghast, and she was furious with herself. Cecil had ceased to be an ideal for whom no sacrifice was too great: he merely represented a sudden and violent change in the order of her inner life; and if his personal fascination and his incalculable advantage of a previous ten years' sojourn in her imagination had accomplished this revolution and kept him master of the field for three additional years, the reaction to a strong and long-fostered individuality was but the more violent. What she wanted she was scarcely able to define, but she felt sure that she wanted several dozen things that she would never have as the wife of Cecil Maundrell.

She searched diligently for his faults, and was obliged to confess that they were few and would play a small part in the balancing of accounts. He was, if exacting, the kindest of husbands; if not amusing, he was always interesting; although moody, he showed no sign of ceasing to be a lover; if devoted to sport, she had never, in her most feminine moments, been able to persuade herself that he was not several times more devoted to her; and she had the most profound admiration for him both as a man and as an intellect. His only imperfection was that he was a strong and dominating personality with whom a woman must live as a second self or not at all; and Lee felt her-

self a fool. But, unfortunately, the supreme tragedies in the lives of two people who love and are
happy have often their genesis in no facts that can
be analysed and disposed of.

Of one desire, Lee was acutely conscious; to get
away from her husband for a time and return to California — to that stupendous country of many parts
where she had been Herself, where she had stood
alone, where she had munched consecutively for
twenty-one years those sweets of Individuality so
dear to the American soul. And, this desire suddenly defined itself, she wanted to be volatile, she
wanted to be free from every responsibility; she
wanted, in short, to get out of the rôle of a serious
factor in the life of a serious man.

And Cecil? She made no excuses for herself, attempted no self-delusion: she looked down steadily,
although with eyes of horror and disgust, at those
depths of selfishness peculiar to the soul of woman —
more so to the souls of women of the younger civilisations. He was practically blameless, and she was
meditating a punishment meet for a brute of a husband. He loved her and needed her, and she was
condemning him to the acutest suffering she could
devise, short of her own death. Nevertheless, if the
situation were to be saved at all, she must get away
from him, she must be Herself for a time — for a
year. After that? Doubtless she would love him
the better. Certainly she would never love any
other man. Her prediction that hatred of her husband might be the result of three more uninterrupted
years of him and of England had been a mere verbal

expression of nervous tension; even in the present adventurous and overworked state of her imagination she knew that she loved him, and would so long as consciousness survived in her. If she could have had that most plausible of all excuses, the death of affection and passion, she would have felt quite ready to justify herself. As it was, there were no limits to her self-abasement. And, logically, there were no limits to her unreasoning anger with her husband.

She wanted her Individuality back; that was the long and the short of it.

Regarding Randolph, she felt a certain disquiet. He had not betrayed himself by so much as a glance, but her woman's instinct told her that he still loved her. There was nothing to apprehend, however, beyond a possible scene at a remote period. If he was playing a big game it was for heavy stakes, and he would not show his cards for many a day. It was more than possible that he hoped everything from a return to the scene of her girlish freedom and triumphs, and from her withdrawal from her husband's influence; but he would watch and wait for the crucial moment before suggesting the facile American specific for matrimonial jars. He was very clever, and she did not doubt that if he were playing for the supreme desire of his life he would be sufficiently unscrupulous. But he was a gentleman and he would not demand her hand as the price of the Abbey's rescue. If she had never met Cecil Maundrell she believed that she could have loved him, for he understood her. He was, now that he had found himself, a charming and companionable man, with no raw edges to irritate the most sensitive romanticism; and her Individuality would have flourished like a green bay-tree. And he had plenty of brains and was just serious enough. She could never have given him the half of what she had given Cecil Maundrell, but there would have been no violent and humiliating reactions from too much high-thinking and attempting to realise a serious man's ideal. Now, neither he nor any other man but her husband could satisfy her for a moment; but as she had no desire to do Randolph any more harm than she had done him already she determined to take Mary Gifford to California with her and give that odd and attractive young person all the advantages of propinquity and comparison.

Emmy's peccancy was but a final reason for her desire to separate herself for a time from her present life. She was charitable, but she was fastidious. Had Emmy been an outsider she might have had twenty lovers; but the proximity disgusted her.

CHAPTER XVII

OF course Cecil did the worst thing possible for himself: he appeared just as she had finished elaborating her case and before she had started upon the argument between her higher and her pettier self which she had dimly contemplated. As he ran up the stair she rose nervously to her feet, regretting for the first time that she had not a room of her own in which she could lock herself. They had continued to put up with the trifling inconveniences of the tower because its isolation and historic associations made it a tenacious symbol in their own romance.

She sat down as he entered.

"I just missed you," he said anxiously, "and some one told me that you had not been in the drawing-room since dinner. Are you ill?"

"No; and I am glad you have come up. I want to ask you something."

He sat down beside her and took her hand.

"What is it?" he asked. "Something has gone wrong?"

"I want to go back to California for a year."

"But, my dear, I can't get away. I should be mad —"

"But you can let me go. Mrs. Montgomery wants to take me back with her."

If he had given her time she would doubtless have approached the subject with tact and many delicate subterfuges; but her mind was wearied and possessed.

He stared at her incredulously.

"I really mean it. The only reasons I can put into shape are that I am desperately tired of this everlasting round of English life, and homesick for California."

"Are you tired of me?"

"No; but I believe that a short separation would be better for us both. I can't make you understand, for you have never cared to understand me. I adapted myself, and you took me for granted—"

"Have you been playing a part?"

"Heaven knows I have been serious enough. It is that as much as anything else — I want to cease being serious for a while."

Cecil continued to stare at her. His tan had worn off, and he paled slightly. When a man after several years of married life is suddenly informed that he does not understand his wife the shock is trying to his mental faculties and to his patience.

"I do not know you to-night," he said coldly. "I have seen you in a number of moods, and occasionally in a temper, but I have never before seen you when you were not — sweet."

"I don't feel sweet. I wish I did. I hate to hurt you."

Cecil seized the suggestion. "You have certainly hurt me; and nobody could know better than you how much. What *is* the matter with you?"

"I want a change, that is all."

"I'm afraid I've really done something quite abominable, although I don't remember — and it isn't like you not to speak out."

"I haven't a fault in the world to find with you. I wish I had!"

"I don't understand you," he said helplessly. "And as I am so dense, perhaps you will be good enough to explain. I really think I have the right to demand it." He would have liked to shake her, for he had not yet been made to realise that she was in anything but a surprisingly nasty temper.

Lee was quite sure that he had the right to demand a full explanation, and she cast about for the phrases which would point it best. But her reasons put their tails between their legs and scampered to the back of her brain, where they looked petty enough. So she began to cry instead.

Cecil took her in his arms instantly, excoriating himself for his desire to shake her. "You are ill; I know you are ill," he whispered, "and you are so unused to it that it has quite demoralised you." Then, his knowledge of women being primitive indeed, he descended to bribery. "I am going to ask father to give you my mother's jewels; I never knew he had them — that there were any — till the other day. There are some wonderful pieces."

Lee pricked up her ears, then despised herself and sobbed the harder. Suddenly, she shrank visibly from him, slipped from his embrace and walked over to the fireplace, turning her back to her husband. It had flashed into her mind that

Randolph's arms had been round her that morning.
She had thought no more of it at the time than if
they had been Mrs. Montgomery's or Coralie's; but
of a sudden her quiescence seemed an act of infi-
delity, if for no other reason than because Cecil
would be furious if he knew it. She decided that
she certainly must be growing morbid, and she
resigned herself to being just as unpleasant as her
resources permitted.

Cecil went over to her and wheeled her about
sharply. There was no question about his pallor
now; his very lips were white. "That was the first
time you ever shrank from me," he said. "What
does it mean?"

"I mean that I *will* go to California."

"That 's not the point."

"I simply can't explain, but I 'll try to in my
letters. I promise that if you don't understand me
now you shall before I get back."

"I have no time to read a woman's novels about
herself. I once read several volumes of women's
'letters.' There never yet was a woman who could
write about herself unself-consciously; she is always
addressing an imaginary audience. Say what you 've
got to say now, and have done with it. If I 've
failed in anything I love you well enough to do all
I can — you know that."

"You told me when you proposed to me that you
would hate understanding a woman's complexities,
that she had no right to have any, that a woman
must become a mere adjunct of her husband."

"I don't remember ever having said anything of
284

the sort.   But if I did — I very dimly realised at
that time all that you would become to me.   Now I
would do anything in my power to keep you as you
have been these three years."

Lee almost relented; but her conscience was in
a state of abnormal activity.   It had reminded her
that she had talked her husband over with another
man, and that the act was both disloyal and in bad
taste.   She would have given all she possessed to
return her confidences where they belonged, much
as she had needed the relief.   She hated Randolph
Montgomery and she hated herself.   So she stamped
her foot at Cecil.

"I *wish* you would let me alone," she exclaimed.
"If I feel like it later I 'll explain, but I won't say
another word to-night."

There was really nothing for Cecil to do but to go
out and bang the door, so he went out and banged it.

CHAPTER XVIII

LEE slept more soundly that night than she had expected, and awoke the next morning feeling very much ashamed of herself. Her determination to leave England for a time was unaltered, but she would have given a great deal to have come to an amicable understanding with Cecil. She had treated him abominably, and he was the last person she desired to wound. When she was in exactly the right temper she would make herself as legible to him as she could, and, as he was the quickest of men, he would understand as much as any mere man could, and would agree that the separation — she might reduce it to six months — was advisable for them both. He would do a good deal of thinking during her absence and the result could not fail to be happy.

She went out on the moor to luncheon and was so amiable and charming and so pointedly bent upon charming no man but her husband that Cecil's brow cleared and he sunned himself in her presence. But he was seriously disturbed, and she saw it. She had awakened him roughly out of what was doubtless beginning to look like a dream, and he was not the man to close his eyes again until he had quite determined of what stuff his dreams were made. But when they were alone he pointedly avoided the subject.

The Gearys arrived next morning, and it seemed to Lee that the whole Abbey was filled with Coralie's light laughter. She wanted to see everything at once, and the four Californians spent the entire day moving restlessly over the house and grounds.

"Just think," cried Coralie, flitting about the ghostly gloom of the crypt. "I 'm in an *Abbey* — an old stone thing a thousand years old — oh! well, never mind, a few hundred years more or less don't matter. It 's *old*, and it 's stone, and it 's carved, and it 's haunted, and grey-hooded friars were once just where I am. I think it 's lovely. Is n't it, Ned? Is n't it?"

But Mr. Geary smiled with the true Californian's mere toleration of all things non-Californian. Coralie knew that smile, and tossed her head.

"Well, thank Heaven I 'm not quite so provincial as that!" she cried with sarcasm. "I 'm going to keep you abroad three years. *I never in my life* saw any one so improved as Randolph."

Whereupon Mr. Geary coloured angrily and strode off in a huff.

"Tell me some more," demanded Coralie. "Don't slam the door, Teddy. Has n't there ever really been a hooded friar seen stalking through this crypt at night?"

"They do say — You know all the dead earls lie here for a week; and on alternate nights the tenantry and the servants sit up. Those people are superstitious, and they vow that they see shadowy forms way over there; of course lamps are hung on the columns near by — perhaps I can show you a whole chest full of the silver lamps that have been used for centuries. They make the rest of the crypt fairly black, and it is easy enough to imagine anything. The interment always takes place at midnight, by torchlight, even when there is a moon; and there is popularly supposed to be an old abbot telling his beads just behind the procession."

"How simply gorgeous! Of course I don't want Lord Barnstaple to die, but I should *love* to be in at that sort of thing. When Mr. Geary died of course he was just laid out in the back parlour — drawing-room I shall always call it hereafter; poor Mrs. Geary has never been out of California since she left the immortal South — and he really did look so uninteresting, and his casket was so hideously expensive. But an earl — laid out in a crypt — of an ancient Abbey — with tenantry kneeling round and shivering at hooded friars in the background — I 'm really alive for the first time! Is there an Abbey we could rent anywhere? I 'd only want it for about six months, but I 'd have a simply heavenly time so long as the novelty lasted."

"It would take you six months to get used to the size of it," said Randolph, "and by the time it had begun to fit perhaps you would feel that everything else was commonplace." He spoke to Coralie, but he looked at Lee.

She smiled and brought her lashes together. "Sometimes there are things one wants more than magnificence," she said. "Well — Emmy must be awake. I'll go and speak to her about Tom."

For Tom was in London and had asked his sister to make known that he desired an invitation to the Abbey, and had come to England merely to look upon its future *châtelaine.*

Lee found Lady Barnstaple in one of her freshest and fluffiest wrappers and in one of her ugliest tempers — attributable doubtless to the fact that Mr. Pix, after three days of hard shooting, had been obliged to go to London on business, and had not yet returned.

"Ask all California if you like," she said crossly, "but tell them to keep out of my way. I know their airs of old."

"It's not at all likely that your guests would put on airs with you. For the matter of that you have the rank that all good Americans approve of —"

"Some people are putting on airs with me," said Lady Barnstaple darkly.

This was an obvious opportunity to approach a delicate subject, but Lee shrank from it. Moreover, the thing would have run its natural course before her return and one more unpleasantness been avoided. Lady Mary's advice was wise and appealed to her present craving for a long period of irresponsibility. So she said instead:

"I think of going to California for a visit — with Mrs. Montgomery, about the middle of October."

Lady Barnstaple raised her eyes and stared at her daughter-in-law. Even in the pink light it was evident that she changed colour. She dropped her eyes suddenly.

"California is a long way off," she said dryly. "I wonder Cecil consents; but these little separations are always advisable. How long shall you stay?"

"A year, possibly. I am going to take Mary Gifford with me if Mrs. Montgomery will invite her — as of course she will."

"Oh, do marry her to Randolph Montgomery! It would be an act of charity."

"How pleased she would be! But I think it can be managed, particularly as Tiny likes her; and Mrs. Montgomery would be sure to fall in love with her and conceive it her mission to modify her voice."

"Well, I hope she 'll stay in California. I 'm sick of her. I 'm sick of the rudeness of English people, anyhow."

"You have cultivated their rudeness with a good deal of energy. It seems to me that most Americans cultivate that attribute more successfully than they cultivate any others of the many English attributes they admire so profoundly," Lee observed.

"Well, I wish you 'd let me alone!" shrieked Lady Barnstaple. "Don't speak another word to me to-day."

Lee hastily retreated and sent off a telegram to Tom, then went out in search of the others. She found them by the lake feeding the swans.

"The swans and the peacocks make it all just perfect!" cried Coralie. "I want Ned to sit up all night with me in the crypt to see if there won't be a ghost, and he won't do it."

"As if there were such things," said Mr. Geary disdainfully.

Lee turned to Randolph. "You look a whole generation older than Ned," she said, with the sensation of having just made the discovery of how much improved he was. "I believe you could almost bring yourself to believe in a ghost."

He smiled and opened her parasol. "And you, I am afraid, have taken on at least a century — without being aware of the fact. I am afraid you will realise it when you return to California."

"I want California more and more every day."

"We shall see. The changes of association are very subtle. I can only hope they are not so deeply wrought in you as they sometimes appear to be — that you will really enjoy your year in California, I mean."

They were walking toward the fell, and the others were some distance behind.

"I am going to ask Aunty to invite Mary Gifford to go back with us. She is my best friend here and she is simply dying for a change."

"I am sure mother will be delighted. She will undertake her reformation at once."

"That is what I told Emmy. How do you like her — Mary, I mean?"

"She interests me very much, if only to see how wide she can open her mouth."

"No, but seriously — Mary is such a problem to me."

"Well, she's a beauty, like a blue and white moonlight in mid-winter; and has a tantalising sort of elusiveness. I detest Englishwomen as a rule, but I never met a woman before who talked so loud and at the same time suggested an almost exaggerated shrinking and modesty. The combination is certainly striking."

"It isn't that she's really cold," said Lee, with the deep subtlety of her sex, "but she's never met the right man. I only hope she won't fall in love with you, but she admires you tremendously."

"Ah!"

"Do pay her a lot of compliments and show her a lot of little attentions; Englishwomen get so tired of doing all the work. But don't make love to her."

"I have no intention of making love to her," said Randolph; but if he had a deeper meaning he kept it out of his eyes — those eyes which had lost their nervous facility of expression, and rarely looked otherwise than cold and grey and thoughtful.

Tom arrived next morning talkative, restless, and irresponsible; but although he frankly avowed himself as much in love as ever, he hastened to add that he would not mention it any oftener than he could help. For several days Lee neglected the other guests and devoted herself to her old friends. The last three had certainly brought the breezes of the Pacific with them, and they talked California until Lady Mary, who had joined them several times, declared she could stand it no longer.

"I'll go with you gladly if Mrs. Montgomery will take me; and I intend to make love to her, you may be sure," she said to Lee, " but I really can't stand feeling so out of it. And besides you are all so intimate and happy together, it's almost a sin to intrude. You're looking much brighter since they came."

" It has done me good to see them again, and it's made me want to go back more than ever."

"I can understand. But it's a pity Cecil can't go with you. He's looking rather glum. Is that what's the matter with him?"

" I am not sure," said Lee uneasily. " I'm going to have a talk with him on Sunday. I did say something about it on Monday night, but of course — well ——"

" It's hard to persuade an English husband that he's got to conform to the American habit of matrimonial vacations and plenty of them." Lady Mary laughed. " Speaking of vacations, Mr. Pix is taking rather a long one, but I believe he returns on Monday. I can't quite make out, but I fancy the men have rather snubbed him — as much as they decently can. He must feel frightfully out of it. I only hope he won't lose his temper. He's got a nasty one, and if he let it go he's underbred enough to shriek out anything. I saw with my own eyes that Lord Barnstaple avoided playing with him the night before he left. Of course Lord Barnstaple carried it off as he does everything, but I think the man noticed it all the same."

" Then I wish he had pride enough to keep out of the house, but of course he has n't."

" Your Californians now are so different. They are quite *comme il faut* ——"

" Mary Gifford, you are really intolerably rude ! "

" Upon my word I don't mean to be. And as you know, I want to marry one." She paused a moment, then raised her cold blue eyes to Lee's. " I too have a will of my own," she announced, " and when I make up my mind to do a thing I do it. I am going to marry Mr. Montgomery, and whether you go back to California or not I am going with my future mother-in-law."

" Of course I shall go; and it is seldom that a woman — particularly a beauty — fails to get a man if she makes up her mind to it. He is interested; there's that much gained."

CHAPTER XIX

MRS. MONTGOMERY arrived the next day without Tiny, whose children were ailing. As the following day was Sunday, and as Mrs. Montgomery would hardly let Lee out of her sight, the definite understanding with Cecil had to be postponed. She had seen practically nothing of him since Tuesday. Mr. Geary and Mr. Brannan laughed at the bare idea of tramping about all day carrying a heavy gun, nor did they, nor Coralie, fancy the idea of luncheon on the moor. They wanted Lee to themselves, and they had a little picnic every day. Mrs. Montgomery was too old for picnics, and Lady Mary announced her intention of taking the good lady on her own hands. Before sunset she had bewildered and fascinated her victim, and by noon the next day had received the desired invitation.

"I wish I could have had the bringing up of her," said Mrs. Montgomery earnestly to Lee. "She's really very peculiar, and has shockingly bad manners, but with it all she is high-bred; it's really very strange. With us it's either one thing or the other. And she's so sweet. I'm sure if I scold her a little after a while she won't mind it a bit."

"I'm sure she'll take it like an angel," said Lee,

who had told Mary what she was to expect, and could still hear that young lady's loud delighted laugh. "And be sure you're good to her. She's very much alone in the world."

Lee's conscience hurt her less at this deliberate scheming than it might have done a few weeks since, for she had by this time convinced herself that Mary was really in love with Randolph; and she was certainly a wife of whom any man might be proud.

On Tuesday evening as Lee and her friends were descending the fell — on whose broad summit they had laughed the afternoon away, and Lee had been petted and flattered to her heart's content — she paused suddenly and put her hand above her eyes. Far away, walking slowly along the ridge of hillocks that formed the southeastern edge of the moor, was a man whose carriage, even at that distance, was familiar. She stared hard. It was certainly Cecil. He was alone, and, undoubtedly, thinking. She made up her mind in an instant.

"I see Cecil," she said. "I'm going to bring him home. You go on to the Abbey." And she hurried away.

Doubtless he had been there for some time, and had sought the solitude deliberately: the men were shooting miles away; apparently even sport had failed him. She made tight little fists of her hands. Her morbidity had not outlasted the night of her momentous interview with her husband, but her old friends had both satisfied her longings for previous conditions, and rooted her desire for a few months' freedom. It was true that, with the exception of Randolph, they bored her a little at times, but the fact remained that they symbolised the freest and most brilliant part of her life, and that they were in delightful accord with the lighter side of her nature. Cecil, outlined against the sky over there in the purple, alone, and, beyond a doubt, perturbed and unhappy, made her feel as cruel and selfish as she could feel in her present mood. She rebelled against the serious conversation before her, and wondered if she had slipped from her heights forever. They had been very pleasant.

Cecil saw her coming and met her half-way. She smiled brilliantly, slipped her hand in his, and kissed him.

"You are thinking it over," she said, with the directness that he liked.

"I have been thinking about a good many things. I have been wondering how I could have lived with you for three years and known you so little. I hardly knew you the other night at all, and I never believed that you would care to leave me."

"Cecil! You are so serious. You take things so tragically. I *can't* look at it as you do, because I have seen women going to Europe all my life without their husbands. One would think I was wanting to get a divorce!"

"Are you trying to make me feel that I am making an ass of myself? I think you know that I have my own ideas about most things, and that I am not in the least ashamed of them. I married you to live with you, to keep you here beside me so long as we both lived. I have no understanding of and no patience with any other sort of marriage. And I think you knew when you accepted me that I had not the making of an American husband in me."

"I never deluded myself for a moment. And you must admit that I have been English enough! Believe me when I say that a brief relapse on my part is necessary ——"

"I cannot understand your having a 'relapse' unless you are tired of me."

"I am not in the least tired of you; no one could ever tire of you. It is all so subtle —— "

"Don't talk verbiage, please. There are no subtleties that can't be turned into black and white if you choose to do it. I can quite understand your being homesick for California, and I 've fully intended to take you back some day. But you might wait. I have kept you pretty hard at the grind, and if it were not for all the political work I 've got to do this autumn and winter, I 'd take you over to the Continent for a few months. And after a year or two we shall do a great deal of travelling, I hope: I want more and more to study the colonies."

"That is one reason I thought it best to go now — you are going to be so busy you won't miss me at all. When you 're travelling about, speaking here and speaking there, you 'll be surrounded by men all the time. You won't need me in the least."

"It is always the greatest possible pleasure to me to know that you are where I can see you at any moment, and that you have no interests apart from my own."

"That is just the point. I should like a few trifling ones for a time. If you want it in plain English, here it is — I want to be an Individual for just one year. I made a great effort to surrender all I had to you, and you must admit that I was a success. But reaction is bound to come sooner or later, and that is what is the matter with me."

Cecil stood still and looked at her. "Oh," he remarked. "That is it? Why did n't you say so at once? I ought to have expected it, I suppose. I saw what you were before I married you — about the worst spoiled woman I had ever met in my life. But you had brains and character, and you loved me. I hoped for everything."

"And you can't be so ungrateful as to say that you have been disappointed."

"No. I certainly have not been — up to a week ago: I thought you the most perfect woman God ever made."

Lee flushed with pleasure and took his hand again.

"I would n't make you unhappy for the world," she said. "Only I thought I could show you that it was for the best. We are what we are. Brain and will and love can do a great deal, an immense amount, but it can't make us quite over. We bolt our original self under and he gnaws at the lock and gets out sooner or later. The best way is to give him his head for a little and then he will go back and be quiet for a long time again. But ——" she hesitated for so long a time that Cecil, who had been ramming his stick into the ground, turned and looked at her. "If I can't make you agree with me," she said, "I won't go."

"But you would stay unwillingly."

"Oh, I do want to go!"

"Then go, by all means," he said.

CHAPTER XX

DURING the following week Lee was not so absorbed in her friends that she would have been oblivious to a certain discomposure of the Abbey's atmosphere, even had Mary Gifford not called her attention to it. Some of the guests had given place to others, but the Pixes, Lady Mary, and the Californians still remained. Of course they were all scattered during the day, but the evenings were spent in the great drawing-room and adjoining boudoirs and billiard-room, and it was obvious to the most indifferent that there was a discord in the usual harmony of the Abbey at this season. Lady Barnstaple's temper had never been more uncertain, but no one minded that: Emmy was always sure to be amusing, whether deliberately or otherwise; that was her rôle. Nor was any one particularly disturbed by the increased acidity of Lord Barnstaple's remarks; for when a man is clever he must be given his head, as Captain Monmouth had remarked shortly before he left; "and some pills are really cannon balls," he had added darkly.

Mr. Pix was the disturbing element. He had managed to keep an effective shade over the light of his commonness in London, for he did not go out too much and was oftener in Paris. Moreover, Victoria, who was painfully irreproachable, had provided a sort of family reputation on which he travelled. But in the fierce and unremitting light of a house-party he revealed himself, and it was evident that he was aware of the fact; his assumption of ease and of the manner to which his fellow-guests were born grew more defiant daily, and there were times when his brow was dark and heavy. Everybody wondered why he did not leave. He handled his gun clumsily, and with manifest distaste, and it was plain that he had not so much as the seedling of the passion for sport. Nevertheless he stuck to it, and asserted that he longed for October that he might distinguish himself in the covers.

If the man had succeeded in giving himself an acceptable veneer, or if he had had the wit to make himself useful financially to the men with whom he aspired to associate, he would have gone down as others of his gilded ilk had gone down; but, as it was, every man in the Abbey longed to kick him, and they snubbed him as pointedly as in common courtesy to their host they could.

"I am actually uneasy," said Lady Mary to Lee one evening as they stood apart for a moment in the drawing-room. The guests looked unconcerned enough. They were talking and laughing, some pretending to fight for their favourite tables; while in the billiard-room across the hall a half-dozen of the younger married women were romping about the table, shrieking their laughter. But Victoria Pix, looking less like a marble than usual, stood alone in a doorway intently regarding her brother, who was also conspicuously alone. And although Emmy was flitting about as usual, there was an angry light in her eyes and an ugly compression of her lips.

" I wish it were the last of September," replied Lee.

" So do I — or that we were in California. I feel as if some one had a lighted fuse in his hand and was hunting for dynamite. It's really terrible to think what might happen if that man lost his temper and opened his mouth."

" I don't want to think of it. And where there are so many people nothing is really likely to happen; there are so many small diversions."

But she broached the subject to Cecil as they were walking along the corridors to their tower some hours later. Apparently they were the best of friends again, for Cecil was not the man to do anything by halves. He had not even returned to the subject; and if he were still wounded and unquiet he gave no sign.

" I wish that horrid Mr. Pix would go," said Lee tentatively. " He's so out of it, I wonder he does n't."

" I can't imagine what he came for. I never saw a man look such an ass on the moors."

" He must get on your father's nerves."

" I fancy he does. I suppose Emmy asked him here. She could hardly avoid it, she's so intimate with Miss Pix. By the way, that woman actually talked at dinner to-night; you may not have noticed, but I had her on my left; I suppose I'm in Emmy's bad graces for some reason or other. But she really seemed bent on making herself entertaining. She has something in her head, I fancy. If less of it were snobbery she would n't be half bad."

"Fancy what you escaped. If you had never come to America they might have married you to the Pixes."

"The person has yet to be born who could do my marrying for me," said Cecil; and there was no doubt that he knew himself.

CHAPTER XXI

THE next afternoon as Lee was taking tea with the other guests in the library she happened to glance out of the window, and saw Lord Barnstaple returning from the moors, alone. It was an unusual occurrence, for he was an ardent and vigorous sportsman. Ten minutes later she became aware that a servant in the corridor was endeavouring to attract her attention. She went out at once and closed the door. The servant told her that Lord Barnstaple desired an interview with her in his own sitting-room; he feared interruptions in her boudoir.

Lee went rapidly to his rooms, curious and uneasy. She felt very much like running away, but Lord Barnstaple had been consistently kind to her, and was justified in demanding what return she could give him.

He was walking up and down, and his eyebrows were more perturbed than supercilious.

"I want to know if you will give me a little help," he said abruptly.

"Of course I will do anything I can."

"I want that bounder, Pix, put out of this house. I can't stand him another day without insulting him, and of course I don't want to do that. But he is Emmy's guest and she can get rid of him—I don't care how she does it. Of course I can't speak to her; she would be in hysterics before I was half through; and would keep him here to spite me."

" And you want me to speak to her? "

" I 'm not asking you to undertake a very pleasant task; but you 're the only person who has the least influence over her, except Cecil — and I don't care to speak to him about it."

" But what am I to say to her?   What excuse? "

Lord Barnstaple wheeled about sharply. " Can't you think of any? " he asked.

Lee kept her face immobile, but she turned away her eyes.

Lord Barnstaple laughed. " Unless you are blind you can see what is becoming plain enough," he said harshly. " I 've seen him hanging about for some time, but it never occurred to me that he might be her lover until lately.   I don't care a hang about her and her lovers, but she can't bring that sort to the Abbey."

" I can tell her that everybody is talking and that the women are hinting that unless she drops him she 'll be dropped herself."

" Quite so.   You 'll have a nasty scene.   It is good of you to undertake it without making me argue myself hoarse."

" I am one of you; you must know that I would willingly do anything for the family interests that I could."

" You do belong to us," said Lord Barnstaple with some enthusiasm. " And that is what Emmy has never done for a moment.   By the way," he hesitated, "I hate to mention it now, it looks as if I were hastening to reward you; but the fact is I had made up my mind to give you my wife's jewels. They are very fine, and Emmy does not even know of their existence. I suppose it would have been rather decent of me to have given them to you long ago: but —— "

Lee nodded to him, smiling sympathetically.

"Yes," he said, "I hated to part with them. But I shan't mind your having them. I'll write to my solicitors at once to send them down; I've got to pass the time somehow. For Heaven's sake come back and tell me how she takes it."

"I don't suppose I shall be long. I have n't thanked you. Of course I shall be delighted to have the jewels."

"You ought to have the Barnstaple ones, but she's capable of outliving the whole of us."

CHAPTER XXII

AS Lee walked along the many corridors to her mother-in-law's rooms she reflected that she was grateful Lord Barnstaple had not refrained from mentioning the diamonds: their vision was both pleasing and sustaining. She was obliged to give serious thought to the coming interview, but they glittered in the background and poured their soothing light along her nerves.

Lady Barnstaple had but just risen from her afternoon nap and was drinking her tea. She looked cross and dishevelled.

"Do sit down," she said, as Lee picked up a porcelain ornament from the mantel and examined it. "I hate people to stand round in spots."

Lee took a chair opposite her mother-in-law. She was the last person to shirk a responsibility when she faced the point.

"You have seemed very nervous lately," she said. "Is anything the matter?"

"Yes, everything is. I wish I could simply hurt some people. I'd go a long ways aside to do it. What right have these God-Almighty English to put on such airs, anyhow? One person's exactly as good as another. I come from a free country and I like it."

"I wonder you have deserted it for five-and-twenty years. But it is still there."

"Oh, I don't doubt you'd like to get rid of me. But you won't. I've worn myself out getting to the top, and on the top I'll stay. I'd be just nothing in New York. And Chicago — *good* Lord!"

"You've stepped down two or three rungs, and if you're not careful you'll find yourself at the foot —"

"What do you mean?" screamed Lady Barnstaple. "I've half a mind to throw this teacup at you."

"Don't you dare to throw anything at me. I should have a right to speak even if I did not consider your own interest — which I do; please believe me. Surely you must know that Mr. Pix has hurt you."

"I'd like to know why *I* can't have a lover as well as anybody else."

"Do you mean to acknowledge that he is your lover?"

"It's none of your business whether he is or not! And I'm not going to be dictated to by you or anybody else."

Lady Barnstaple was too nervous and too angry to be cowed by the cold blue blaze before her, but she asserted herself the more defiantly.

"I have no intention of dictating to you, but it certainly is my business. And it's Lord Barnstaple's and Cecil's —"

"You shut up your mouth," screamed Lady Barnstaple; her language always revealed its pristine simplicity when her nerves were fairly galloping. "The idea of a brat like you sitting up there and lecturing me. And what do you know about it, I'd like to know? You 're married to the salt of the earth and you 're such a fool you 're tired of him already. If you 'd been tied up for twenty years to a cold-blooded brute like Barnstaple you might — yes, you might have a little more charity —— "

"I am by no means without charity, and I know that you are not happy. I wish you were; but surely there are better ways of consoling oneself —— "

"*Are* there? Well, I don't know anything about them and I guess you don't know much more. I was pretty when I married Barnstaple, and I was really in love with him, if you want to know it. He was such a real swell, and I was so ambitious, I admired him to death; and he was so indifferent he fascinated me. But he never even had the decency to pretend he had n't married me for my money. He 's never so much as crossed my threshold, if you want to know the truth."

"People say he was in love with his first wife, and took her death very much to heart. Perhaps that was it."

"That was just it. He 's got her picture hanging up in his bedroom; won't even have it in his sitting-room for fear somebody else might look at it. I went to see him once out of pure charity, when he was ill in bed and he shouted at me to get out before I 'd crossed the threshold. But I saw *her*."

"I must say I respect him more for being perfectly honest, for not pretending to love you. After all, it was a square business transaction: he sold you a good position and a prospective title. You 've both got a good deal out of it —— "

"I hate him! I hate a good many people in England, but I hate him the most. I'm biding my time, but when I do strike there won't be one ounce of starch left in him. I'd do it this minute if it was n't for Cecil. What right has he got to stick his nose into my affairs and humiliate the only man that ever really loved me ——"

"If you mean Mr. Pix, it seems to me that Lord Barnstaple has restrained himself as only a gentleman can. He is a very fastidious man, and you surely cannot be so blind as not to see how an underbred ——"

"Don't you dare!" shrieked Lady Barnstaple. She sprang to her feet, overturning the tea-table and ruining her pink velvet carpet. "He's as good as anybody, I tell you, and so am I. I'm sick and tired of airs — that cad's that's ruined me and your ridiculous Southern nonsense. I'm not blind! I can see you look down on me because I ain't connected with your old broken aristocracy! What does it amount to, I'd like to know? There's only one thing that amounts to anything on the face of this earth and that's money. You can turn up your nose at Chicago but I can tell you Chicago'd turn up its nose at you if it had ever heard of you. You're just a nonentity, with all your airs, and all your eyes too for that matter, and I'm known on two continents. I'm the Countess of Barnstaple, if I was — but it's none of yours or anybody else's business who I was. I'm somebody now and somebody I'm going to stay. If I've gone down three rungs I'll climb up again — I will! I will! I will! And I can't! I can't! I can't!

I have n't a penny left! Not a penny! Not a penny! I 'm going to kill myself——"

Lee jumped up, caught her by the shoulders and literally shook the hysterics out of hĕr. Then she sat her violently into a chair.

"Now!" she said. "You behave yourself or I'll shake you again. I'll stand none of your nonsense and I have several things to say to you yet. So keep quiet."

Lady Barnstaple panted, but she looked cowed. She did not raise her eyes.

"How long have you been ruined?"

"I don't know; a long while."

"And you are spending Mr. Pix's money?"

"Yes, I am."

"Do the Abbey lands pay the taxes and other expenses?—and the expenses of the shooting season?"

"They pay next to nothing. The farms are too small. It 's all woods and moor."

"Then Mr. Pix is running the Abbey?"

"Yes he is—and he knows it."

"And you have no sense of responsibility to the man who has given you the position you were ready to grovel for?"

"He 's a beastly cad."

"If he were not a gentleman he could have managed you. But that has nothing to do with it. You have no right to enter a family to disgrace it. I suppose it 's not possible to make you understand; but its honour should be your own."

"I don't care a hang about any such high-falutin' nonsense. I entered this family to get what I wanted, and when it's got no more to give me it can be the laughing-stock of England for all I care."

" I thought you loved Cecil."

The ugly expression which had been deepening about Lady Barnstaple's mouth relaxed for a moment.

" I do; but I can't help it. He's got to go with the rest. I don't know that I care much, though; you're enough to make me hate him. What I hate more than everything else put together is to give up the Abbey. And you can be sure that after the way Mr. Pix has been treated——"

" Mr. Pix will leave this house to-night. If you don't send him I shall."

" You're a fool. If you knew which side your bread was buttered on you'd make such a fuss over him that everybody else would treat him decently——"

"I have fully identified myself with my husband's family, if you have not, and I shall do nothing to add to its dishonour. There are worse things than giving up the Abbey — which can be rented; it need not be sold. The Gearys would rent it to-morrow."

" If you think so much of this family I wonder you can make up your mind to leave it."

Lee hesitated a moment. Then she said: " I shall never leave it so long as it needs me. And it certainly needs somebody just at present. Mr. Pix must leave; that's the first point. Lord Barnstaple and Cecil must be told just so much and no more. Don't you dare tell them that Mr. Pix has been running the Abbey. You can have letters from Chicago to-morrow saying that you are ruined."

"If Mr. Pix goes I follow. Unless I can keep the Abbey — and if I've got to drop out —— "

"You can suit yourself about going or remaining. Only don't you tell Lord Barnstaple or anybody else whose money you have been spending."

"I'd tell him and everybody else this minute if it weren't for Cecil. He's the only person who's ever really treated me decently. And as for the Abbey —— "

She paused so long that Lee received a mental telegram of something still worse to come. As Lady Barnstaple raised her eyes slowly and looked at her with steady malevolence she felt her burning cheeks cool.

"He wouldn't have the Abbey, anyhow, you know," said Lady Barnstaple.

"What do you mean?"

"I heard you jabbering with Barnstaple and Cecil not long since about the Abbey and its traditions, but either they hadn't told you or you hadn't thought it worth remembering — that there is a curse on all Abbey lands and that it has worked itself out in this family with beautiful regularity."

"I never heard of any curse."

"Well, the priests, or monks, or whatever they were, cursed the Abbey lands when they were turned out. And this is the way the curse works." She paused a moment longer with an evident sense of the dramatic. "They never descend in the direct line," she added with all possible emphasis.

"I am too American for superstition," but her voice had lost its vigour.

" That has n't very much to do with it. I 'm merely mentioning facts. I have n't gone into other Abbey family histories very extensively, but I know this one. Never, not in a single instance, has Maundrell Abbey descended from father to son."

Lee looked away from her for the first time. Her eyes blazed no longer; they looked like cold blue ashes.

" It is time to break the rule," she said.

" The rule's not going to be broken. Either the Abbey will go to a stranger, or Cecil will die before Barnstaple is laid out in the crypt —— "

Lee rose. " It is an interesting superstition, but it will have to wait," she said. " I am going now to speak to Mr. Pix — unless you will do it yourself."

" I 'll do it myself if you 'll be kind enough to mind your business that far."

" Then I shall go and tell Lord Barnstaple that you have consented —— "

" Ah ! He sent you, did he? I might have known it."

Lee bit her lip. " I am sorry — but it does n't matter. If to-day is a sample of your usual performances, you can't expect him to court interviews with you."

" Oh, he 's afraid of me. I could make any man afraid of me, thank Heaven ! "

CHAPTER XXIII

LEE returned to her father-in-law more slowly than she had advanced upon the enemy. She longed desperately for Cecil, but he was the last person in whom she could confide.

Lord Barnstaple opened the door for her.

"How pale you are!" he said. "I suppose I sent you to about the nastiest interview of your life."

"Oh, I got the best of her. She was screaming about the room and I got tired of it and nearly shook the life out of her."

Lord Barnstaple laughed with genuine delight. "I knew she'd never get the best of you," he cried. "I knew you'd trounce her. Well, what else?"

"She promised to tell Mr. Pix he must go to-night."

"Ah, you did manage her. How did you do it?"

"I told her I'd tell him if she did n't."

"Good! But of course she'll get back at us. What's she got up her sleeve?"

"I don't think she knows herself. She's too excited. I think she's upset about a good many things. She seems to have been getting bad news from Chicago this last week or two."

"Ah!" Lord Barnstaple walked over to the window. He turned about in a moment.

"I have felt a crash in the air for a long time," he said pinching his lips. "But this last year or two her affairs seemed to take a new start, and of course her fortune was a large one and could stand a good deal of strain. But if she goes to pieces —— " he spread out his hands.

"If Cecil and I could only live here all the year round we could keep up the Abbey in a way, particularly if you rented the shootings; but our six months in town take fully two thousand —— "

"There's no alternative, I'm afraid: we'll all have to get out."

"But you would n't sell it?"

"I shall have to talk it over with Cecil. The rental would pay the expenses of the place; but I can't live forever, and when I give place to him the death duties will make a large hole in his private fortune. I have a good many sins to repent of when my time comes."

He had turned very pale, and he looked very harassed. Lee did not fling her arms round his neck as she might once have done, but she took his hand and patted it.

"You and Cecil and I can always be happy together, even without the Abbey," she said. "If Emmy really loses her money she will run away with Mr. Pix or somebody. We three will live together, and forget all about her. And we won't be really poor."

Lord Barnstaple kissed her and patted her cheek, but his brow did not clear.

"I am glad Cecil has you," he said, "the time may

come when he will need you badly. He loves the Abbey — more than I have done, I suppose, or I should have taken more pains to keep it."

Lee felt half inclined to tell him of Randolph's promise; but sometimes she thought she knew Randolph, and sometimes she was sure she did not. She had no right to raise hopes, which converse potentialities so nicely balanced. Then she bethought herself of Emmy's last shot, which had passed out of her memory for the moment. She must speak of it to some one.

" She said something terrible to me just before I left. I 'd like to ask you about it."

" Do. Why did n't you give her another shaking?"

" I was knocked out: it took all my energies to keep her from seeing it. She said that Abbey lands were cursed, and never descended from father to son."

Lord Barnstaple dropped her hand and walked to the window again.

" It has been a curious series of coincidences in our case," he said, " but as our lands were not cursed more vigorously than the others, and as a good many of the others have gone scot free or nearly so, we always hope for better luck next time. There is really no reason why our luck should n't change any day. The old brutes ought to be satisfied, particularly as we 've taken such good care of their bones."

" Well, if the Abbey has to go, I hope the next people will be haunted out of it," said Lee viciously. " I must go and dress for dinner. Don't worry; I have a fine piece of property, and it is likely to increase in value any day." She felt justified in saying this much.

"You had an air of bringing good luck with you when you came. It was a fancy, of course, but I remember it impressed me."

"That is the reason you didn't scold me for not bringing a million, as Emmy did?"

"*Did* she? The little beast! Well, go and dress."

CHAPTER XXIV

AS Cecil and Lee were descending the tower stair an hour later he said to her:

"Don't look for me to-night when you are ready to come home; I am coming straight here after dinner. It's high time I got to work on my speeches."

She slipped her hand into his. "Shall I come too and sit with you?"

He returned her pressure and did not answer at once. Then he said: "No; I think I'd rather you did n't. If I am to lose you for a year I had better get used to it as soon as possible."

She lifted her head to tell him that she had no intention of leaving him for the present, then felt a perverse desire to torment him a little longer. She intended to be so charming to him later that she felt she owed that much to herself. But she was dressed to-night for his special delectation. If Cecil had a preference in the matter of her attire it was for transparent white, and she wore a gown of white embroidered mousseline de soie flecked here and there with blue.

They were still some distance from the door which led into the first of the corridors, for the stair was winding, worn, and steep, and, in spite of several little lamps, almost dark. Cecil paused suddenly and turned to her, plunging his hands into his pockets. She could hardly see his face, for a slender ray from above lay full across her eyes; but she had thought, as she had joined him in the sitting-room above a few moments since, that he had never looked more handsome. He grew pale in London, but a few days on the moors always gave him back his tan; and it had also occurred to her that the past two weeks had given him an added depth of expression, robbed him of a trifle of that serenity which Circumstance had so persistently fostered.

"There is something I should like to say," he began, with manifest hesitation. "I should n't like you to go on thinking that I have not appreciated your long and unfailing sacrifice during these three years. I was too happy to analyse, I suppose, and you seemed happy too; but of course I can see now that you were making a deliberate — and noble — attempt — to — to make yourself over, to suppress an individuality of uncommon strength in order to live up to a man's selfish ideal. Of course when I practically suggested it, I knew what I was talking about, but I was too much of a man to realise what it meant — and I had not lived with you. I can assure you that, great as your success was, I have realised, in this past week, that I had absorbed your real self, that I understood you as no man who had lived with you and loved you as much as I — no man to whom you had been so much, could fail to do. I am expressing myself about as badly as possible, but the idea that you should think me so utterly selfish and unappreciative after all you have given up — have given me — has literally tortured me. I don't wonder you want a fling. Go and have it, but come back to me as soon as you can."

She made no reply, for she wanted to say many things at once. But it is possible that he read something of it in her eyes — at least she prayed a few hours later that he had — for he caught her hard against him and kissed her many times. Then he hurried on, as if he feared she would think he had spoken as a suppliant.

When she joined him in the corridor the Gearys were waiting for them, and Coralie immediately began to chatter. Her conversation was like a very light champagne, sparkling but not mounting to the brain. Lee felt distinctly bored. She would have liked to dine alone with Cecil and then to spend with him a long evening of mutual explanation and reminiscence, and many intervals. She answered Coralie at random, and in a few moments her mind reverted with a startled leap to the pregnant hours of the afternoon. Could she keep Cecil ignorant of the disgrace which had threatened him? Had Pix gone? Would Emmy hold her counsel? She had forgotten to ask Lord Barnstaple to keep away from her; but such advice was hardly necessary.

"Where on earth did you disappear to this afternoon?" Coralie was demanding. "I hunted over the whole Abbey for you and I got lost and then I tried to talk to *that* Miss Pix and she asked me all about divorce in the United States — of all things! I wonder if she's got a husband tucked away somewhere — those monumental people are often bigger fools than they look. I told her that American divorces were no good in England unless they were obtained on English statutory grounds — we'd known some one who'd tried it. She looked as mad as a hornet, just like her brother for a minute. And he fairly makes me ill, Lee. Just fancy *our* having such people in the house. I must say that the English with all their blood —— "

"Oh, do keep quiet!" said Lee impatiently. Then she apologised hurriedly. "I have a good deal to think about just now," she added.

Coralie was gazing at her with a scarlet face. "Well, I think it's about time you came back to California," she said sarcastically. "Your manners need brushing up."

But Lee only shrugged her shoulders and refused to humble herself further. She was beset with impatience to reach the library and ascertain if Pix had gone.

He was there. And he was standing apart with his sister. His set thick profile was turned to the door. He was talking, and it was evident that his voice was pitched very low.

As the company was passing down the corridor which led to the stair just beyond the dining-room, Lady Barnstaple's maid came hastily from the wing beyond and asked Lee to take her ladyship's place at the table.

It seemed to Lee as the dinner progressed that with a few exceptions every one was in a feverish state of excitement. The exceptions were the Pixes, who barely made a remark, Cecil, who seemed as usual and was endeavouring to entertain his neighbour, and Lord Barnstaple, whose brow was very dark. Mary Gifford's large laugh barely gave its echoes time to finish, and the others certainly talked even louder and faster than usual. Randolph alone was brilliant and easy, and, to Lee, was manifestly doing what he could to divert the attention of his neighbours. Before the women rose it was quite plain that they were really nervous; and that the influence emanated from Pix. His silence alone would have attracted attention, for it was his habit to talk incessantly in order to conceal his real timidity. And he sat staring straight before him, scarcely eating, his heavy features set in an ugly sneer.

"I'm on the verge of hysterics," said Mary Gifford to Lee as they entered the drawing-room. "That man's working himself up to something. He's a coward and his courage takes a lot of screwing, but he's getting it to the sticking point as fast as he can, and I met him coming out of Emmy's rooms about an hour before dinner. I ran over to speak to her about something, but I was not admitted. He looked as if they'd been having a terrible row and he was ready to murder some one. I'm in a real funk. But if he's meditating a *coup de théâtre* we can baulk him for to-night at least. It's a lovely night. Get everybody out of doors and then I'll see that they scatter. I'll start a romp the moment the men come out."

"Good. I'll send up for shawls at once. I'll tell Coralie to look after Lord Barnstaple; she always amuses him. Then—I'll dispose of Mr. Pix."

"Oh, I wish I could be there to see. He'll sizzle and freeze at once, poor wretch. Well, let's get them out. I'll deposit Mrs. Montgomery in the Sèvres room, and tell her to look at the crockery and then go to bed."

Lee had intended to return with Cecil to the tower and inform him that his bitter draught was to be sweetened for the present, but Pix must be dealt with summarily. If she did not get him out of the house before Lord Barnstaple lost his head there would be consequences which even her resolute temper, born of the exigencies of the hour, refused to contemplate.

The women, pleased with the suggestion of a romp on the moor, strolled, meanwhile, about the lake, looking rather less majestic than the swans, who occasionally stood on their heads as if disdainful of the admiration of mere mortals. When the men entered the drawing-room Lee asked them to go outside immediately, and Coralie placed her hand in Lord Barnstaple's arm and marched him off.

Lee went down to the crypt with them, then slipped back into the shadows and returned to the drawing-room. Pix had greeted her suggestion with a sneer and a scowl, but it was evident that his plans had been frustrated, and that he was not a man of ready wit. He had sat himself doggedly in a chair, obviously to await the return of Lord Barnstaple and his guests. He sat there alone as Lee re-entered, looking smaller and commoner than usual in the great expanse of the ancient room, with its carven roof that had been blessed and cursed, and the priceless paintings on the panels about him. The Maundrells of Holbein, and Sir Joshua, and Sir Peter seemed to have raised their eyebrows with supercilious indignation. He was in accord with nothing but the electric lights.

As Lee entered he did not rise, but his scowl and his sneer deepened.

She walked directly up to him, and as he met her eyes he moved slightly. When Lee concentrated all the forces of a strong will in those expressive orbs, the weaker nature they bore upon was liable to an attack of tremulous self-consciousness. She knew the English character; its upper classes had the arrogance of the immortals; millions might bury but could never exterminate the servility of the lower. Let an aristocrat hold a man's plebeianism hard against his nostrils and the poor wretch would grovel with the overpowering consciousness of it. Lee had determined that nothing short of insolent brutality would dispose of Mr. Pix. And for sheer insolence the true Californian transcends the earth.

"Why have n't you gone?" she asked as if she were addressing a servant.

Pix too had his arrogance, the arrogance of riches. Although he turned pale, he replied doggedly:

"I 'm not ready to go and I don't go until I am. I don't know what you mean." He spoke grammatically, but his accent was as irritating as only the underbred accents of England can be.

"You know what I mean. You saw Lady Barnstaple this afternoon. She told you you must go. We don't want you here."

"I 'll stay as long as I——"

"No, my good man, you will not; you will go to-night. I have ordered the carriage for the eleven-ten train to Leeds, where you can stay the night. Your man is packing your box."

"I won't go," he growled, but his chest was heaving.

"Oh yes you will, if you have to be assisted into the carriage by two footmen."

He pulled himself together, although it was evident that his nerves, subjected to a long and severe strain, were giving way, and that the foundations of his insolence were weakened by the position in which she had placed him. He said quite distinctly :

"And who's going to feed this crowd?"

"My husband and myself; and I'll trouble you for your bill."

"It's a damned big bill."

"I think not. I have no concern with what you may have spent elsewhere. I shall ascertain exactly when my mother-in-law's original income ceased and I know quite as well as you do what is spent here; so be careful you make no mistakes. Now go, my good man, and see that you make no fuss about it."

The situation would unquestionably have been saved, for the man was confounded and humiliated, but at that moment Lord Barnstaple entered the room.

"My dear child," he said, "I was a brute to leave this to you. Go out to the others. I will follow in a moment."

Lee, who was really enjoying herself, wheeled about

with a frown. "Do go," she said emphatically. "Do go."

"And leave you to be insulted by a cur who does n't know enough to stand up in your presence. I am not quite so bad as that." He turned to Pix, whose face had become very red; even his eyeballs were injected.

"I believe you have been told that you cannot stay here," he said. "I am sorry to appear rude, but — you must go. There are no explanations necessary, and I should prefer that you did not reply. But I insist upon you leaving the house to-night."

Pix jumped to his feet with hard fists. "Damn you! Damn you!" he stuttered hysterically, but excitement giving him courage as he went on: "and what 's going to become of you? Where 'll you and all this land that makes such a h—l of a difference between you and me be this time next year? It 'll be mine as it ought to be now! And where 'll you be? Who 'll be paying for your bread and butter? Who 'll be paying your gambling debts? They 've made a nice item in my expenses, I can tell you! If you 're going to make your wife's lover pay your debts of honour — as you swells call them — you might at least have the decency to win a little mor 'n you do."

He finished and stood panting.

Lord Barnstaple stood like a stone for a moment, then he caught the man by the collar, jerked him to an open window, and flung him out as if he had been a rat. He was very strong, as are all Englishmen of his class who spend two-thirds of their lives in the open air, and his face was merely a shade paler as he turned to Lee. But she averted her eyes hastily from his, nevertheless.

"Doubtless that man spoke the truth," he said calmly, "but she must corroborate it," and he went towards the stair beyond the drawing-room that led to his wife's apartments.

Lee ran to the window. Pix was sitting up on the walk holding a handkerchief to his face. No one else was in sight. Presently he got to his feet and limped into the house. Lee went to the door opposite the great staircase and saw him toil past: it was evident that he was quite ready to slink away.

She sat down and put her hand to her eyes. It seemed to her that they must ache forever with what they had caught sight of in Lord Barnstaple's. In that brief glance she had seen the corpse of a gentleman's pride.

What would happen! If Emmy lost her courage, or if her better nature, attenuated as it was, conquered her spite, the situation might still be saved. Lord Barnstaple would be only too willing to receive the assurance that the man, insulted to fury, had lied; and, above all, Cecil need never know. There was no doubt that Lord Barnstaple's deserts were largely of his own invoking, but she set her nails into her palms with a fierce maternal yearning over Cecil. He was blameless, and he was hers. One way or another he should be spared.

She waited for Lord Barnstaple's return until she could wait no longer. If he were not still with Emmy —and it was not likely that he would prolong the interview — he must have gone to his rooms by the

upper corridors.   She went rapidly out of the drawing-room and up the stair.   She could not be regarded as an intruder and she must know the worst
to-night.   *What* would Lord Barnstaple do if Emmy
had confessed the truth?   She tried to persuade herself that she had not the least idea.

CHAPTER XXV

HE was sitting at his desk writing; and as he lifted his hand at her abrupt entrance and laid it on an object beside his papers she received no shock of surprise. She went forward and lifted his hand from the revolver.

"Must you?" she asked.

"Of course I must. Do you think I could live with myself another day?"

"Perhaps no one need ever know."

"Everybody in England will know before a week is over. She gave me to understand that people guessed it already."

"*This* seems such a terrible alternative to a woman — but ——"

"But you have race in you. You understand perfectly. My honour has been sold, and my pride is dead: there is no place among men for what is left of me. And to face my son again! Good God!"

"Can nothing be done to keep it from Cecil?"

"Nothing. It is the only heritage I leave him and he'll have to stand it as best he can. It won't kill him, nor his courage; he's made of stronger stuff than that. And if I've brought the family honour to the dust, he has it in him to raise it higher than it has ever been. Never let him forget that. You've played your part well all along, but you've a great deal more to do yet. You'll find that Fate didn't steer you into this family to play the pretty rôle of countess —— "

"I am equal to my part."

"Yes: I think you are. Now — I have an hour's work before me. I can't let you go till I have finished. You are a strong creature — but you are a woman, all the same. You must stay here until I am ready to let you go."

"I want to stay with you."

"Thank you. Sit down."

He handed her a chair, and returned to his writing.

Lee knew that if he had condemned her to the corridor under a vow of secrecy she should have paced up and down with increasing nervousness. But she felt calm enough beside him. He wrote deliberately, with a steady hand, and out of the respect he commanded she felt as profound a pity for him as she would feel when she stood beside him in the crypt. The soul had already gone out of him: it did not even strike her as eerie that the vigorous body beside her would demand its last rites in an hour.

Although taught to forgive her father, she had been brought up in a proper disapprobation of suicide. The impressions rooted in her plastic years rose and possessed her for a moment; but she wisely refused to consider what was none of her business. She did not even argue Lord Barnstaple's case, nor remind herself that she understood him. It was exclusively his own affair, and to approve or condemn him was equally impertinent.

Her chair faced the window. The crystal moon hung low above the park. The woods looked old and dark: night gave them back their mystery. The lovely English landscape was steeped in the repose which the centuries had given it. The great forests and terrible mountains of California may have been born in earlier throes, but they still brooded upon the mysteries of the future. England was worn down to peace and calm by centuries of passing feet. She had the repose of a great mind in the autumn of its years.

Lee melted into sympathy with the country of her adoption. California loomed darkly in the background, majestic but remote, and folding itself in the mists of dreams. It had belonged to her, been a part of her, in some bygone phase of herself. She was proud to have come out of it and glad to have known it, but it would be silent to her hereafter. She was as significantly a Maundrell as if she had been born in her tower; for she was, and indivisibly, a part of her husband.

She was too sensible to waste time in upbraiding herself for her conduct of the past fortnight. It had been as inevitable as exhaustion after excitement, or mental rebellion after years of unremitting study; and the suffering it had caused could easily be transformed into gratitude. The important points were that her reaction had worn itself out, and that the tremendous climax on its heels had forced her prematurely into the consciousness that the three years' effort to be something she had not developed in the previous twenty-one, had changed her character and her brain as indubitably as the constant action of water changes the face of a rock. One month of her old life would have bored her to extinction. Two months and she would have anathematised the continents of land and water between herself and her husband. A fortnight later she would have been in her tower. Solemn as the passing moments were, she could not ignore the prick of ironical relief that her future was to lack the determined effort of the past three years. Her new self would fit her with the ease of a garment long worn. Love had sustained her when she had desired nothing so much as happiness; but she knew that she had hardly known the inchoation of love until to-night. Cecil, in his terrible necessity, had taken her ego into his own breast.

Her thoughts went to him in their tower, writing, like his father, but with far less calm; for he grew nervous and impatient over his work. It seemed a strange and terrible thing that he should sit there unconscious of the double tragedy preparing for him, but she was glad to prolong his unconsciousness as long as she could. And she would be the one to tell him.

Lord Barnstaple laid down his pen and sealed his letters. He stood up and held out his hand.

"Good-bye," he said.

They shook hands closely and in silence. Then she went out and he closed the door behind her. She stood still, waiting for the signal. She could not carry the news of his death to his son until he was gone beyond the shadow of a doubt. It was so long coming that she wondered if his courage had failed him, or if he were praying before the picture of his wife. It came at last.

CHAPTER XXVI

SHE walked rapidly along the corridor toward the tower. But in a moment or two she turned back and went in the direction of the library. It was Randolph's habit to read there when the other guests were playing and romping. To-night's frolic would certainly not have appealed to him. It was more than possible that he was there alone, or in his room; and to-morrow he must go with the others. It might be years before she would see him again, and it would be culpable not to make him a last appeal. If the Abbey was lost it should not be for want of effort on her part.

Randolph was in the library, and alone. He rose with a brilliant smile of pleasure, then stood and looked hard at her.

"Something has happened," he said. "You look as if you had just come back from the next world."

"You are not so far wrong. Lord Barnstaple has just killed himself. Things had come to his knowledge that I hope you may never hear. But he is dead, and to-morrow you will have gone."

They were standing close together.

"You will not return to California with us."

"I would never leave Cecil Maundrell for an hour again if I could help it."

They exchanged a long look, and when it was over each understood the other. Lee looked down; then, in the unendurable silence, raised her eyes again. She averted them hastily. His were the eyes of men who look their last. It was the second time she had looked into a man's soul to-night, and she felt cold and faint. What should she see in Cecil's?

And how was she to speak of the Abbey in the face of a tragedy like this? She turned to go, but her feet clung to the floor. The Abbey was Cecil's, and Cecil's it must remain if its rescue were within the compass of her determined hands. But words were hard to find.

Then she remembered that she had very eloquent eyes, and that Randolph was versed in their speech. She raised them slowly and let them travel about the beautiful old room, then out to the cloisters under whose crumbling arches hooded shadows seemed passing to and fro; then raised them once more to his with an expression of yearning and appeal.

"Is it true that Lady Barnstaple is ruined?"

"She has not a penny."

There was another silence, so intense that they heard the echo of a laugh, far out on the moor.

Randolph picked up a book from the table, and examined its title, then laid it down again, and turned it over.

"I have never yet broken my word," he said.

Lee flashed him a glance full of tears and tribute. Then once more that night she shook hands with a man who was sick with the bitterness of life.

She left the library and went rapidly down the corridor. As she passed Lord Barnstaple's door she noted with gratitude that there was no sign of discovery. If the blow could be softened it was by her alone.

She was traversing the last corridor but one when her eyes were arrested by the chapel and the churchyard on the hill. She paused a moment and regarded them intently. A week from to-night she and her husband would follow Lord Barnstaple up that hill to the vault beneath the chapel's altar. She had hardly realised his death before, but that solitary hill, cold under the moonlight, cold in its bosom, coldly biding its Maundrells, generation after generation, century after century, made the tragedy of the earl's death one of the several sharply-cut facts of her life. They were five; she counted them mechanically: the violent death of her father, her meeting with Cecil, the death of her mother, her union with her husband, the violent death of her husband's father. There was certainly a singular coincidence between the first and the last.

As she continued to look out at the graveyard, dark even under the moon, and wondering if the next great fact in her life would be the birth of a child, to be borne up that hill supinely in his turn, following the father who had gone long since, she became aware that the word coincidence was swinging to and fro in her mind, although the other words of its company had gone to their dust-heap. She frowned and reproached herself for giving way to melancholy; then reflected that she would be less than mortal if she did not . . . the reiteration of the word annoyed her, and in a moment she had fitted it into her conversation with Lord Barnstaple that afternoon.

Her stiffening eyes returned to the hill, and their vision stabbed through the mounds to the bones of the abbots, whose brothers had cursed the Abbey. It had been but a coincidence perhaps, but it had worked itself out with astonishing regularity.

Lee became conscious that she was as cold as ice. The Abbey was saved to the Maundrells. Was Cecil dead? Had he died before his father? Nothing could be more unlikely, for he was the healthiest of men, and there was no one to murder him.

She shook herself violently and took her nerves in hand. Two years ago she would have flung off the superstition as quickly, but to-day the old world and all its traditions had taken her imagination into its mould. Had Pix — or that silent, persistent, unfathomable woman, his sister ——

She ran towards the tower, gripping her nerves; for if Cecil were there she would have need of all her faculties. It was no part of her programme to burst in upon him and scream and stammer her terrible bulletin. But she was a woman, frightened, horrified, overwrought with hours of nervous tension. When she reached the stair her knees were shaking, and she climbed the long spiral so slowly that she would have called her husband's name could she have found her voice. She wished she had asked him to write in her boudoir, whose open door was as black as the entrance to a cave; but he was — should be — in his own little sitting-room above.

She climbed the next flight with something more of resolution; courage comes to all strong natures as they approach the formidable moments of their lives. At the last turning she saw a blade of light, but the door was too thick to pass a sound. When she reached it her fear and superstition, and the obsession they had induced, left her abruptly, and she opened the door at once. Cecil was writing quietly.

THE END.